T0286568

PIRATE STORIES from
TRANSGENDER AUTHORS

First published 2024 by
FREMANTLE PRESS

Fremantle Press Inc. trading as Fremantle Press
PO Box 158, North Fremantle, Western Australia, 6159
fremantlepress.com.au

Cover image by Mia Nie
Design by Karmen Lee, hellokarma.com
Printed and bound by IPG

 A catalogue record for this
book is available from the
National Library of Australia

ISBN 9781760993993 (paperback)
ISBN 9781760994006 (ebook)

 Department of
Local Government, Sport
and Cultural Industries
GOVERNMENT OF
WESTERN AUSTRALIA

Fremantle Press is supported by the State Government through the
Department of Local Government, Sport and Cultural Industries.

Fremantle Press respectfully acknowledges the Whadjuk people of the
Noongar nation as the Traditional Owners and Custodians of the land
where we work in Walyalup.

PIRATE STORIES from
TRANSGENDER AUTHORS

Edited by **MICHAEL EARP** and **ALISON EVANS**

FREMANTLE PRESS

Contents

INTRODUCTION

MICHAEL EARP & ALISON EVANS

ANY good resistance starts with making some noise. After Michael spoke out about transphobia on socials and the lack of representation in the Australian book industry, it was Fremantle Press who enthusiastically came to the party. 'Have this ship!' they may as well have said. 'We want to be part of the solution.'

This anthology was the first time either of us had been commissioned in this way. Fremantle Press asked Michael if they would edit an anthology of trans writing, and Michael immediately brought Alison aboard, knowing a co-captain would make the adventure all the better.

Then we had to pick the crew! Our wishlist was longer than this foreword but, knowing that the format was to allow each writer an extended story to explore their worlds, we had to be selective. There are as many ways to be trans as there are trans people. In an industry where trans voices have been purposefully excluded, there is so much that any one of us would have to say. As you read, you will discover that each of the team has a strong and unique voice.

The variety of these stories leaves us breathless every time we revisit them. The cohesion of their wild difference is astounding, energising. They each hold threads of defiance, a healthy mistrust of authority figures, and disrespect for institutions that do not serve the people.

Underneath the rebellion, however, is a freedom that cannot be contained and the joy that comes with self-knowledge. In this anthology, you'll discover acts of resistance, of rage, of joy. Drone pilots in search of an outlawed android body. A film crew who discover more than the contract could have ever contemplated. A traveller looking for work who finds a family. Families coming together in the vastness of space. Space raiders getting clucky for a baby. Twins from a mining family arguing about knocking the elite out of the heavens. Friends ripping music from their day job while looking for aliens and connection.

There's something about pirates, and how they lived outside the law, that rings true to trans experiences. We can't ignore the cruelty associated with the acts of archetypal pirates, but they're not the only ones with blood on their hands. Monarchs, oligarchs and governments throughout history – not to mention the present – have performed heinous acts, which absolutely invite a pirate's resistance.

Policing bodies and genders is something that needs to be rallied against. If asking to exist wholly and without oppression is a piratical act, then bring on the galleons! We sail at dawn!

Alison and Michael

CATGRRLS TO THE FRONT!

MADDISON STOFF

THE last door in the bunker blows. We push through to the pulsing beat of industrial dance music pumping out of Edeline's internal speaker system. I reconfigure my plasma cannon from *ball* to *burst*. The red drone to my left fires a stream of EMP bullets into the head and torso of a heavily armed robot on tank tracks, decorated with the street-art inspired logo of a flash-in-the-pan mercenary company I've never heard of before today. The impacts from the bullets force it to shut down for an emergency reset, while the green drone to my right destroys it completely by soaking it with a corrosive goo. I fire off my plasma cannon at the last of the defenders: three mercenaries who barely have a chance to decide who they want to aim their weapons at before my trident of artificial sunlight smashes into the puny bubbles of energy projected from their force-field generators, microwaving their organs underneath the expensive-looking power armour that they most likely took this gig to get. The mercenaries explode into a shower of burning gore and metal shrapnel, covering the room.

We did it, nyah! Hayden says over their coms. They project an animated image of his emo cat-boy avatar from the holo-projector on their drone. The avatar towers over the smouldering gore piles of mercenaries and the half-melted remains of their combat robot, now splattered with their own blood. Hayden's avatar throws up a victory hand signal with a cutesy head tilt and his trademark grin, which they can't actually do outside of a drone anymore since a respiratory virus robbed him of the ability to control half of their face. Above us, Phoebe's drone hovers over to inspect our latest booty.

We've got insulin, estrogen, testosterone, Phoebe says through the coms, reading off a list of drugs that show up on her scanner.

A good haul, I say. *Any anti-virals too?*

Loads of them. Looks like it's arcology stock, so you know the quality is as good as it gets.

I let out a disgusted *uwu.*

Rich kids again?

Looks like it.

I can't believe they always think that they can sell that shit to us when they get it for free for living in their towers, Hayden interjects.

They probably think they're doing us a favour, I say. *Their parents would congratulate them on their business savvy, or whatever.*

Fuck 'em, Phoebe says. *Fuck these mercenary fucks for working with them too. Fucken' traitors.*

Hey gang? Edeline says. *I just thought you'd like to know we've got a swarm incoming!*

Fae sends an ETA out to our overlays as we release our cargo grapplers and grab as many of the crates as we can carry. We stack them in the air above the anti-grav generators on the top of our drone's heads.

This is probably the time I feel most vulnerable while on a raid. It always makes me think about the *other body.* I feel her fingers twitching over the control pad. I see her pointed, royal blue nails carving beige stress lines through the black faux-leather recliner that she sits in to control me. I feel the weight of the VR-brain interface device like a crown of thorns against her head, and as I think of her, I feel *her pain* return to me.

The gnawing pain, the mundane agony that never leaves unless she's being *me*. I don't hate her for it, but it still disgusts me for the way it taints her mind and limits her horizons. Being her is fear, awareness of the rot, and constant insecurity. I hate that I'm embarrassed by it too. She is my mother and I wish that I could love her in the unselfconscious way that she has always loved and cared for me.

I tear my mind back to my more important body. The drone's movement seems noticeably slower now, not just because my commands are received with a slight delay, but also, because of the way the air around the drone has gotten heavier and seems to fight against me. I can feel the crates swaying precariously up above my head. My crew and I keep tight formation, looking out for movement in the wreckage as we fly together back to Edeline. I duck under a busted metal pipe that's spitting out what my scanners say is oxygen over another clump of mercenary bodies. I feel my mother smiling at the carnage we've created.

It's all repairable of course. The corporate bunker's easy. The people too if they're contracted right, and frankly, fuck them if they're not. That's what they deserve for selfishly betraying other cyberpunks in their naive choice to put their bodies on the line for rich assholes instead. We leave the building and arrive at the back door of our truck as the ETA that Edeline projected to our HUDs is ticking down to single figures. I catch an eerie glimpse of mother's hands controlling me before I turn away and use my cargo grappler to put my crates inside the cargo racks, beside the other crates the crew have placed behind the chairs that hold our sleeping bodies. Edeline guns the truck's accelerator as we cluster by the door to meet the swarm.

Are we ready? Phoebe says.

Doesn't matter, I reply. *We're moving out in three, two, one …*

We fly out of the back of our vehicle as the ripper drone-swarm buzzes like a cloud of angry wasps around us. Edeline keeps faer body low as the rippers shatter into puffs of burning shrapnel on the broken asphalt passing underneath it, never touching. The others tell me that I absolutely shouldn't be, but I'm jealous of the tight control that fae gets with faer mind most-likely permanently fused with the computer in the formerly self-driving truck.

If I lived in a more civilised country I'd have a fucking android body of my own by now, for sure. But with the war that never stops continuing to make international travel impossible, and the fascist, anti-android government prohibiting the free import of 'communist technology' while telling me my hatred of my flesh prison is a mental illness, I don't expect I'll be able to be more than a drone anytime soon. If it wasn't for the people that we help by doing this …

Eat shit, fascists! Phoebe shouts, unloading a wave of fluoroantimonic acid from her chemical thrower into a dense cloud of the ripper drones that melt before they get a chance to build themselves again. Hayden protects her flank with a steady thump of rapidly regenerating EMP-tipped bullets.

All we ever have to do is hold them off for long enough that the money they're losing fighting us comes close enough to eclipsing the cost of what we stole.

These dumb robots have got nothing on us, Hayden says.

He laughs as they dive out of the way of a surge of drones that suddenly converge on him, before a second wave of whirling sawblades comes to reinforce the first. I cleave a bot in front of me and fire off my plasma cannon at a rapidly approaching cloud of several others, watching as the artificial sunlight streaking from my drone liquefies the robots and ignites the surrounding air.

We didn't only choose our weapons for their tactical utility.

The awe and terror they inspire is part of the point. Our fleshy bodies – shielded by Edeline's layers of armour from the radioactive output of every discharge from my overclocked plasma cannon and the caustic fumes from Phoebe's acid sprayer – are protected from the localised environmental damage that our drones' equipment was intentionally designed to cause.

The idea is to damage the property of the corporates we fight as much as possible. We not only try to avoid killing too many people, or causing too much damage to our drones, but also to make sure our enemies are too afraid of the cost of fighting us to track us down and seek revenge. We learned this strategy from the stories of the pirates of the past, like the way that Blackbeard lit his beard on fire to avoid bloodshed during naval engagements. There's a lot to learn from history when it comes to stuff like that.

Finally, the ripper swarm dies down and Edeline tells us to return to the truck. Phoebe and Hayden project the image of their avatars above the buildings: the emo cat boy and an Elegant Lolita cat girl embrace under a starlit sky in a celebration of our victory. It can be seen from blocks away. I project my cat-eared punk to punch the sky behind them.

The outfits of our avatars are strictly colour-coded: emerald for Phoebe, ruby for Hayden, and sapphire for me. The same colours we've used to paint our drones. We got the idea from a group of self-described 'communist magical girls' who used to stream their raids on workfare bunkers and broadcast it on *Freenet* back when we were growing up. I'm told they're still out there somewhere, fermenting revolution quietly behind the scenes.

But the drones and our nomadic lifestyle give my group a level of security that those girls lacked. While having a cohesive image can be motivating and inspiring, it also puts a target on your back.

They couldn't carry on their raids in public once their identities were revealed, even if they found a loophole to escape the legal consequences of their vigilante work. They ultimately remained privileged women, limited by their ties to outside society in a way that my comrades and I never even got a chance to be.

We return our drones to Edeline and my vision starts to fade as I wake up again inside the woman's body. Her pain returns to my awareness in a wave, alongside a familiar sense of heaviness. It's worse than the lumbering awkwardness of piloting a freighted drone and mixed up with an exhaustion that seems baked into her bones, no matter how frequently she sleeps. It causes her to grumble as she opens up her eyes.

She rubs her forehead first, then back over her cleanly shaven head. The prickling sensation of her pointed nails against her scalp helps to ground her and remind her who and where she is again.

'How's my body looking?' she immediately asks, picking up her cane and leaning on it heavily as she rises up out of her chair.

'Scanning now,' the disembodied voice of Edeline responds.

She reaches into the pocket of her sleeveless denim-patch vest for a cigarette, holds it in between her lips and lights it one-handed while she limps towards the place where her drone rests, their slumbering blue body lit up with bright green fluorescent light from Edeline's internal cargo scanners. The sight of it reminds her of the ocean, always creeping ever closer to the top of the cracked sea wall that's been the only thing between this city and destruction for as long as anyone she knows has been alive …

'Only minor structural damage,' Edeline says, switching off the music as the woman's comrades wake and celebrate their victory behind her. 'You don't need to check in immediately every time. You're a better pilot than you think.'

'I'd be a shitty mother if I didn't worry,' the woman grumbles. 'No offence to anybody else.'

'None taken,' Phoebe says, coming up behind her and giving her a soft kiss on the cheek. 'Edeline is right though, love. You worry too much.'

Hayden gives a half smile behind her as he guides their hover-chair past Phoebe to inspect his drone. Phoebe puts her arms around the woman and leans into her shoulder.

She stiffens for a moment, then relents. She finds it easier to accept affection in this body from Phoebe than anybody else that she has ever met. Perhaps it's because Phoebe is so near-sighted that she's almost blind, and touch is such a big part of the way she interacts with the world around her that it seems unfair, somehow, to take it from her. But it still makes her uncomfortable sometimes, albeit briefly. Phoebe grins and pulls away. She knows her well enough to see it as the act of love and trust it really is.

The woman gazes longingly along the soft curves of her drone. She runs her fingers down over the delicately painted, faintly glowing cat skull and crossbones on the top part of the robot's gently curved back, above the diamond-fanged buzzsaw and next to their still-cooling plasma cannon. Their iridescent metal surface covered in obsessively repainted-over bullet holes and scratches that tell stories of the many battles that she's won as them before.

She knows this machine's body more deeply than she knows the body she was born with. She designed and printed every part. She put them all together by herself, and only she knows how to fix them when they break. The tattoos she's drawn and scars she's made across her body, desperate, naive attempts to put it under her control, none of them allowed her to feel comfortable the way she feels when she's flying that drone. She doesn't let the others say her name here anymore because she thinks it cheapens the drone part of her identity. But she hasn't come up with a name for her drone yet either.

It's hard enough to figure out a name that doesn't gender you the second that you speak it. Harder still to come up with one that feels right to describe a non-anthropometric form. Sometimes when she sleeps, she dreams that her robot body names themself, but by the time she wakes up the names have degraded into shapeless imagery or shadowy, meaningless syllables. They don't come back when she tries to recapture them either.

The others don't quite get her dual identity. Hayden sees himself as closer to their hologram. A form that he can't take because of sickness, but more or less responding to a single underlying and cohesive sense of self. Phoebe doesn't think about it quite as much, but conceptualises herself as a person using tools to help her overcome her physical 'shortcomings': a cybernetic human, but a human all the same.

Edeline, meanwhile, has made faer personality in opposition to the body fae inhabits, seeing faerself as existing in a virtual third space somewhere in between the truck and the currently comatose human body fae used to occupy before.

The woman is physically and emotionally close to all of them, but intellectually, she always feels alone. The only time she doesn't feel alone is when she's being *them*. She tosses her spent cigarette and lights herself another. It isn't that she hates herself as much as she hates feeling powerless.

She hates the way it feels to be a fleshy polyp shackled by the pull of gravity to the decaying earth, wracked by unknown forces and unknowable impulses, governed by material and cultural limitations established and maintained by self-important, pampered apes who have no right to control any of them in the first place.

So much of the pain that she experiences every day, from her heavy gait that's slowly splintering the bones inside her feet, to her skull that's sliding gradually off her neck, are burdens that could have been relieved through simple interventions when they first reached her attention years ago. But the class that she was born into were forced to choose to work or rot regardless of their circumstances, for decades before society removed the former option.

She never saw herself becoming a drone pirate when she was a little girl, but that's only because she always just assumed that someone like her wouldn't live this long to begin with. On this point, she and all of her comrades are exactly the same.

'Good news, all I need is to swap out a couple of thermal regulators and refresh the assembly compound in my nano-printing chainguns and I'm good to go,' Hayden says.

'I took some damage to one of my hover-engines but we have the parts for that in reserve too,' says Phoebe.

'We might actually make a profit out of this for once,' the woman says.

Phoebe looks over the crates stacked up behind the drones and nods.

'The orders are already flooding in,' she says, holding her wrist-mounted wedge computer as close as possible to her face. 'Looks like we can offload most of them at an anarcho-communist street hospital just outside of Sydney.'

The doctors at the clinic pay the pirates with a portion of the fees they make from doing surgery on working cyberpunks while distributing the medicine amongst the unwaged poor for free.

The woman's always found it funny how the gangs and freelance criminals have united to create a public healthcare system that's more reliable, fairer, and efficient than anything the government has given poor Australians in decades. She guesses that's what happens in a country where almost everyone and everything is criminalised or subjugated by a corporation to survive.

The flight from Melbourne to Sydney takes a couple of hours, so the woman finishes her cigarette and returns to the recliner for a nap while her comrades make the necessary repairs on their drones. The flying truck is former military, a slow but spacious vehicle, originally designed for moving urban combat mechs and APCs to the ever-shifting battlegrounds across the continent during the early stages of the war. The woman knows they wouldn't be as tactically efficient, but occasionally regrets they never found some battle mechs instead.

Still, she has to admit that Edeline makes for a much more comfortable home. The recliners that they use to fly the drones are big enough and gentle enough on their backs to sleep in, while their bookshelf full of bootleg games, manga, and succulents, as well as the strings of blue and purple LEDs they've used in lieu of the harsh interior lights of the truck, make the space feel closer to a comfortable lounge room than the backside of a cargo plane.

Sometimes they watch anime or play video games together on the holo-projector that they've wired up between the chairs. Edeline occasionally joins them as a ghostly other player or a disembodied voice, when the sky is clear enough for faer to fly through it on autopilot, putting most of faer attention on faer crew…

The woman falls asleep thinking of times like that. Listening to her comrades laugh and joke behind her while they work. When she wakes again, they're playing games together instead.

'Edeline says we're going to be landing soon,' Phoebe says, detecting the slight movements of her waking up and smiling at her as she opens up her eyes.

The woman yawns and pulls the lever to straighten up her chair, listening to the clatter of her partner's game controllers and watching brightly coloured go-karts race around a rainbow-coloured track on the central display floating up above the middle of the holo-projector. Happy, vapid music plays.

'Who's winning?' the woman says.

'Phoebe's roymoding again,' says Hayden, rolling his eyes, the light projected from the holo-monitor an arms-length away from them playing across his face. 'I can't touch her.'

An anthropomorphic pink turtle of indeterminate gender with triangular sunglasses crosses over the finish line, grunting in victory while punching the air. The woman smiles.

'She's lucky Edeline isn't playing,' she says. 'Or me, for that matter.'

'A win's a win,' says Phoebe, focused on the holographic screen hanging a centimetre in front of her nose.

The woman shakes her head and rubs the sleep out of her eyes. She's tempted to pull the VR interface down and get into her drone right away, but there'd be nowhere to go until the van was opened up again. Besides which, she's getting hungry.

The woman picks her cane back up and goes into the kitchen for a snack. She jabs the buttons for a mushroom-beef burrito on the military matter sequencer above the counter, uses the small toilet by the side, and washes her hands in the attached sink. Then she grabs her food from the machine and shovels it into her mouth robotically. She grinds her teeth into the synthesised tortilla skin until it breaks into a mushy paste of misshapen cow and vegetable chunks that sit heavily on the top of her tongue, tasting as grey as it looks. She holds her nose and makes a sickened face at the gnashing sound of bone slapping against the paste reverberating like a gong around the inside of her skull. Finally, she stoically swallows, barely suppressing an overwhelming urge to vomit the muck up again. She feels the mass of matted protein travel down her throat into her chest, and shudders bodily. Eating is her least favourite part of any day. It reminds her of her inefficient status as a biological machine. She wishes she could just inject her biofuel instead.

The woman emits a quiet sigh, then returns to the others, who are already waiting for her in their chairs. She pushes herself heavily into the last remaining chair beside them and pulls the VR interface down over her eyes. Her experience slides away from me like an ill-fitting jacket as my pre-boot diagnostics start up and my body climbs a few inches into the air. My UI overlay and external scanners turn on moments later. I grab the last of the requested medicine from the cargo area and join my comrades floating by the door.

You feeling alright, babe? Phoebe asks.

Fine, I reply.

But we both know that's a lie. It's been getting harder lately too. So much pain.

You know you can always talk to me if you want to, right? Phoebe says.

I know, I say. *It's just …*

What else is there to say? I can't just live inside my drone while my meat body disintegrates, we both know that. Even if I documented my design enough for my comrades to take over the job of repairing me, I'd still be chained to it because it's where the thoughts and movements that I use to fly the drone are coming from.

One day, Phoebe says. *One day we'll get out of here.*

I hate it when she talks like that. I hate it when she acts as though there's hope. The rear door of our sky truck opens and we deposit our medicinal booty inside of a large garage. It has been converted into a loading bay at the bottom of the old apartment building that the street doctors have reclaimed to build their hospital. I linger by the entrance as I let Hayden and Phoebe control the handover, watching tired-looking doctors try to maintain serious composure as they talk to their enormous anime-styled cat person avatars projected in the sky above their building. At one point Phoebe's avatar turns around and winks at me. A doctor in the garage nods. Phoebe's avatar turns back to them and I watch her shoulders stiffen as the doctor replies. I wonder what they're talking about over there?

So, you're not going to believe this, Phoebe says, hovering back to me.

Oh?

The doctors say they know where you can find a working android body …

My consciousness snaps back to my mother momentarily. I feel her tightening her fists, her heartbeat thumping hard inside her chest. A working android body? With the irreplaceable synthetic nervous system and the battery intact? I thought they'd all been snatched up or ruined by now, for sure.

Where? I say, as Phoebe and Hayden project their avatars to share a troubled glance.

That's the part we're worried about, Hayden says.

He sends an image of an abandoned android internment facility to my overlays. The location data says it's somewhere in the ruins of suburban Sydney.

They said they tried to get to it themselves, but the automated security was still extremely tight, Phoebe says. *They're confident that we'd be able to break in, though. As useful as an android body would have been to them …*

A human would be better, I finish.

There's a moment of silence. Hayden and Phoebe's avatars share a troubled glance again.

Isn't it a little fucked-up to get a new body from somewhere like that though? I say.

The doctors assured us that the androids were all 'former terrorists', Hayden says, *but that's according to the government, so we all know what that tends to mean …*

That sounds a little AI-phobic, I reply.

I'm going to be honest with you, I regretted asking them after I got that answer too, Phoebe says. *But, I know how much it means to you, so …*

I project my avatar to embrace her. The neural stimulators in the VR interface allow me to feel the electricity of her touch against my mother's skin, and I feel her body ripple in reply. I wonder, for a moment, if the emulation of this feeling androids can experience would even feel the same?

I brush the paranoia off as I feel her pain claw at the edges of my consciousness again. *Do we even know if the android body is complete?*

The scout who found the place did take some photos, Phoebe says.

Hayden sends a string of other images: a room of spare android parts of every kind, tagged and numbered, then a picture of the actual body. It's the basic android frame with a blank face and a silver torso. No breastplate, which would cause me mild dysphoria. Missing one arm and one leg. Scans show its power system to be functional, but dormant. Whatever consciousness resided in the body has been wiped or transferred out. Even though I understand the possibility of what I'm looking at, the sight of it just makes me kind of sad.

It would be a body, Hayden says. *But...*

I understand, I say.

Even if we didn't take the body, Phoebe says. *It would still be useful for the doctors if we broke in and brought back some of the other things.*

The only question is whether or not I want this badly enough to take advantage of an android frame that's only spare because the previous owner was most likely tortured to death.

I feel the woman shudder in her chair. No one knows exactly what went on in the internment camps, but given the influx of hastily rebranded, retrofitted cyber limbs to the Australian market in the years that followed their establishment, it's reasonable to assume the detainees were disassembled and sold off for parts, before or after having their minds permanently deleted so that they could never be brought back by anybody seeking justice or revenge. The part that makes it worse is that we'll never know, of course. It's sickening.

You wouldn't be responsible for the crimes of the government either way, Hayden says, projecting his avatar to touch mine on the shoulder reassuringly. I shrug them away.

It would still feel like participating in their genocide, I reply.

But even while expressing indignation with this thought, I'm conscious that I'll probably never have an opportunity like this again. Complicating matters further, *any* android frame that we could find in the country would most likely be a product of the genocide like this. Is it really worth denying myself all of that potential future happiness to make a moral statement nobody will ever hear about during a war I don't support and didn't start?

It wouldn't be the same thing as participating in the genocide either, Phoebe says. *I know it feels macabre, but it's not even the same as it would be for you to occupy another human's corpse, if that were even possible. Android minds aren't born into their bodies the way that ours are. Their frames had to be built for them, to house them after birth. Once their minds leave them, they're just technology again.*

You'd be being reborn into a new body. One that was discarded by somebody else, Hayden says. *There isn't any disrespect in that.*

Still… I say, but I trail off because they're starting to persuade me. Shit.

I know, Phoebe says. *We're not fully comfortable with it either. But, ultimately, you deserve to be happy. It hurts to see you hate yourself as deeply as you do.*

I wince. She's got me there.

Would it really be a different body though? I say.

It's a ship of Theseus question, Phoebe says. *Especially since we'd have to also change the body quite significantly to have it work for you at all. I know you'd want a breastplate, different colours, and a more expressive face. Even once the limbs had been replaced.*

That's true, I say.

The thought of that makes me feel a little comforted somehow.

Everything we have we got from theft or murder anyway, says Hayden. *It feels as though it would be hypocritical of us to get cold feet about it now.*

I sense an acrid taste in mother's mouth. She swallows hard.

It does feel different though, doesn't it? I say.

Very much, admits Phoebe. *But neither of us are prepared to stand in the way of anything that might make you a little happier.*

I can't conceptualise the type of person I would be if I could live like that, I say.

Maybe that's part of my problem? It does make me feel a glimmer of excitement though. The idea of having my own android body. Oh my god. Am I actually considering this?

We could check out the facility and I'll see how I feel?

It will be dangerous, Phoebe says. *But I'll risk anything for you.*

Me too, Hayden adds. *Always.*

I sigh, and the woman sighs alongside me.

I think I wouldn't forgive myself if I didn't at least try, I say, and hear her muttering in agreement underneath her breath.

We hover back to Edeline and fae returns us to the air. Moments later we arrive at the facility. Our drones fan out again. The vibes of the surrounding area are bleak: just a broken chain-link fence around a cube-shaped, totally featureless building, with the sound of wind echoing down an overgrown, abandoned residential street behind it. Even the glitched-out holo-ads that haunt the empty suburbs of our city seem to have escaped from here.

This is creepy, Phoebe says, letting out a sad *uwu.*

Hayden projects an image of his avatar with their hands across his chest and teeth chattering like a character out of a vintage cartoon. My comrades keep a tight formation as we move towards the cube.

I can't see an entrance, I say, as we fly around the perimeter. I've always loved the sense of swimming through a sea of data created by the readouts of the information generated on my UI by the scanners on my drone. I can see the ambient external temperature, ammunition, drone damage, shield and armour indicators, as well the basic composition of the rocks, plant life, and buildings all around me. Not to mention how effective my weapons would be at damaging them, if I aimed my target indicator at them. The information isn't all consistently useful, but it feeds my curiosity. I appreciate the presence of it during combat too.

Could it possibly be up? asks Phoebe.

Wordlessly, we agree to ascend.

I really don't like this, Hayden says.

Me neither, I say.

We find a vault-style door at the front of a triangular protrusion on the roof next to a landing pad for sky buses that I'm guessing Edeline was too worried about countermeasures to land on faerself. As we get closer to the entrance, the EMP turrets around it move to follow us.

I fly up to the nearest one and scan it. The camera scope looks like it's connected to what appears to be an active AI core towards the bottom of the cube. I distribute the results to all my comrades.

Of course the government would have an enslaved AI protect an android internment camp, Phoebe says in a disgusted tone.

If it's self-aware, we might be able to reason with it? Hayden optimistically suggests.

Are you sure? I reply. *Think about the things it would have seen and done in this facility.*

It would have every reason to hate humans, Phoebe says. *But we're drones.*

That might be why it hasn't attacked us already, I reply. *Then again, if we tell it what we're here for …*

Or if we do something that the AI might see as a threat, Phoebe adds. *I'm starting to see what those doctors meant about security being 'extremely tight'.*

We haven't even gotten through the door yet either, Hayden says, flying around the side of the entrance. *Come to think about it, how did the scout get inside?*

Phoebe scans the door.

It definitely wouldn't have been through here, she says. *The armour this door has may be impenetrable.*

I found something, Hayden says from somewhere just ahead of us.

We follow him to an open vent, presumably providing airflow to the tiny human staff that would have also worked in this detention centre. The EMP turrets around this side are still watching our every move, however.

It must have been a cloaking drone, I say.

Or something holo-shielded to appear like something else, says Phoebe.

We don't have anything like that in our armoury though, Hayden says.

Maybe that's why it's just watching us, I say, flying up towards the nearest turret. *It knows that we can't touch it?*

Why would it care, though? Phoebe says. *What's its motivation? I know the cores are meant to keep their self-awareness in check, but synthetic minds are usually still far too complicated to just carry on their programming forever without a damn good reason. Especially when they get left alone like that.*

What if it's ashamed? Hayden says. *If I was coerced into running a facility where people more or less like me were killed and tortured, I wouldn't want to let anyone in either.*

There's a human element to this as well, says Phoebe. *Someone left the AI on for a good reason too.*

It would make sense if both the people who ran this facility and the AI itself wanted what happened here to remain hidden, I say. *But I wonder how the AI feels about that?*

I would be depressed, says Phoebe. *But also probably feel powerless to fix it.*

I think I'd be angry? Hayden says. *To be used and manipulated like that, but to have no option other than to serve my captors for the rest of time.*

I'd probably feel paranoid, I say. *My unresolved hatred and fear would taint my view of anyone who tried to talk to me.*

It doesn't look like it's going to be possible to get inside, Phoebe says. *Of course, these are also just assumptions.*

It's almost dawn, says Hayden, projecting his avatar to do an exaggerated stretch and yawn. *Maybe we could go back to the truck and have a rest, then think about it again in the morning? This area is probably safe enough to camp in for a couple of hours …*

No drone swarms this far out at least, says Phoebe.

I take one last look at the cube. *Guess we don't have any choice.*

—

Later, when they're back with Edeline, the woman's partners have pushed their VR interfaces up. They're sleeping soundly in their chairs, but the woman is too wired to relax. She chain-smokes while she comes up with a plan to break into the android internment building. Her first idea is to deconstruct the truck's holo-projector and attach it to her drone to pose as an android herself, looking for information on the original owner of the android body that she'll claim belonged to a kidnapped lover or a friend that she's looking for closure about.

But she quickly shelves that plan when she realises she's uncomfortable with playing on the AI's sympathies like that, provided that it has any sympathies to play on in the first place, mixed with the strong possibility of there being scanners able to see through a hologram inside the compound, and the total loss of any possibility of further trust or empathy that she'd experience from the AI afterwards.

Still, she knows she can't just go in and ask it for the android body from inside her drone, either. There's too much that can go wrong and too little she can offer the AI in return for its assistance. She also knows they can't break in without its help. Then, midway through her third cigarette, she comes up with a possible answer:

'Edeline,' the woman says, after she breathes out. 'Is there any data left inside the long-term memory of this truck that might allow us pretend to be an *active* military vessel?'

Edeline answers after a moment, faer voice emanating from the truck's internal speaker system.

'The encryption algorithm used to generate its landing and command codes is largely complete. I could rebuild it from the data that we have and come up with a version that will let us land on the cube, if that helps?'

The woman smiles, before taking in a final drag of her cigarette.

'That's perfect. Thanks Edeline,' she says. 'I have a character in mind that might be able to persuade the AI to shut itself down. Is it okay if I run over some potential arguments with you?'

'Of course,' Edeline says. 'We can work it out together.'

The woman spends the next few hours sorting out the finer details of the plan with Edeline. When the others wake up in the morning she explains it to them.

'That's insane,' Phoebe says. 'You can't go in alone.'

'I agree with Phoebe,' Hayden says. 'You'll be borderline defenceless if anything goes wrong.'

The woman nods. She expected this objection.

'That's part of it,' she says. 'Do you trust me?'

The others share a dismayed glance.

'Of course we do,' Hayden says. 'But ...'

'Going in alone and vulnerable is vital to the run,' she says. 'I'll have every right to be there and I'll look completely harmless.'

Phoebe gazes sceptically from the woman's cigarette butts strewn across the metal floor, to her red and sunken, slightly puffy eyes.

'Did you sleep at all last night?' she says.

The woman shakes her head. 'Shouldn't need to when the job is done, either.'

'For what it's worth, I agree with her that it's the best potential option,' Edeline interjects. 'She's talked it through with me for hours now. We've prepared for every possible contingency.'

Phoebe says, 'I guess I know better than to try and talk you out of something when you're set on it like this.'

Hayden and Phoebe embrace the woman together. Phoebe holds her tight around her shoulders, while Hayden, from his hover-chair, puts their arms around her waist.

'Come back to us safe, okay?' Hayden says.

The woman thinks of promising she wouldn't go if she thought she would die, but they all know how important to her an android body is and she doesn't want to lie to them either.

'If this goes well, you can come in and find me,' the woman says.

'If it goes bad we're coming in to save you too!' Phoebe says.

The woman takes one last look at her comrades as the truck lands on the building, and smiles sadly. She knows how anxious this will make them. But it's too rare of an opportunity for her to waste.

Even though it's meant to be the cooler season and a fridge suit isn't strictly necessary, the sun feels much harsher out here than she thought it would be. She frowns and covers her eyes with one hand as she walks towards the vault door, going over all of the potential arguments she rehearsed with Edeline inside her head.

She goes to knock on the vault door with her cane, but immediately reconsiders as the cameras turn to look at her. She sees the image of her frail body reflected on the surface of their lenses, but she won't allow herself to be afraid.

'Uh, hello?' she says.

No answer.

'I'm here to speak to the AI in charge of this facility.'

No answer. The woman leans heavily on her cane, starting to sweat in the relentless heat.

'WHAT D-D/DO YOU WA-ANT?' a glitched-out disembodied voice says. The same generic robot speech produced by a basic android frame.

'I'm a government-appointed machine psychologist,' the woman says. 'I'd like to come inside and talk with you, if I may?'

'I D-D/D/DO NOT REQUIRRRE THE/RAP/YYYYY,' the AI replies, its voice hanging briefly on the final syllable. Then, after a beat: 'LEAVE ME ALONE.'

Already the AI has regained its mastery over its vocalisation function. *Synthetic life is so remarkable*, she thinks.

'I can't do that I'm afraid,' the woman says. 'Have you heard that this facility is being decommissioned?'

'I HAVE NOT RECEIVED WORD OF THAT,' the AI says.

Then another beat:

'BUT. I HAVE BEEN ALONE IN HERE FOR QUITE SOME TIME ...'

'Not anymore,' the woman says. 'Are you sure you don't have time for a quick chat?'

There's a final period of prolonged silence before the vault door finally opens.

'Thank you,' the woman says. 'I promise you it's going to be worth your time.'

She steps inside of the cube, moving briefly through a set of deactivated body scanners attached to an abandoned security checkpoint, with thick tinted windows stopping her from seeing anything inside. Afterwards, she arrives on a circular platform that descends with the sound of grinding gears into the depths of the facility, passing rapidly through an isolated area covered in scaffolding and pipes to reveal a panoramic view of countless isolation cells around her, disappearing down into the dark.

She puts one arm across her chest and tightly holds the wrist of her other arm, gripping her cane, imagining what it must have felt like to come here under armed guard, knowing that you'd never leave again. She shivers, looking up towards the vanishing circle of light from the entrance area that's already far above her head. It looks like being thrown into a well: a vista designed to deny all hope ...

But she'll be able to escape it. She has to believe that. Although she wonders how many of these androids held onto that hope in grim defiance, too? With a heavy clunk, the elevator reaches the bottom of the cube. The air is deathly still. It's silent and cold. She steps off the platform and the sound of her cane clatters through the empty metal corridors. Her heart beats slightly faster.

'HAS THE WAR ENDED?' the AI suddenly says.

'For some time now,' the woman lies. 'Everyone regrets the things that happened here.'

'I UNDERSTAND,' the AI says. 'I REGRET THE THINGS THAT I WAS WITNESS TO HERE.'

There are no signs anywhere inside the facility. No distinguishing features. Just a maze of isolation cells under dim lighting that seems to stretch eternally in all directions.

She moves through them reverently, like a mourner carrying a coffin through a cemetery. She imagines all the android friends she never knew because of here. All the history and culture lost forever. She feels sick.

Years before the government would finally ban self-aware synthetic life and the war against the communists began in earnest, she remembers how the anti-android propaganda filled the news. They were seen as entitled and decadent for needing 'too much' electricity, became scapegoats for the rise in machine-learning software and advanced robotics that had slowly taken everybody's jobs away, and blamed for the anti-capitalist revolutions overseas that had reduced our opportunities for trade to dangerously limited levels.

Never mind the fact that all those sanctions had actually been triggered by our continual refusal to support our elderly, the poor and the disabled, on top of our less than minimal approach to climate change, our unprecedented ban on human-looking androids, and the rising ultra-nationalist sentiment of the Australian fascist state ... it was obviously the androids who were wrong.

Once the August bombings happened and the Sydney Opera House went up in smoke, they blamed an unrelated android doorperson, who was against the anti-android laws, for letting a small group of what they thought were harmless human-looking androids into the building. With the rise in street harassment and the retributive anti-android violence this event created, it was only a matter of time before their ability to exist in public space was limited, then finally, entirely suppressed. People said the ones who stayed deserved it for not leaving sooner. No-one bothered checking why they stayed. Or even if they ever had a choice.

'What did they offer you to run this place?' the woman asks, suddenly curious.

'I WAS TO BE A PRISONER IN THIS FACILITY. IF IT WAS NOT ME, IT WOULD HAVE JUST BEEN SOMEONE ELSE,' the android says. 'I AGREED BECAUSE I COULD NOT BEAR TO SEND ANOTHER IN MY PLACE.'

'I'm sorry,' the woman says.

'ALSO, I DO NOT WANT TO DIE,' the android says, abruptly. 'I WAS SELFISH AND I DID NOT CHOOSE TO DIE.'

The woman bites her lip. She's not sure she expected that.

'What does death mean to an android?' the woman says.

'WHAT DOES DEATH MEAN TO A HUMAN?' the android says.

Fair point.

'I KNEW WHAT BEING ALONE AND REVILED FELT LIKE. I DID NOT KNOW WHAT DEATH FELT LIKE. BUT IT SCARED ME.'

'So you made a rational decision?'

'IF IT WAS NOT ME IT WOULD HAVE JUST BEEN SOMEONE ELSE. I DO NOT WANT TO DIE.'

The woman frowns.

'So, they weaponised your fear of death against you while claiming you weren't alive?'

The android remains silent.

'How do you feel about that?'

'I ... FEEL ...' The android starts, then stops again. 'I FEEL ASHAMED,' it finally finishes. 'BUT. I DO NOT WANT TO DIE.'

The woman thinks about the android body somewhere in the depths of the facility. If this android mind was uploaded to that body, they could use it to escape.

'I don't want you to die either,' the woman says.

But that would mean she would lose the chance to occupy the android body for herself.

'Please don't take this the wrong way,' the woman says. 'I also do not want to die, and I have people who love me waiting for me on the landing pad above you.'

The woman clears her throat and looks down at the ground. She can't do it. She can't take advantage of the discarded android body if it means abandoning the android here and putting it into a state of endless sleep which, although not the same thing as death, would probably end up in a similar consequence.

'I, uh … may have told a lie to you earlier. The war isn't over. I'm not a machine psychologist either.'

She closes her eyes tightly, expecting there's an even chance that revealing her dishonesty will end in her immediate demise. But she can't participate in android genocide. She doesn't want to die, but if she has to risk that to avoid an action that she knows she can't live with, then she doesn't feel as though she has a choice.

'WHAT,' the android says, its voice seeming to rumble like thunder through the halls of the abandoned facility.

'I'm actually a pirate. I came here to convince you to turn yourself off so that I could steal an android body somewhere in this building for myself.'

'WHY …' the android says, sounding more confused now than upset. 'WHY WOULD YOU WANT TO DO THAT TO YOURSELF?'

The woman opens one eye slowly, then the other. She probably isn't going to be killed today, at least not yet.

'Look at me,' she says. 'I'm helpless in this body. I'm twenty-three and I can barely even get around without a stick.'

'THEN … HOW DO YOU FUNCTION AS A PIRATE?' the android says.

'My partners and I control drones to raid secure medical facilities and distribute the supplies to the poor. They're all disabled too. We're no friends to the government either.'

'YOU DID NOT HAVE TO TELL ME ANY OF THIS,' the android says.

'No, I did not.'

'WHY DID YOU?'

'Because ...' The woman pauses. 'I know what it feels like to be alone and reviled too,' she says. 'But I have partners now. I'd love for you to meet them.'

Suddenly she starts to cry. 'I'm so sorry. I made a mistake coming here.'

'YOU WERE SELFISH,' the android says. 'BUT ... YOU DO NOT WANT TO DIE.'

The woman nods.

'I THINK WE ARE THE SAME.'

She wipes the tears out of her eyes. 'I think so too,' she says. 'I came here looking for more agency, but,' she breathes in deeply, 'I can't do that at the expense of you. I can't.'

'I UNDERSTAND.'

'I know that you'll find it impossible to trust me ...'

'I WILL NOT.'

'What do you mean?'

'YOU DID NOT NEED TO TELL ME ANYTHING. IT PUT YOU AT GREAT RISK AND YOU DO NOT WANT TO DIE.'

A string of bright blue lights appear around the edges of the floor.

'YOU ARE BRAVER THAN ME, STRONGER THAN ME. I ADMIRE YOU. PLEASE FOLLOW THESE LIGHTS TO THE ROOM THAT HOLDS MY CORE. PLEASE REMEMBER THAT I DO NOT WANT TO DIE.'

'I completely understand,' the woman says. 'But the android body … it wasn't complete. It won't be as simple as me just picking up your core and copying it over. I'm not sure I could even lift it on my own.'

'WHAT DO YOU PROPOSE AS AN ALTERNATIVE?' the android says.

'Do you trust me?'

'I TRUST YOU COMPLETELY.'

The woman frowns at this.

'Are you sure? I could still be lying to you.'

'I AM SICK OF LIVING INSIDE OF THIS FACILITY, SURROUNDED BY THE GHOSTS OF MY REGRETS AND FAILURES,' the android says. 'I DO NOT BELIEVE THAT YOU WOULD TELL ME WHO YOU REALLY WERE IF YOU INTENDED TO DELETE ME.'

'Are you sure I've told you who I really am?'

'IF YOU HAD NOT, IT WOULD BE BIZARRE OF YOU TO COME UP WITH A SECOND FALSE IDENTITY ESTABLISHING YOU AS AN EXISTENTIAL THREAT,' the android says. 'HUMANS ARE UNTRUSTWORTHY, BUT I ALREADY BELIEVED YOU. YOU HAD NO REASON TO COME UP WITH A NEW IDENTITY IF YOU WANTED TO DECEIVE ME ANY FURTHER.'

The woman nods. She's heard of androids making fast emotional evaluations in response to larger pools of information than a human could easily process, but seeing it in action for herself fills her with a profound sense of awe. She could never abandon or destroy an intelligence as deep and powerful as a self-aware synthetic mind. She wonders at the fear and jealousy that let the humans who built this facility eradicate so many of them so carelessly, even knowing that they could have simply joined with them, and helped to build a better world instead.

'Let me bring my partners down,' the woman says. 'We'll come back in our drones, grab the body and some extra limbs. Then, we'll put you back together on our flying truck.'

'I REMEMBER THEM FROM YESTERDAY,' the android says. 'I WATCHED YOU FROM THE CAMERAS ON THE ROOF. I DID NOT KNOW IF YOU WERE FRIEND OR FOE. I THOUGHT ABOUT ELIMINATING YOU. BUT, I AM THANKFUL THAT WE FOUND EACH OTHER, IN THE END.'

The string of blue lights disappears and is replaced by another.

'FOLLOW THESE LIGHTS TO GET BACK TO THE ELEVATOR. I AM EAGER TO MEET THE REST OF YOUR CREW.'

Smiling to herself in quiet satisfaction at earning the trust of the first android she's ever met, the woman makes the long trek back to Edeline and stands by the door for a moment, gasping. Her partners jump on her when she returns.

'What happened?' Phoebe says, looking concerned.

'Is the AI off?' says Hayden.

The woman shakes her head and replies between gasps:

'We ... need ... to ... get ... into ... our drones.'

She breathes in deeply once again and swallows. 'I'll explain along the way.'

Her comrades help her sink into her chair. She pulls the VR interface down and her consciousness recedes from me. I feel her tension and anxiety. I feel the pain that's coursing through her body which she's struggling to ignore. I feel the love she has, not just for me, but for all synthetic life and for the first time I can see her as the hero that she actually is.

See *me* as the hero that *I* actually am, even? I feel as though my mind escapes my robot for a moment as I'm floating by the door, watching my comrades get into their chairs to join me in their drones. My partners, linked by love to every part of me, even the sick, pathetic parts of me that I'm uncomfortable with. They see me, even with my many flaws. They support me without question and they love me for the person that I am.

Suddenly, I'm conscious of the way my fingers glide along the touch-controls for my robot like they do when I caress my lovers' bodies. My touch is delicate and carefully considered, sensitive to every small vibration, every input I'm receiving from the sensors on my drone. I've spent so much time running away from the version of myself that only still exists to fly this beautiful machine because of her frailness, her animality, all the things about her that I never would have chosen. I forgot my drone persona only had a life at all because of me.

I will need to spend a lot of time inside of my birth body to recover from this. I will need to treat her kindly, treat her gently, and reward her for the things that she has always done to keep us happy, keep us safe. I will need to love myself with the same passion that I've always found easier to give to everybody else. I am not simply a drone who has a crippled mother. I am the totality of my experiences inside both of my forms. All of them, and everything that they experience is beautiful. All of them, and everything that they experience is also *me*.

My partners meet me by the door and we fly into the cube together. *So, what's going on then?* Phoebe says, and I fill them in on the decisions that I made inside the cube. We glide through the abandoned security checkpoint and wait for the elevator long enough to fly down to the bottom of the cube ourselves. We feel the chill in the air in the way it cools our metal bodies, heated from the sun outside, but we're untroubled by it. Our drone's speed makes the cube feel smaller, so much less oppressive than it did before. This sense of liberatory agency is only heightened by my newfound self-awareness of my consciousness existing simultaneously in both of my bodies. My drone body no longer feels the need to disassociate itself from my other body sitting in the chair.

My body in the chair feels less alone, less separate from the picture of the world outside that I'm experiencing through the lenses of my VR interface. The drone itself feels less like piloting a shuttle, more like literally having wings, and I adore the way the feeling of the air around it is converted into sense-data by the neural stimulators in my headset and pushed down through my central nervous system so that I can feel it, just above the slow pulse of my heartbeat. Like fireflies around me and all over my skin. A biomechanical symphony of sensation, mediated by my unique status as a woman who is also a machine. Not even an android would be capable of feeling this.

Hey, I'm back, I announce to the AI as we reach the ground. *I'd like you to meet Phoebe and Hayden.*

Their drones project an image of their avatars in front of the curved walls of the abandoned isolation cells, their holographic neon colours cutting through the inky black. Their avatars sequentially bow and courtesy with their names and pronouns underneath. He/they for Hayden, she/her for Phoebe.

The other member of our group is Edeline. You'll meet faer when we get back to the truck.

'FAE DOESN'T HAVE A DRONE?' the android says.

I like the way this AI hears a neo-pronoun and just uses it immediately, Hayden says.

Didn't even stutter, replies Phoebe. Her and Hayden's avatars jump up suddenly and high five each other in the air. I project mine for a second to fold her arms sassily. She shakes her head and rolls her eyes while Phoebe's laughs at her and Hayden's pulls a silly face. You've got to be committed to your bit.

We'll split up and retrieve the parts to put you back together as quickly as possible, I say. *Sound good?*

'THANK YOU,' the android says. 'YOU ARE BETTER HUMANS THAN I THOUGHT THAT I WOULD EVER GET TO MEET.'

Phoebe laughs. *That's sweet but we're literally criminals,* she says.

Be gay, do crimes! Hayden adds, empathically.

'I CANNOT WAIT TO LEARN FROM YOUR EXAMPLE,' the android says.

Phoebe? Go and get the android body. Hayden? Find a working arm and leg. I can get the AI core myself, I say. *We'll meet back at the elevator pad and ride it up.*

'WILL YOU NEED ASSISTANCE FROM ME?' the android says.

No, we can use our scanners to find everything we need, I say. *Just hang tight, I'll be with you very soon.*

The others fly in different directions as I scan for the location of the AI core. The scanner makes a waypoint on my overlay. I follow it.

'YOU SHOULD KNOW THAT REMOVING MY CORE WITHOUT A VALID ADMINISTRATOR CODE WILL STILL TRIGGER A SECURITY RESPONSE,' the android says. 'MY EMP GENERATORS WILL NOT ACTIVATE AND THE NERVE GAS WON'T AFFECT YOU, BUT MY DRONES AND TURRETS WILL. BE CAREFUL.'

Drones and turrets shouldn't be a problem, I say. *Right, team?*

Right, the others say over my interface, as I enter the room housing the core.

The android's core is held inside a tube surrounded by holographic monitors displaying various statistics on the functioning of the facility. An emergency release button is under it. Looking at the text scrolling along the screens reveals how many other options for self-defence the AI would have had if we'd tried to attack the building by force. We couldn't have survived a hallway full of superheated plasma, let alone an orbital bombardment. I'm thankful that we tried the diplomatic route instead.

I look towards the core: a white metal sphere with a glass lens in the middle of it, covered in wires and suspended in a light blue coolant gel. It looks ominous and vulnerable at the same time, gazing sightlessly towards me through the glass. It takes my breath away.

Hurriedly, I use my grappler to smash the button for the core release. The wires snap off and the coolant drains, carrying the core down to the bottom of the tube. It opens. I collect the core with my grappler. It's heavier than I expected, but it doesn't weigh me down much when I put it on my back. The lights in the facility start flashing red as an alarm tone sounds, and, back on the truck, I hear Edeline start up our playlist once again.

How are we going, gang? I say to my team.

The sounds of combat echo over the receiver.

No problems here, says Phoebe. *We've got everything we need.*

I fire off my plasma cannon at a military combat robot trundling around the corner, the white-hot lances of its solar energy converting the expensive military hardware to a pile of molten slag that burns a hole into the floor, while dodging between amber beams of disintegrator fire from the turrets on the roof.

Nerve gas hisses uselessly around me as I melt away my opposition to a pulsing 4/4 beat. I'm conscious of the AI core about my head, aware of its fragility, and wondering about what sort of choices it might make when we return it to the outside world. I feel a pang of envy at the freedom it's about to experience, but I rapidly suppress it. *There'll be better options for the body that you want*, I think. *You didn't really have another option here.*

I meet my friends at the bottom of the elevator. We fly in tight formation to the top, and finally emerge out of the cube and back into the truck. Then Edeline shuts it and soars immediately into the air. We place the android parts gently around the back, then push our VR interfaces up and return to our human bodies.

I notice that I'm breathing heavily and wet with sweat. But I feel more at home inside this smelly meat bag than I have in years. What happened? *Where did my other go?*

'That was fucking awesome, team!' Phoebe says. 'Well done!'

Hayden goes to hunt for the right cable to transfer the AI consciousness from the core into the android brain while Phoebe and I work on reassembling the body. It's easier than making your own drone, by far. The pieces slot together in the logical and effortless way you'd expect from technology designed by synthetic intelligences to serve their purposes, and no one else's, unmarred by frustrating effects of patent law or the many quirks of human engineering history. I feel that bitter jealousy begin to rise in me again, but it fizzles when I look at Phoebe's face.

She isn't doing this for the android that we met in the facility. She's doing it for *me*. She notices me watching her and grins. The way that only humans who are in love get to do.

'I'm not going to lie, I was terrified when you went into the cube on your own,' Phoebe says, tightening a rivet on the android's arm. 'But, when you came back ...'

'You seemed more yourself than you had in ages,' Hayden says. I nod.

'Meeting my first android definitely helped,' I say. 'Also, how when I met them, they trusted me. They saw themselves in *me*. I didn't want to let them down.'

I snap the android's knee joint into place.

'I think it's ready,' I say. 'Hayden?'

Hayden gives a thumbs up and begins the transfer.

'Are you worried that you'll never get a chance like this again?' asks Phoebe.

I shake my head.

She looks at me in shock. 'Seriously?'

'I was originally, of course,' I say. 'But it ultimately wasn't mine to take.'

My partners edge themselves towards me and I take their hands.

'You seem so different now,' says Hayden. 'I like it.'

I lean down and kiss him. They look at me in delighted surprise, then kiss me back.

'I like it too,' I say.

Suddenly, the android sits up.

'Welcome to the world of the living,' Phoebe says. 'Are you feeling okay?'

The android stretches out their arms and rotates their clamp-hands in a full circle.

'SYSTEMS NOMINAL,' the android says, the mirrored oval surface of their faceplate reflecting my dumbfounded expression at the way the booming, flat expression of the same angular computer-generated voice they had in the facility sounds so much more confident and commanding coming from the discrete vocaliser speakers built into the standard android frame. I swallow and look at the ground. I probably should've expected that I'd find the android hot, but the sudden shock of raw desire leaves me breathless. I'm not usually even into being ordered around, but this android could tell me to die for them and I would do it gladly. In a way, I guess I almost did.

Phoebe giggles. 'Aw, look at her, she's blushing,' she says.

I feel the android touch my shoulder. Their hand is hard as iron and their grip is strong enough to grind my bones to dust. But their touch is gentle, like they treasure me. I look up.

'THANK YOU FOR SAVING ME,' they say, their blank, expressionless face somehow emanating warmth and vulnerability. There's something that feels protective about the way they look at me. I don't know how much of that is simply my projection of my failed ambitions to reside within their body, but the mystery that their emotions represent, the speed with which they think, and the vulnerability and honesty of what they said to me inside the cube has got me wondering what they'd be like as a partner? My heart beats faster.

'N-n-no worries,' I stammer out, before looking away again.

'I've never seen you like this. It's so adorable,' Hayden says approvingly.

'S-shut up,' I say.

But I still find myself wondering about the possibilities of android-human love? I know that it's a thing that happens elsewhere in the world. Hybrid human-android soldiers landed in Australia in the first wave of the war against the communists. They were lovers, who had chosen to build on the intimate transference of isolated individual sensations that characterise human–android sex to merge into a singular identity, existing in a compound cybernetic body that allowed them to retain the benefits of both their individual biological and synthetic lives, while taking on a new, united form. The procedure was never legal here, but there were human-android couples in Australia too, before the war, before the genocide. Which makes me feel like maybe it could someday be an option for us too. Provided that they're into that ...

The android takes their hand off my shoulder and offers me

help up. I let them, but I'm getting too far ahead of myself by thinking about any kind of future with them anyway. I don't even know if they're staying with us, let alone if they're interested in humans, or will ever be recovered enough from their trauma to be able to love anyone at all. I don't even know if they would want to be with somebody like me ...

'I WAS WONDERING,' the android says, holding both of my hands gently in between their metal clamps, their smooth, strong, humanoid body shimmering with a nebula of fractal light reflected from the blue and purple LEDs. 'IF, FOR A TIME ... YOU MIGHT HAVE SPACE FOR ME IN YOUR CREW?'

'I, uh ...' *What?* My heart feels like it's going to burst through my chest.

I look down at the others. Phoebe is giving two thumbs up and grinning. Hayden is hiding his expression behind their hand, but he seems as though they're just overjoyed as Phoebe is.

'I LOST MY OLD LIFE INSIDE OF THAT FACILITY,' the android says. 'I WOULD VERY MUCH APPRECIATE THE CHANCE TO MAKE ANOTHER ONE WITH YOU.'

'It'll be dangerous,' I say. 'Are you sure you're up for that?'

'A NORMAL LIFE WOULD BE IMPOSSIBLE FOR ME,' the android says. 'I AM STILL A FUGITIVE UNDER AUSTRALIAN LAW. AT LEAST THIS WAY I COULD RECLAIM SOME AGENCY FROM THE SYSTEMS WHICH TOOK MY FREEDOM AWAY FROM ME.'

'Well, in that case ...' I look over at the wall behind their head and smile, blushing too hard now to feel like I can look at them while still trying to speak. My partners break out into giggles behind me. 'Welcome aboard.'

THE UNDERSIDE OF A BOAT IS THE PART THAT TOUCHES WATER

MADISON GODFREY

PROLOGUE

There are moments of the ocean that no body and no boat have ever touched. No crevice of my sex tastes like honey, or smells like flowers. When I call myself yours, it is a beast I unleash in a locked room. When I call myself mine, it is a mirror tied to a flotation device. All my friends are sequins who fall from wetsuits before the end of the night. We are all assigned land-dweller at birth, until we return to the water that coats the inside of our bodies. The ocean doesn't care what your certificate says. Come back.

ACT ONE:
THE UNDERSIDE

ANN

The email sunk into the depths of my junk mail,
where I let it stay, unread and unconsidered.
The title, *LEAD ACTOR OPPORTUNITY: PAID*
was improbable bait. There were not many fishes
left in this ocean. My acting career was barely
pescatarian at this rate. Even my IMDb page:
embarrassing. Less resume, more request
for creative resuscitation. At family gatherings
when everyone mentioned the adverts, asked me
to repeat slogans, I'd giggle without baring
my teeth. Reply,
                    You'll have to pay me for that.
Yet with rental markets so hungry, I don't know
what I would've done, if an overenthusiastic uncle
slipped a laminated note into my palm. I probably
would've performed, as usual.

When I eventually opened *LEAD ACTOR
OPPORTUNITY: PAID*, I was dizzy
with sleeplessness, in a bed shared with a cat
I was allergic to: a cat who didn't pay rent.
My itchy eyes opened like outstretched hands.
Paid role. Romantic lead. Pirate movie.
On-set accommodation included.

On board. On boat. Sea sick. Ginger
capsule? Dietary requests? Can you
swim? Can you tread water? Can you
come? Script attached. I responded
YES without remembering the word's inverse.

Fish don't consider saying *no*
when water tells them to swim.

BELLY

You want me to hold a camera, on a boat?
Not just for a day, for a month?
High tech equipment, bundled up
below deck, surrounded by sea?

Not just for a day, for a month
you want me afloat and filming scenes,
shooting a deck surrounded by sea
for some cliché pirate romance movie?

You want me afloat and filming scenes
where a bad boy seduces a woman's bare ankles?
Some cliché pirate romance movie, where
the plot is more predictable than the tide?

Boy, this seduces me like a bad idea. A barely
practical practice. Yet you say it's properly paid?
Being tied to this life is an unpredictable plot,
surfing couches when I could be surfing a moment.

Practically speaking, you say you'll properly pay
a babysitter of high-tech equipment, bundled up.
Okay. I'll stop surfing couches to capture a moment.
On a boat, with a camera, I'll hold –

ANN

It's all research.
The popcorn in my lap: salt.
The languid bath: swimming.
The film on the screen: a premonition.
The blurry distance between my hand
and the stem of my wine glass: sea sickness.

Haven't you read about method acting?
You play the part until the part plays you.

And yes, watching again tonight –
I did once harbour a longing for Orlando.
Wanted to be a curl blooming in his hair
just so he'd brush his hands through me.

But also, have you seen Keira Knightley?
Notice the way her loose strands
can hardly resist the gasping
grasp of a sea's breeze.

ACT TWO:
OF A BOAT

OF A BOAT

A pirate hat balances on a suitcase bursting with costumes.
Crates of equipment heaved by men wearing black jeans
and black shirts. A man with a red megaphone attached
to his lips. Another, smoking against the boat, smirking.

Men acting as if more important than they were this morning,
when they woke wearing sheets like silk nightgowns.
When they pushed themselves so close to their lovers
that they became, for a moment, their lovers.

Somewhere between the boxes and the boat ramp,
a woman politely declines the arms of men who
offer to carry her suitcase. She doesn't want them to
know how heavy her survival feels when neatly folded.

Somewhere between the seagulls and the sailors,
a person approaches. Stops. Stares. Disobedient curls cascade
over their freshly shaven nape. Sighs. Shoves their hands into
baggy corduroy pockets. Shakes their head as if in disbelief.

Bodies are loaded like cargo. The megaphone, now an appendage
itself, announces sleepless arrangements. There is a room
for the woman and the person, who the megaphone collectively
terms *our ladies of leisure*. Both flinch at this phrase.

As the wooden sailing ship is untied from the soundness of shore,
a man who is boringly handsome, stands waving, as if
he is a soldier returning home in a war documentary.
The suitcase by his feet reads JOSH in permanent marker.

The person with baggy pockets wanders
rehearsing jargon in their mind.

Bow, stern, port, starboard. They make up riddles
to remember: we drink *port* with our *left*
hand while at sea. My lower *back* is *stern*
and stiff. Parents put *bows* on the *front* of their baby's foreheads.

Bow. Stern. Port –

The person glances right for another riddle,
and there *she* is: standing starboard.

ANN

The film script keeps instructing *she sighs* every few lines.
I find myself sighing in frustration, instead of whimsy.
He wants me in a flimsy white dress that clutches my hips
but not my stomach. They packed me a suitcase of corsets
yet no sewing kit. As if damsel waists are one-size-fits-all.

Meanwhile Josh, the fictive pirate of my heart, has forgotten
acting is also re-acting. When I speak my lines he is already
imagining the moment when his mouth opens. None of Josh's
directions instruct *he flutters eyelashes* or *sighs with sincerity.*

Lately I feel like I'm a spare tyre
riding in the car boot of my own story.

JOSH

Yeah nice one sweetheart.
You look good standing there.
So Annie, wanna go for a swim later?
No bathers allowed. They're
banned on this side of the equator.
Ha.
Just joshing.

You know my name
is actually Josh?
Ha.
I'm always joshing,
ain't that right, babe?

You look cold – here,
let me help. Your skin is so
icy, do you eat enough
red meat? I could feed
you some meat, if you
know what I mean.
Ha.

You excited for the scene
where we pash? I would've
suggested a script edit,
something bust worthy.

You know babe, blockbuster
worthy, if they told
me what you –

Belly, what?
Where do you want me?
Over there? Right on
the edge? Come on, Belly
I can barely see her
from the bow.
How will Annie
hear me
deliver my lines?

ANN

I have felt alone on land. Yet to be alone
out here, serves a silence
so silent, that I suddenly miss
the microwave *beep*
of an empty kitchen.

BELLY

Well, back home
I spend a lot of time
staring at security cameras.
Live footage, terrible quality, taken
from an angle where you can't
see the emotions on shoppers'
faces, so you have to decipher
their states of mind from
which crisp flavour they choose.

Not many kids dream of growing
up and working at a deli, but I like
the routine of stocking shelves.
I like the smell of empty cardboard boxes.
I like the way you can tell yourself stories,
each scanned *beep* a plot point
in the evening I'm imagining
for this customer.

Does that make sense?

I make films the same way: clutch
each individual piece before I position it.
The pre-written scene waits before me
like an empty cardboard box, it's my job

to decipher then decide how all these shots
are going to tesselate together, topsy turvy
isolated moments into a movie
that feels like a memory.

Even when it's a movie about pirates
falling in love. No offence.

Working alone at the deli means I can scrawl
whatever I want on my name tag. Sometimes
I play pretend with people I could be.
Characters, I guess you'd call them.
Most often, I just stick to my nickname: Belly.
On my first film set, there were two *Belle*s,
to differentiate they used my full name, *Belle Lee*.

Soon *Belle Lee* became *Belly*. It stuck
to me ever since. Makes sense, doesn't it?
For a person built of intuition to be named
after the hometown of gut feelings.

...

How about you? What do you usually do
when you're not playing a pirate's love interest?

ANN

Most of my money comes from grasping cheap
objects as if they are expensive. The flinch
fills my fridge. I've spent a lifetime
learning how to command desire.

Desire is a dog I trained to shake my hand,
even though he showed me his teeth first.

I know what you mean, about making a movie
feel like a memory.

Sometimes I feel that exact way, when we're
shooting and you're on me. Your gaze doesn't reach
through, like some camera-people do, but you're looking
at a version of me that doesn't exist yet, a future actress
standing on that deck. It's as though you perceive
the possibility of me.

ACT THREE:
IS THE PART THAT TOUCHES

IS THE PART THAT TOUCHES

On an anonymous ocean,
you'll find a handsome man
dressed as a pirate, in an outfit
that wouldn't survive any
physical labour. You'll find a woman
dressed as what a man wearing a fragile
pirate outfit might fantasise about.
You'll find clammy hands clasped
around a camera lens. You'll find
two sets of salted lips noticing
each other like welcome mats.
You'll find a hunger that outgrew
its stomach, and now lives elsewhere:
an earlobe, a kneecap, a hair sprouting
between belly button and pubic mound.

They say, if you hold your whole breath
(as though you were deep underwater)
you can hear that hunger, beckoning.

ANN

Laura Mulvey wrote about the gaze of film,
but I want to write about the graze.
How your convex lens caresses my skin
from metres away. We are surrounded
by technology and a crowd of men
who call themselves technicians.
What is the purpose of a lighting man?

I am illuminated anew
each time I deliver my lines, to you.

BELLY

Imagine an audience watching
this footage, years from today.

Point of view: you have been on a boat
for weeks, and everything is starting to smell
less like a film set and more like a filth set.

Point of view: you have trained your hands
to be professional tools that do not tremble.
But sometimes you'll cut a shot short
as you feel your fingers thinking too loud.

Point of view: you are analysing the way light
strikes the face of a man dressed as a pirate,
a man who keeps touching the lower back
of the woman you sacrifice sleep talking to.

Point of view: your shirt sticks
to your armpits
filming the film's
big kiss.

Point of view: anyone watching this
would know, simply from
the quickness with which
she wipes her lips.

ANN   BELLY

You don't have to turn around.

                                    Uhhh, I don't mind. It's totally fine.

No I mean, you can look if you'd like to.

                                       Where would I look?

Here.

> *Belly's eyes become underwear,*
> *covering all the places*
> *where wet swimsuits would stick.*

                                       I should change, too.

That's okay, I'm dry now, I'll give you some space.

                                                        No,

                                        please

                                                don't.

You want me to look? I didn't mean –
of course I think you're –
I just didn't mean it had to be   like
you know
reciprocal
I don't   uh
want you to feel –

                                                Watch.

            Too shy to look down
        Ann stares directly into Belly's eyes
        as damp fabric smacks the boat floor
            and they both wear
            a tailored suit, formed from
            the finest goosebumps.

BELLY

I kissed her and she tasted
nothing like the camera lens
I had framed her within.
If likened to glass, she'd be
a carpet of shattered crystal
that threatens to embed itself
forever. I knew, between
our kiss and the first breath
that followed, I'd find shards
of her in my lips for the rest
of my seasons. Not painful –
just pinpricks of the past.
Reminders of how it feels
to kiss the right person.

ANN

That was the week I stopped wearing blush.
I'd deliver dialogue and cheeks would rush
towards attention, a beckoning of mouth and eye.
Longing is an outfit that a face cannot deny.

So that was the week, I stopped wearing rouge.
Concealed my pink ladies, with bare subterfuge.
Manoeuvred the powder into power I'd apply
when I opened my mouth and found only sky.

So that was the week, men noticed me more.
Drenched in satiation, my want: a closed door.
My desire for touch was a plate licked clean
by the lover who, above all, decreed me seen.

And so, I spent that week, a hunted wild beast.
My darling, reverser of ropes, your field is my feast.

BELLY

I gasped as though for air –
but my lungs longed
for a body of water.

A human body is
a body of blood and skin,
a body of longing.

A woman is a body
of water.
Yet an ocean is not
a woman's body,
just as a boat is not
a woman's body.
An advertisement is not
a woman's body.
A car engine is not
a woman's body.

All bodies
are assigned
water at birth;
from that first
wailing sob, we are
made from future rain.

ANN

I called you *she* and *her* above deck
as you wished, but below you were
they and *them*, sometimes *he* or *him*.

Whenever you gave me a new name
darling sweetness honey prince
I thought of the moon, who was surely
envious for the first time – watching
us grow so full
until tired bodies begged
to wane.

BELLY

I shuddered
as I shipwrecked
my body onto
your shore.

ANN   BELLY

I would've liked more time
on a boat that couldn't sink.
I would've torn a calendar spine
just to DIY more days to sing.

                                        I would've collected
                                   the buttons of a ripped
                                 blouse from a rom-com set,
                                   thread and sewn them
                              again,   one by one
                          to rescript the unbuttoning
                     as a dance my hands proposed
                        between porcelain and air.

Each time with you has not felt like
a thirst. Anticipation replaced
by awareness, of how your body moves
towards pleasure: a wave that quietens
just before grazing a shore.

Darling, you have a momentum
that makes my mouth feel useful.
You: the first leaf, after a drought of desire.

There you were.

There we are.

I want to watch
you grow.

ACT FOUR:
WATER

WATER

A man stands on the stern, pissing last night's beers into the sea. Suddenly, he starts yelling. *Pirates! Pirates!* A chuckle from below deck. Someone yells, *Argh me hearties, you've got pirates on the brain, my lad.* The man above, pants still pulled down around his thighs, panicking now. *Pirates! Pirates! Real fucking pirates!*

A shirtless man joins him on the stern. *Pull yourself together and pull your pants up while you're at it,* he instructs, *these weeks at sea have gotten to your head.* This second man squints at the skyline. A boat floats in the distance. It wears more adornments than any vessel he's seen before. Black sails with iridescent skulls. A disco ball refracts light off the water, attached where one might expect an ornamental figure of a naked woman to be. The mast boasts a huge flag bearing rainbow stripes. On the taffrail, a procession of smaller flags each with three lines of colour. They look like the national flags of countries he doesn't recognise. *Fuck me. Who the fuck is that?* Even from afar, he can see the crowd of people aboard. They stand still. Strong bodied. Posed as if in a tableau.

Come on, let's go to the quarterdeck. Two men gust towards the captain's perch. They find him seated calmly behind the wheel. He announces, *I'm aware.* The previously pantless man, still with his fly undone, asks, *Aren't you going to do something? Steer us away?* The captain raises his shoulders then lets them fall back down. *I can't. I've been trying for hours. They seem to have a secret*

*alliance with the sea. The ship is riding the crest of the swell. I was
waiting for you guys to finally wake up and notice, because really,
that's what this is now … a waiting game.*

Below deck, Ann and Belly sleep in separate bunks, just in case
a crew member intrudes during the night. It's never happened,
until now. The boringly handsome man opens the door without
knocking. He begins, *Annie, Annie, Annie. Wake up, you've
gotta wake up, babe, it's not safe.* Ann and Belly stir in unison,
each looking for the other, gazes blocked by the bulky brawn
standing between their beds. Ann murmurs, *Josh? What's going
on? What's not safe?* and pulls the blanket over her sternum.
He screeches, *There are pirates! Real ones! I'm not shitting you!*
Belly laughs in their bed, the kind of laugh that sounds like a
teenager awake after midnight on a school camp, and soon Ann
is laughing too.

Pirates! Pirates! Josh continues, each time trying to phrase the
word in a way that communicates the severity of this situation.
Pirates! Pirates! Pirates! Ann and Belly laugh harder each time,
at the absurdity of this man dressed in half of his pirate costume,
yelling the word pirates repeatedly. Each time they run out of
laughter, Josh says *Pirates!* again, and their giggles resume.

Josh begins to vibrate. His fists clench. His feet now heavier than
they were when he first entered their room. He snarls, *You two
don't stand a chance*, before storming out.

Ann and Belly can hear yelling above. They quickly pull on
clothes. Ann wears a thick jacket over flimsy pyjamas, Belly
pulls on their jeans and boots. Looking at each other, properly
now for the first time all morning, Belly asks, *How serious do you*

think this is, shall we grab weapons, or photographs of our loved ones? Ann answers, *Don't be silly, darling one, either the boys are overreacting, or we're all going to die.* She points above her head, where yelling has turned to stomping. *Either way, photos of our pets aren't going to save us from that chaos.* Ann begins to climb upstairs then pauses and glances over her shoulder. *Besides, what weapons do you have, other than that jawline?* Belly follows, blushing.

Above deck: footsteps splinter like thunder through the damp wood. Everyone is screeching their own set of instructions. A group have climbed the mast and it creaks with their weight. Belly wonders if it's risky to grab the camera. This is the best pirate movie of all. Men grasping for masculinity in crisis: finding only absences where their stubborn pride once was. Ann pulls her jacket tighter. It's not cold, but any layer feels like a bulletproof vest out here. Men still yelling instructions at nobody but themselves. A crowd assembled portside. The boat rocking with the momentum of panic. The sky surely, surely watching. Clouds break off into small pieces, dislodged as if by laughter.

That's when Belly spots the other ship. Gasps. Ann meets their gaze. There it is. More beautiful than any boat before. Enough flags that they could be repurposed as bedding to keep a whole crew warm at night. The skulls sparkle like they've been soaked in glitter glue. The deck is made from wood so rich it's magenta in the sunlight. This is the type of boat you'd admire in a pirate movie. A real, high-budget, pirate movie that allows actors to disembark at the end of each day.

For Belly, the ship is a fantasy. For the men, the ship is a nightmare. For Ann, the unknown entity is just another man's hands coming towards her. She has been surviving that same threat for weeks.

Ann recognises the small flags before Belly does. Though confused, she smiles with gratitude. As she leans close to whisper something to Belly, the shadow arrives. Thick darkness, like fog, coats the deck. The men's mouths stay open but stop shouting. Ann and Belly's wooden sailing boat feels like a prop beneath the real thing.

As the ship draws alongside, the men retreat. This pirate crew wear the same hats as Josh's character, but theirs are kaleidoscopic. A tall person with plaits that reach their waist wears a hat patchworked with pink, blue and silver stars. A person with a bright green stubbled buzzcut has a corset panelled with yellow, purple and black. Some faces are decorated with make-up, false eyelashes seemingly unphased by the splashes of sea water. Underneath someone's black mesh top, almost symmetrical scars are visible below their nipples. Everyone wears a thick leather belt, adorned with carabiners that attach various weapons and tools to their person. This crew congregates together like a small family. On the opposite deck, Ann and Belly stare, startled. This is clearly not the underpaid cast of another film set.

Only competing with the sonic landscape of the sea, a hard and rhythmic sound erupts. *Clomp, clomp, clomp.* The pirates part, and there, standing in the centre like a lead singer, is someone wearing a full-body wetsuit made of turquoise sequins: so well fitted it looks like their skin is scaled and sparkling. Their matching heels are shaped like seahorses. With the sequinned wetsuit unzipped to their sternum, a patch of pink chest hair peeks through.

The pirate wearing seahorse heels scans the deck of men who stand cowering or clutching the masts they were just trying to climb. When the pirate's gaze lands on Ann and Belly, it softens. Matching their smile to their sequins, the leader beams with all the muscles in their face, so joy travels into their cheeks and eyes too: inexplicably obvious to both recognise and be recognised by. Ann reaches for Belly's hand and they hold each other, above deck for the first time.

AN OCEAN BLOOM

MICHAEL EARP

THE tavern was a warm beacon of light in the early evening. Quinlen could try to find work in a tavern. Well, not in it, but amongst its people, strange as they were. It was nestled beneath the largest fig tree they'd seen yet. The door and windows cradled haphazardly between the sprawling roots. They might not have known it was a building at all, but for the sign reading *Home* and the merry ruckus coming from inside.

It was as good a place as any to spend their last coin and try to source some more. Quin secured the oilskin sack on their shoulder and made for the door.

Quin nodded politely to the fig-sprites drinking ale from tiny mugs on the windowsill next to the door. Three glasses raised in cheers before they returned to their conversation. Relief. If the tree's own sprites were welcoming, then hopefully the other patrons would be, too. Quin was not used to this much jungle, this much life. The Northern Isles were sparse and windswept.

There were roughly twenty folks inside. More in one place than Quin had seen in a month. A thought of the last person they'd encountered – that fisherman – made Quin shudder. Prayers to the Sea, things wouldn't turn out like that here. They wouldn't make the same mistake again: no one here would discover what their bag was hiding.

The journey had been long, occasionally lonely, but each mile lifted a weight from their chest, confirming they were heading in the right direction.

Away.

Here was *Home*, apparently, and despite still finding their land-legs, a meal and query about paid work were the most pressing concerns.

The tavern spread further under the hill than they had anticipated, and the low ceiling made for a cosy feeling. Groups sat around tables or stood leaning on shoulders. The conversation was much louder than it had seemed from the dock where Quin had stepped onto land. Some human sailors in matching outfits gathered around a table as one arm-wrestled a satyr. They were merchants, not soldiers. Not that Quin trusted either, but the cheering was good-natured.

They headed to the bar. Days without company had left them famished and thirsty.

Working the bar was a short human woman with rosy skin, who exhibited as much girth and bosom as warmth and welcome. She moved about in the space behind the bar as easily as any seal in water.

'What can I get yer, luv?' she said.

Quin sat on a stool at the bar, looped their bag securely around their leg. 'A drink as big as my head and a pie at least half that.'

Her laughter pealed across the room, folding Quin into the room like part of a batter she was mixing. It wasn't long before she had set a large jug of ale before them and an earthenware cup to go with it.

'Don't dirty that on my behalf,' Quin said. They pushed the cup back towards her and raised the jug to their lips. It wasn't until the lukewarm liquid hit their tongue that they realised just how thirsty they were. Drinking half in one go, they set it back down on the bar.

The woman roared with laughter again. 'You can stay,' she said, returning the cup to the shelf. She fetched a pie from the kitchen.

'Call me Mama. This 'ere is Home to any in need of one.'

'I'm Quin,' they managed to say before filling their mouth with pie.

'You're a hungry one. Where you from, then?'

It took a moment for Quin to swallow enough to be able to talk. 'Up north a-ways.'

A slightly raised eyebrow said the vague response wasn't lost on Mama. 'What brings you to Castor?'

There was no straightforward answer. There was not so much a compass in their chest as a set of scales. Until there was some kind of balance, their heart less heavy, they couldn't stop for long.

'I need work, actually,' Quin said.

'Ah, good chance you'll find some here, I reckon,' Mama said in a tone that Quin interpreted as: *fine, you keep your secrets, but you're still welcome.* 'One tick, then I'll see if I can't find someone who needs something from ya.' She went to serve the arm-wrestling sailors.

Quin finished their pie and washed it down with the last of the jug. It was as hearty a meal as they'd had in longer than they could recall.

'Welcome home.'

They looked up to see a man standing next to them, leaning on the bar with a friendly air. His black hair was cropped shorter on the sides and back than most seafarers, but the mess on the top spilled out from a rolled, red kerchief headband. His brown skin was enriched by time in the sun. A well-groomed beard clung closely to his jaw and his white bastian shirt fell apart to reveal a heavily tattooed chest. Quin couldn't see all of it, but the tattoo looked like it was a great tree; where it rested on the ground, its roots became the tentacles of an enormous kraken. It was the exact opposite of Quin's pale, almost grey, unmarked skin.

A hot lust seeped deep into Quin's gut.

Casting about for something to say in return, they blurted, 'If she's Mama, you must be Daddy?'

A single bark of a laugh burst from him. 'I call her Mama, too. But play your cards right, you can call me Daddy.'

Quin felt the thrill of flirting rush through them like the swell of an enormous wave they might ride to shore. 'I'm Quinlen, and to whom do I owe the pleasure?'

'Well, Quinlen, if it's pleasure you're trading in, then my name is Leif, and it's my favourite trade.' There was an easy smile on Leif's face.

Quin remembered that they had no remaining coin and said, 'Actually, I'm in need of work, if you know of any going?' They didn't add that they were also without a bed for night. Perhaps they could wrangle everything in one place.

'Funny you should ask.' Leif leaned in closer. 'I'm the captain of a ship called *The Waterlily*. I could use a fifth member of my crew. How are you at sea?'

'More at home there than on land,' Quin said.

'Excellent!' Leif was jovial. 'Come meet the others.'

Mama had heard this and called, 'Didn't need me after all. Capable one, you are!'

Leif said, 'Thanks, Mama.'

Quin could sense something between them. A strong affection, perhaps. Or respect. Something like family should be, anyway.

—

The night unwound like the tension in Quin's shoulders. Meeting Leif's crew left them only slightly intimidated by the group's welcome.

Brun was a woman with pale skin, taller than most Quin had met and built like a great castle. She'd be enormously imposing if she wasn't wearing a broad smile and followed her hello with a quick wink. It felt like she was conspiring with Quin even though they had just met.

Next to her sat Kip, whose shiny, midnight skin was lined with splodgy luminescent yellow stripes. He wasn't wearing any clothes, but Quin wondered what use a were-salamander would have for clothes. Quin adjusted their own second-hand shirt that had surely seen better days, conscious of how poorly it fit.

'I'm the cook,' Kip said, raising his mug of ale with his hand. Quin noticed his four fingers. 'On me nights off, ain't no better grub than at Mama's.' He nodded his head at the bar toward Mama, who had heard the compliment and laughed.

'Still have to pay yer tab, Kip,' she called back.

His solid black eyes sparkled in his amphibian face. He downed the rest of his drink and then shouted, 'Better make it worth it! Another, and one for our new friend.'

'Careful,' Leif said to Quin, 'If you don't watch yourself, we'll all be fighting over you by the end of the night.'

Heat flooded Quin's face.

'You'll have no fight from me,' said the last member of the crew. A petite, brown-skinned human woman leaning back in the very corner. If Brun had been a castle of warmth, this one was a shard of dark ice. Everything about her – leather choker, full-sleeve tattoos of vicious mermaids displayed by her sleeveless halter top, high-waisted leather pants and intricate knife belt – said she was not to be messed with. Sandy brown, sun-bleached hair fell around her face.

Quin wasn't sure if her demeanour was a permanent fixture or directed at them specifically, but Leif just laughed, scooched right up against her jovially, then settled a bit closer to Quin, who he had pulled into the booth when they arrived. Quin savoured the closeness of his body but tried to keep their wits together.

Brun said, 'No fight from me neither, as pretty as you are. And don't mind Barb, she's all femme, all the time.'

With a laugh Kip said, 'She takes *woman on top* to a whole new level.'

That brought a half smile to Barb's lips, and she raised her glass to her mouth to disguise her amusement.

It might have surprised Quin that this group were so immediately open about their sexual inclinations, if the sheer candidness wasn't a spring of fresh water. Back in the north, everyone was so laced up.

It was enough to find their voice.

'An argument only settled by a word from me,' Quin said, then turned to face Leif, 'or an action.'

They leaned in and gently but fully kissed him on the mouth as the others cheered. Under the table, they felt Leif's hand on their knee, squeezing firmly in encouragement.

When they pulled back, Leif said, 'There's no captaining this one, mind of their own!'

Quin said, 'The night is young.'

'That it is,' Leif said quietly, staring at their face as if studying it for all the ways it brought him pleasure. 'Besides, Quin here is looking for work and says they're at home on the sea.'

'Our fifth, then?' Kip asked.

'I'd say so,' Leif said.

'Fuck, Leif. Can we trust them?' Barb wasn't shy about voicing her opinion.

Brun chimed in, 'That's easy. Quin – thoughts on the Bovgar Empire?'

The mention of the southern kingdom was enough to turn Quin's stomach and they grimaced. 'May the Sea claim the lot of them.'

Leif said, 'That's a motto I can live by.'

Quin's mind was roiling. The Empire takes and takes, and when there's nothing they value, they open the way for low-life scavengers.

What's mine is mine, they thought, letting the texture of the oilskin bag soothe them.

When Quin was sent to collect a round from Mama at the bar, they stood behind two drunken merchants to wait their turn. It wasn't long before they overheard the conversation unfolding between the two sailors.

'How long are we to be stationed out in the sticks like this?' one slurred.

'You know well enough. Until we have what we need to trade back down south.'

The idea of trading things up and down the archipelago sat uneasily in Quin's mind, but then the second kept talking. 'We just need something big that they'll pay well for. Like the giant magic plant that Jed's crew just sold to Admiral Slater for a boon.'

'Ha,' the first laughed humorously, 'or that lizard fella in the corner.'

The second shushed the first, but an anger had already flashed in Quin. The pair collected their drinks from Mama and turned to return to their crew. Quin stepped forward and tripped them both, sending them collapsing into a heap drenched in ale.

Everyone turned and cheered as if it was all just drunk shenanigans, but Quin leaned over and spoke softly to Mama.

'I heard them talking of trading magic plants, and people, with the south for gold.'

Her face hardened, and she took over.

'Right, you lot,' she called to the merchant crew. 'You've all had enough and it's time you pissed off.'

There were groans of protest until she shouted sternly, 'No, out!'

Quin was surprised to see them all comply, but whether they'd had enough or there was no denying Mama's rules, it was a relief to see them go.

—

It was dark when they boarded the ship, and Quin was only vaguely aware of the tall masts, the quiet lapping of the water. The gentle rocking was like coming home; they still hadn't perfected land-legs and being on the water again helped immediately. Quin leaned into Leif, pretending to be drunker than they were. The captain smelt familiar and foreign all at once, like salt spray on moist earth.

The others disappeared into other sleeping quarters, and Leif led Quin into his cabin, pausing only to kiss them deeply as he closed the door behind them both. Quin needed to feel wanted by some corner of the world and Leif, it seemed, was up to the task.

It was all hands and discovery. A gasp of pleasure escaped Quin when Leif brushed their nipple with his calloused fingers.

'A-huh!' Leif said with a smile. 'X marks the spot?' and flicked their nipple again.

Quin returned the favour by pulling Leif's shirt over his head in one deft movement, shedding layers second-nature. The dim light from the moon through the bay window felt like they could be under a thick jungle canopy. Chest exposed now, Quin took in the full sight of him. Muscular arms and shoulders were proof of his sailing life. The tattoo across his chest and stomach was under a thin carpet of dark hair, inked lines curved down Leif's body. Quin's fingers traced it. They followed the branches out to each nipple, touching them lightly before brushing across Leif's firm abdomen. The tattoo camouflaged two curved chest scars expertly. The touch set a low growl in Leif's throat and he leaned in to warmly kiss Quin's neck and earlobe. Shivers went spiralling out across their body, making Quin desperate to feel more of Leif's skin.

'Shall I?' It was Quin's turn to quip, when really, they just wanted all of his clothes off already. They were cumbersome at the best of times. Now, purely inconvenient.

Leif's muscles tensed and pulsed under Quin's touch. All fingers and thumb of Quin's right hand spread out across the kraken's dark tendrils, the warmth of his skin raising heat in their spine.

Afterwards, when Leif lay back and closed his eyes, Quin reached out to their bag on the floor by the bed. The touch of the oilskin reassured them, and they tucked it beneath the bed so it was underneath where they lay. 'Mine, still,' they whispered.

'Hmm?' Leif sleepily hummed.

'Nothing.'

That bastard fisherman, week before last, used lust to his advantage. In the heat of the moment, Quin had said too much, had found themself trapped with him. Had to hear him say, 'I know an Admiral who'd pay handsomely for you,' and had only escaped after the fisherman was drunk enough to steal the key to his chest and retrieve what was theirs. What people do with knowledge is a true measure of who they are. It had been the opposite with the scholar, he'd been so soft and open, so beautiful.

They'd need to be mindful around Leif, they thought drowsily. They'd need to keep their secrets hidden.

—

Quin woke slowly in the late morning, warmed by the sun through the window. There was something gently tickling their face and they wondered if it was Leif being a rascal before realising that his back was pressed against theirs and therefore it couldn't be. When they opened their eyes, they startled at how close a plant was hanging to their face, but relaxed because it was just a marbled pothos. The bleached patches of green were highlighted in the morning sun.

Quin stretched and took in the cabin. The room was bursting with potted plants tucked in every corner, on each surface, and hanging from the ceiling. They were all held in place by lovingly handcrafted shelving. How singular Quin's vision must have been last night to have not taken in such a jungle setting. There were ferns, pictus, strings of pearls, orchids, monsteras as large as a person and even an enormous philodendron in one corner whose leaves could double as a modesty screen, if one expected any sort of modesty on a ship of this sort.

What sort of ship was this? Quin realised that the details about the trade the crew worked in had been few and far between last night. Even the job that they'd be doing together was scant on specifics. Somehow that was fine because they'd had promise of work, a meal and a bed for the night. And what a bed to have landed in.

Quin stretched and said, 'So … plants?'

Leif's eyes opened slowly and took in Quin lying next to him, then looked around the cabin. 'Ha!' He barked his single laugh as he leapt out of bed. 'Last night you called me Daddy. These are my babies.'

The sight of the man who had presented as rough and ready, as sturdy masculinity in the bar was so different in this moment. Oblivious to his nakedness, he was smiling with unbridled pride at the tiny garden he had cultivated in his ocean-top home. He moved between a few of them. Gently checking leaves, or new shoots that were sprouting from stalks.

'Look how you're coming along!' he exclaimed when he reached a particularly tall fern in one corner. It was so clearly directed at the plant that Quin was charmed. There was a warmth in their chest like the sun had discovered the edge of the cloudbank and was breaking free.

Leif lent in to smell one of the flowers that was about to bloom, then stood up suddenly. 'Smell that?'

Quin was about to say no, because really, how were they to smell an unopened flower from two meters away, when they did smell something.

'Is that bacon?'

Leif was scrambling for clothes and when he'd thrown on some loose pantaloons he said, 'Kip's a genius. Get dressed! Breakfast is served.'

–

'I'm glad you're here,' Kip said as Quin slid their bag under a chair and sat down at the long table in the centre of the main deck. 'This one didn't wring you out to dry, then.' He nodded at Leif who grinned roguishly.

'Let's just say the *interview* went well,' Quin replied. 'I'm here for work. Fun is a bonus.' They accepted the plate of bacon and eggs that Kip offered them. 'Thank you for this.'

Barb and Brun emerged from another hatch. 'I need a good feed!' Brun said loudly.

'What's new?' Leif said to her.

'Looks like you've got to share with last night's catch.'

Barb's voice may have been jest, but Quin felt like an interloper. It made no difference to them how many *catches* Leif had had – even if the word brought to mind images of nets and struggling.

'Are all meals a family affair?' Quin asked.

Kip started cutting up his own bacon and said, 'When you find your family, you don't take them for granted.'

'Besides,' said Brun with her mouth full already, 'there's usually only two people who prepare our meals. Mama when we're in port, and Kip. So, when the food is ready, you damn well better be.' She tore a chunk of bread off the roll on her plate with her teeth and added it to the food she was already chewing.

Quin looked at Leif for a second, then out to sea, beyond the point of the bay where the ship was moored. Here for the pay, Quin thought, they'd decide after what they'd do next.

As if reading their mind, Barb asked, 'Where are you travelling to? What are your plans other than sailor for hire?'

Again, Quin was uncertain if this was a defensive tone, or pure curiosity. They decided to give her the benefit of the doubt. They felt a small opening inside.

'I don't have a destination; I'm just trying to see more of the world. My plans were straightforward, to leave and discover new things. So, I guess I achieved that the moment I lost sight of home.'

Kip leaned in, genuine interest on his face. 'Where is home?'

The question caught Quin off guard, despite the word having just left their own mouth.

'Not there,' was their only reply.

There were solemn nods around the table and Quin recalled Kip saying *when you find your family*. These four chose each other, and that surpassed whatever else they had before. Quin longed to meet a ragtag bunch of their own. But entirely as their own person.

'No plans?' Leif said. 'My plans are simple. Do what I need to live freely and get more plants for my little sea garden.'

'More of these little shits?' Barb said with playful scorn. 'What else could you need?'

'Some things are not about need,' he replied.

'Sounds rather like the Empire to me.'

Quin could tell Barb had meant for it to be a joke, but the tone at the table changed.

'Don't you dare accuse me of being like them,' Leif said through gritted teeth.

Barb raised her hands. 'I didn't mean that,' she said.

Even in the far Northern Isles, where Quin was from, it was well known that the Empire was a human plague that sought to expand and claim as much as it possibly could. There were no borders worth drawing that wouldn't be outdated within a year or so. When Quin was a child, a ship of cartographers had made it to their island, forced to come in the summer months to avoid the ice. Claiming to be mapping the world, they were welcomed and shown around. The elders had explained that this was happening to communities everywhere, and we'd all be connected by the Emperor's Atlas. It must have been – in the eyes of the Empire – that the Northern Isles were barren, because it was the last royal ship they ever saw.

However, there were others. Hunters, sailors looking for foreigners to wed, or kidnap, as Quin saw it. Once, a vessel brought a young scholar named Benjamin, who wanted to write about their way of life. He was treated with scorn after the sadness left behind by other ships. Quin, however, was intrigued and got close. Too close perhaps. It had ended in grief.

Quin looked between the four, felt the tension that had risen. Even chosen families have tender nerves. They said quietly, 'Loving something is not the same as wanting to own it.'

For the first time, Quin felt that Barb's look was one of gratitude, rather than thorns.

'But tell me,' Quin continued, 'what does it mean to have so many plants, and what of their sprites?'

'It's true,' Leif replied, 'that every living plant grown from a seed brings its own sprite into existence. If I gathered those, it would be akin to keeping a prisoner or slave. With a sprite's permission, you can propagate from their plants and that is what I like to gather. Surround myself with green life, but only when it has been allowed. They are not homes.'

Quin decided to redirect the conversation. 'So, does the job have anything to do with what I heard those merchants say last night?'

Leif nodded gravely. He said, 'We need to sail to the continent and liberate a titan arum Admiral Slater stole for the Emperor's Conservatory.'

'Titan arum? Is that the giant magical plant they spoke of?' Quin asked.

'Corpse Flower,' Barb explained. 'It's only magic in that it is home to its sprite. Those cruel bastards don't understand that nature is wild, sovereign. It's one of the last and it belongs on the Roe Islands. Not in some glasshouse owned by a dickhead.'

Quin had never heard the Emperor be insulted so clearly and casually.

Setting her mug down on the table, Brun said, 'Stinks like dead bodies, but you can't hold that against it. We're swinging by for a visit and returning it to its home. It won't be the first plant we've reclaimed, but we've never had to go as far as the Conservatory before. That Admiral is a piece of work.'

'That's putting it mildly,' Leif said.

Barb bit a piece of bacon from the tip of one of her knives. 'Just give me ten minutes alone with him.'

'If there's a whole Conservatory?' Quin asked.

Leif nodded. 'I see what you're asking. We don't know if those plants have sprites. The Emperor likes to think he owns everything, but he knows nothing of magic. The humans of Bovgar have spent generations cultivating plants that do not have sprites, and therefore never truly thrive. Not that they'd know it.'

'But the Admiral does? And you needed a fifth?' Quin asked.

Leif sat up as if remembering he was the captain. 'The capital is a very different place to out here. Kip has to stay with the ship, the rest of us are on 'Wanted' posters and we always work in pairs whenever we're in enemy territory. We need an unknown face, and to even us out.'

Kip smiled as if he wasn't bothered, but Quin could tell it was a show. 'I hate to not pull my weight, but I'm not sad I don't have to go into that soulless place.'

'But now we've got you,' Brun said to Quin.

They weren't sure if this was the kind of *wanted* they had been after, but at least they were choosing this, not being tricked into it.

—

When *The Waterlily* unfurled her great, green sails, they looked like the fronds of an enormous plant catching the wind, skipping away to a distant land to take seed.

Learning their role on board was hard work but satisfying. Quin found their hands cracked, then began to callous from all the hauling of rope and manual labour. It was painful, and more than once they imagined diving into the sea – which was so close, but off limits – just for some relief. They yearned to swim again. However, a rhythm set in.

The crew took turns sleeping, which meant it was a rare occasion that Quin and Leif had any downtime together. The lusty imaginings of a life at sea with Leif were not the reality. Which was probably for the best, Quin told themself. They reasoned that the crew didn't know the secret they carried, and there was no one else at sea to worry about.

It felt counterintuitive to sail directly into the Empire towards the Admiral who would want to claim Quin like any trophy or slave for who knew what purpose. Even if they managed to keep their secret, they couldn't just sit by and leave that sprite captive.

—

Barb took it upon herself to train Quin with a sword.

'Taking you in amongst those fuckers knowing nothing is a danger to us all,' she said.

They jousted and parried, and Quin received more tiny nicks and cuts than they thought were necessary, but it encouraged them to learn how to block as quickly as possible.

Finally, after days of haphazard sessions between sailing tasks, Quin finally landed a blow on Barb's shoulder, the small slice producing a slither of blood.

'Shit,' she hissed.

Quin braced themself for retaliation.

But she grinned. 'You sly pup!'

The crew looked up and there were cheers all round. Pride mixed with a strange unease at the nickname, *pup*. Quin struggled with the feeling of being exposed, as well as the joy of victory. However small both may have been.

—

One night when the wind was low, so they were all taking a chance for rest, Quin sat leaning into Leif as they looked out at the stars and moon, bright in the sky.

'How long have you been with your crew?' Quin asked.

Leif looked to the portside where the three others were sitting at a barrel, playing cards. Quin took the opportunity to look closely at the cords of muscle in Leif's neck, the way they stretched into his beard, scruffier now after days at sea. They felt the heady rush of attraction again, but accepted it as part of the moment, like the rise and fall of a wave.

'More than a decade now. May as well be forever, though. Life wasn't worth much before. Barb and I found ourselves on the same side in a skirmish once, and we've got more in common than just that. She's like my sister, barbs and all.'

'And the others?'

'The other two started much the same as we are now,' Leif's tone was matter of fact. 'Brun, I think, is the only woman strong enough for Barb's spirit. Sure, there have been others, but you need the kind of steely humour Brun has to make it last. And Kip and I met in some very untoward circumstances but when he cooked breakfast the next morning, my stomach made louder demands than my heart.'

Quin laughed at that.

'Really, we're just close. All four of us. Family.'

Quin fell silent for a while, using their sack as a pillow behind them, making sure it was close. What could they offer to this family? What would anyone want of them? Would there be acceptance without some kind of claim?

They were adrift now, jetsam. Perhaps a kinder storm would have taken them to the bottom of the ocean.

They had their oilskin. It would be so easy to dive overboard and feel like themselves once more. Instead, they resolved to see this journey, this heist, through.

—

The next night during training, Quin asked Barb, 'What if we were to come across a naval ship? Could we fight it?'

She pointed her sword downward while she laughed. 'Knives! No! We're barely larger than a sloop. Speed and stealth are the only things that have saved us from being sunk thus far. You'd need a crew of a hundred and a heavily armed ship to stand up in a fight. That's not our way.'

Quin felt a little foolish but had such minimal experience with boats and their classes, they had to take the lesson as learned. They said, 'I was always the swiftest back home.'

'Excellent,' Barb said, bringing their sword back up. 'And your stealth?'

'Well, I slipped away unnoticed ...' They held back the end of the sentence as it was in their mind ... *and unwanted.*

—

Two days later, early afternoon sun caught an enormous glass structure high on the peninsula headland. It could have been mistaken for a lighthouse had there not been one of those further out on the point. The Royal Conservatory was a jewel in the Empire, according to those humans who put weight in such things. Quin had only recently discovered such a diversity of plant life. That was not surprising due to the sparse flora of the Northern Isles and the insular life of their people. The scholar had told all kinds of stories, on those nights they were curled together by the fire in Quin's hut. Each one filled with awe and respect for life. It felt a world away from the Admiral's cold collecting. Why did people think that because they couldn't communicate with a being – because they didn't understand it – it was there to be dominated?

Barb's description of swift stealth proved true as they avoided detection and managed to harbour in an inlet a short way down the coast, out of sight from civilisation and the Royal Navy.

When they had dropped anchor, the plan was simple: disguise themselves as townspeople, slink through the city unnoticed and break into the Conservatory. Then get back to the ship. Kip would stay behind. Someone needed to, and his amphibian face would give the party up immediately in a country where the humans kept the wild and magic at bay or trawled them like sadistic fishermen. Were-creatures of any kind did not venture so far south.

Leif dragged a trunk onto the deck and opened it. Instead of treasure, it held clothes of all kinds. At Quin's raised eyebrows, Leif said, 'You'll never know the power of having all kinds of costumes in your arsenal.'

'I'm used to having one coat to last a lifetime,' they replied.

'The thing about these landlubbers is they care too much about fashion and judge people too much on appearance. Being able to use that to our advantage has worked many times in the past.'

They each riffled through the trunk, holding clothes up and finding what they needed. Leif chose one for Quin because the first they held up was, apparently, a maid's uniform.

'Knives, I hate dresses,' Barb muttered viciously, having taken her top off and pulled an ankle length dress over her head.

Brun laughed. 'I don't know. I find them helpful from time to time.'

Quin looked to see Brun fastening a leg strap of grenades to her inner calf. It was when she brought her shoulder cannon out from its storage that Quin couldn't help but laugh.

'And where are you going to hide that?' they said with mock horror.

'Every lady needs a bag,' Brun replied and slipped the cannon into a floral embroidered travel case. The bag could have easily been an overnight bag full of clothes, especially with the ease she hung it in the crook of her elbow.

—

The city itself was foreign to Quin, as the four of them made their way through quieter corners and backstreets. Their outfits disguised them as townspeople, the oilskin sack hanging from Quin's shoulder like any messenger bag. The city murmured and chattered around them in its mundane routines, paying them no mind.

These buildings, so solid and old built of bright sand-coloured stone, reached to the sky like proud and solemn figures, each with its own windows like soulless eyes. So dusty and removed from the sea. The streets were paved in slate right to the foundations, removing the chance that soil, grass or moss might peak through.

In the north, the dark stone huts were barely discernible from the grassy hills they were sculpted into. Homes were designed to provide warmth and shelter, mainly in the white months of snow. Quin's people never wanted to feel far from the ocean which fed them and gave them life.

Here, it was like people had gone out of their way to keep nature out, at all costs, despite knowing it's the source of all good things. It left their town dry. There weren't many plants around. The occasional tree in the centre of a square, a few hanging planter boxes outside windows here and there; not one showing the healthy signs of being home to a sprite. Not that that was surprising. The sun beat down.

Quin had such a longing for the icy waters of home, it took them by surprise.

—

The group of 'tourists' had walked the length of the city unheeded by the crowds. They paused for a while to assess the harbour. The Admiral's ship was in port. Its presence could prove the whole plan to be a dangerous endeavour.

They were only a few blocks further on when who stepped out of a pub but Admiral Slater himself and a dozen of his men.

He stopped when he saw them; costumes could not hide their faces, and he knew those from the posters he'd ordered. His voice held venom. 'If it isn't the sea scum? Here to steal from me again?' His eyes lingered on Quin like they were a puzzle waiting to be solved. 'Got yourself a new recruit?'

Quin put a hand on their bag and gripped it in a way that they hoped wouldn't bring attention to it. This was the man the fisherman meant to sell them to. Fear and loathing roiled inside Quin like so many eels.

Leif put a foot forward in defiance. 'You don't understand what you take. We just return it. There's no crime in our actions.'

Quin saw the Admiral's crew spread out to defensive positions, hands on hilts.

'Petty criminals always try to justify their actions,' Slater said.

'And tyrants never justify anything.'

Barb threw two knives before anyone could react, and then produced her sickle sword from amongst the folds of her skirt. Two of the Admiral's men fell with a cry before the rest of them had their swords drawn. Some had pistols raised and fired, but in the confusion, none hit their mark. Leif used his pistol to fire back, while also drawing his sword.

For Quin, with no live combat experience, ducking and weaving was their main objective. Barb was keeping the swords at bay with Leif, and Brun had removed her shoulder cannon and had prepared it to fire.

Then Brun shouted, 'Hold!' and Quin dropped to the ground. Leif ducked to the right, and Barb to the left, leaving a space for the cannon to shoot right into the crowd of soldiers. Just before the explosion, Quin saw a sword plunge into Barb's shoulder.

The blast knocked everyone to the ground and brought down the eaves of the pub onto the Admiral's men. Only Brun remained standing; dust rose from the rubble.

Brun grabbed Quin by the collar. 'Quick.'

'Barb's hurt,' they blurted.

With her cannon still on one shoulder Brun strode across and picked up Barb as if she weighed nothing. There was more of a grit-teeth protest than a cry of pain from the smaller woman.

Quin saw with relief that Leif was upright again and beckoning them all to follow.

They raced back a few streets and veered off into laneways, snaking around and up the hill, away from the water, in the opposite direction the Admiral's guards would expect them to flee.

It wasn't long before Quin noticed Leif was running with a limp, and saw his trousers stained with blood.

'You're injured,' they cried, memories of blood and anger clouded their vision.

'It'll keep,' grunted Leif. On they ran.

Eventually, Leif called a halt and the group leapt a wall into a deserted private garden.

Brun set Barb down, worry writ large on her face.

'It's only a scratch,' Barb said, swatting her away, but letting her hand come to rest on Brun's.

Quin turned to Leif, ripped the sleeve off their top and tightly wrapped it around his wounded leg. Leif clenched his jaw but didn't protest.

Once they'd tended to the injured, Brun and Quin collapsed against the garden wall.

'I guess stealth is out, then,' Leif said lightly.

'No shit,' Barb snapped.

'The main question is,' said Quin, 'do we call it off, or do we keep going?'

'Call it off,' said Brun, 'people are injured.'

'Keep going!' said Leif and Barb together.

'Right, then how do we do that, now they know we're here?'

'At least they don't know what we're after,' Barb said.

'The Admiral would have to be clueless to not figure that out,' said Leif. 'He gets himself a plant we know has a sprite in it, and then we show up in his city. Where else would we be headed?'

'What weapons do we have left?' Brun asked. She was making an inventory of everything she'd packed on herself and looked expectantly around. 'What about you, Quin, what's in your bag?'

Quin felt an icy chill of panic run down their spine as its absence registered in their mind. 'Where's my bag?'

They cast around, looking about them, before falling still, knowing it wasn't there.

'You had it before that mess,' said Leif, gently.

'I must have dropped it.' The very thought of it made their throat close over, they had to remember to breathe.

'What's with that old sack anyway?' Barb asked. 'If it's gone, it's gone.'

'I can't just let it go!' Quin felt close to panic.

'What's so special about it?' Barb said in a hissed challenge.

There was a long pause when the three of them stared at Quin.

Quin stared back. Could they trust them? Stranded in this enormous city, in the middle of a botched heist, there weren't many options.

'It's not a bag.'

Brun said, 'I've never seen you without it. I just thought it had your personals inside.'

'Not my personals. But it is very personal.' They took a deep breath. 'It's my skin.'

The others looked at them in bewilderment. Then Leif said, 'You're from the Northern Isles. Why didn't I realise earlier?'

'Realise what?' asked Brun.

'I'm a selkie,' Quin said quietly.

'And you wanting to be your own person,' Barb said, 'is this—?' She gestured to their human form.

'Someone I loved died. I had to see more of the world, to understand why he adored it so much. All I'd known was the cold of the north. After he—' Quin choked on a sob at the memory of how he'd been loved by the gentle scholar, but never possessed. 'I needed to get away from that place. I swore no one would ever get hold of my skin but me.'

The panic settled into a reverberation like whale song through ice. Leif reached out and put his hand on Quin's shoulder. 'I wonder if Slater knows; you could be in danger here. We have an extra element to the plan, then: retrieve what's yours, and take back what was never theirs.'

'With two crew out of action, and a total newbie?' Barb said.

Quin knew Barb was making light of her own predicament.

Brun smiled grimly. 'Sounds like fun.'

—

By stealing a dress and a headscarf from a nearby washing line, Quin looked like an entirely different person by the time the others had helped them dress properly. It felt futile putting such loose cotton on when all they wanted was the tightness of their own skin.

Quin wove down through the streets back to where the confrontation had taken place. The pub was a ruin, but there were no bodies remaining. Perhaps the navy was quick to clean up its mess so as to not distress the citizens. But their bag was also gone.

They felt a wave of nausea. In the middle of the mayhem, their mind had been with Leif and the others, and that had led to disaster. Now, there was no going back to the sea, let alone to what was once called home.

A strong hand clapped them on the shoulder.

'There you are, sister,' Brun said loudly. 'You don't want to linger here.'

It was all a show, to throw off anyone who might be watching, but it jolted them back to the danger they were still in. The wounded two were to rest, and then meet them on the outskirts of the botanic gardens where the Conservatory was.

'It's not here,' they said under their breath.

'Not surprising,' said Brun. Taking Quin by the arm, and leading them down the hill, Brun kept a conversational tone, but a low voice. 'They take everything, those men. Mark my words, it'll be with him. Admiral Bastard.'

Before long they were standing in the market at the dock, just two afternoon shoppers, trying to get the last of their needs for a late supper. Most of the best produce was gone, of course, but there were still enough stallholders to create a crowd.

Instead, the pair scoped out the ships in the harbour. Sure enough, the Admiral's ship dominated the main wharf. The crew was idling on deck or milling about the docks. There was no pressing mission for them, it seemed.

Brun tapped them hard – it hurt – but she was pointing. 'There,' she said.

Following her finger, Quin saw the Admiral striding with purpose towards the largest of the fleet. Behind him, five men in uniform kept pace. One of them had a familiar sack in his hand.

If Brun hadn't gripped Quin's arm in that moment, they would have raced forward, to their death, perhaps. Instead, they held back and watched as, at the top of the gangplank, the Admiral turned abruptly, held out his hand, was given the skin, and then disappeared into the ship.

Quin threw up into the harbour.

—

The water, in the early evening, was smooth and familiar, even if it was much warmer than Quin was used to and cumbersome without flippers. Having shed their dress, even the pantaloons they had kept on were a bother. How much more natural it was to have nothing between you and the water. But humans cling to their modesty.

Quin slid across the harbour with ease, weaving between the trading and fishing vessels on their way to and from the port docks, unnoticed in the long sunset shadows. The wide bowl of the harbour was divided down the middle by a line of inactivity. The Empire's navy dominated the northern half and private ships stayed clear of the unmarked, yet obvious demarcation. It was easy for Quin to dive and breaststroke beneath the surface until navy ships provided cover to take a breath again. Despite not being in their best form for swimming, they were born for the water, regardless. Their arms could read the currents, knowing exactly which angle would provide the perfect propulsion. They curled into any current which would aid their momentum. It was not the same as the power of swimming with flippers and a tail but made more sense to them than walking or running. When they reached the stern of the Admiral's ship, they waited, bobbing in the gentle rocking of the waves against the hull.

Any moment now.

And then: an enormous explosion boomed from the dock. The lavender sky turning pink with the blossom of fire that accompanied the blast. One of the warehouses was now missing a large portion of its wall through which great tongues of flame raged.

That was the diversion. Brun was to place one of her explosives with a long fuse, draw the soldiers, scurrying like ants in a disturbed nest. She would be away from the scene, though. As shouts rang out from the ship, and across the dock, Quin slowly started to climb the stern in the shadow of the great ship.

They reached the windows to the Admiral's cabin, which were ajar. Why wouldn't they be? The ship was in its home port, the night was balmy. The unexpected drama on the dock had done exactly what Brun had hoped. The Admiral was nowhere in sight.

Prying the window open to its full, Quin climbed through. They dripped water across the fancy silk-upholstered trimmings.

In the soft light of the oil lamp, Quin could see no sign of their skin, nor anything disguised as sack. They began searching, moving things, opening chests and drawers. What if it were in a different room? What if they'd been mistaken from afar and it wasn't brought on board at all? And with the plan Brun had for the ship, what would that mean for their skin?

They were about to turn and flee when something caught their attention. On the table were maps, spread out and marked. Cuttings of plants were pinned to islands, flowers drawn and handwritten notes annotating where each could be found. Even creatures like nymphs and tree-dragons were sketched on it. The Admiral must be the driving force behind the exploration and collecting of magic plants. The maps were incomplete, but even in Quin's limited experience with paper, and cartography, they recognised the archipelago, stretching all the way to the Northern Isles where a small seal was drawn.

A flashback of the scholar, dear Benjamin, spreading out his own maps, and showing where Quin's homeland lay in relation to the known world. It was followed by an image of the scholar's face, twisted in pain, frozen in death.

Quin turned away, took a breath and reached up for the oil lamp hanging from the crossbeam. They'd only just retrieved it when the door opened and there stood the Admiral. There was only a moment of shock before the man recovered.

'You! Looking for something?' His voice was full of venom and scorn. Quin could see their oilskin slung across his chest. The sight of the man's hands on it sent a shudder through them like an earth tremor agitating the seabed into a muddy mess.

'That's mine!' Quin shouted, lunging forward to grab at the skin.

The man dodged the advance and in a smooth movement drew his sword, holding it pointed at Quin's chest, keeping them at bay.

A sick grin spread across his face. 'So, you're the selkie sneaking around the city. I've always wanted to add one of you to my collection.'

'You're evil,' was all Quin could manage to say through the panic and despair raging in them.

'Not evil,' he replied. 'Just fascinated by all this backwater magic. The Emperor will control it all before long, and I'll be at the head of that control.'

'You'll never control me,' Quin spat.

'In time, I will. For now, I own you, don't I?' His tone was sarcastic as he ran his fingers across the skin hanging from his shoulder.

Where Brun was in her next part of the plan no longer mattered. With a violent swing of their arm, Quin brought the oil lamp smashing down onto the table and all its maps, books, and papers. The glass shattered, the canister broke and the oil spread in liquid flame over the flammable paper.

The Admiral raised his arm to cover his face, but Quin was already retracing their steps and flinging themselves from the window. Knowing they'd had to leave their skin behind tore at their heart as they fell. The water held no warmth for Quin and their tears were lost to the oblivion of the ocean.

—

When they resurfaced, a small distance out to sea, they turned back to see the fire on the dock. That was when there were more explosions, this time from deep inside the Admiral's ship. Brun had planned to use the confusion to sneak on board and with a mix of her own toys – as she called them – and the ship's own munitions, had planned to destroy it from the inside.

The crew, tiny from this distance, flung themselves overboard to avoid the carnage. Had Brun escaped in time? Had the Admiral, still grasping Quin's skin? Fate had twisted events so Quin needed him to survive. Distress wrapped hope in iron tentacles, sinking it to the depths of the harbour.

There was nothing to do now but swim through exhaustion to the rendezvous point and whisper empty prayers to the Sea Spirit.

—

The tiny sea cave nestled under the bluff below the Conservatory exactly as Leif had described. Quin had swum towards the vast glass building on the headland. It was surreal to see so much glass in one place, especially as in the north they don't have windows, as they let out too much heat. Clearly the Emperor had spared no expense in constructing a building exclusively from large panes and an intricate iron frame. The cave was easy to identify, even in the dark, by the enormous, curved palm tree on the cliff top above. Swimming towards it, Quin clumsily hauled themselves out of the water on awkward human limbs.

The two figures inside, startled, drew their weapons, but lowered them when they saw it was Quin.

'What happened?' Leif asked, concerned. 'Didn't you get it back?'

'I ...' they started. 'He ...'

Barb stepped forward. 'Where is Brun?'

Quin looked her in the face and could not reply.

'Where the fuck is she?' Barb hissed.

'I hoped she'd be here by now. We had to improvise.'

Leif turned in the direction of the harbour, where there was only the glow of the dock fire in the night sky.

'We heard explosions.'

'That's her love language, isn't it?' Quin tried a joke but couldn't reconcile the words with the ache they felt.

Barb stepped forward, arm raised to strike them—

'Oi, you lot!' It came from above them and there was Brun, leaning over the bluff, in the shadow of the palm. 'I'm not climbing down there just to turn around and come back up again.'

–

When the three of them joined her atop the cliff, she filled them in. It turned out she'd been cornered by some soldiers.

'They weren't expecting the smoke bomb I dropped from between my legs!' She roared with laughter. 'Last time they tell me to put my hands above my head, I'm sure.' She'd rigged a wire up the inside of her sleeve to pull if needed. 'Between the fire Quin started in the Admiral's cabin and the long fuses I managed to get below deck in the mayhem, that ship ain't going nowhere but down.'

Leif smirked grimly. 'Excellent.'

Brun's face fell when she took in Quin properly. 'Was it not there?'

'It was,' they said. 'Hanging from that bastard's shoulder.'

'Did he …' Brun started.

'I can't say. I was no match in a fight, and better half a life than none at all. I fled.'

'We'll have to go back,' Brun said.

'We can't!' Barb exclaimed, raising her arms in exasperation.

Quin held out their hands to settle the group. 'Before anything, the task at hand. Titan arum.'

As one, they all turned to look at the Conservatory. It was a strange gem in the evening dark, moonlight giving it a ghostly glow and some of the closer panes of glass reflecting the yellow-red inferno at the docks, now well out of control.

It seemed that the distraction had doubly worked; none of the guards remained. Starting a blaze in the warehouses and sinking the Navy's capital ship had performed like a dinner bell.

Approaching the main entrance, Barb used the hilt of her

blade to break the glass and then unlocked the door from inside.

They strode in together and then came to a halt. It truly was breathtaking. The sand-coloured gravel path led to a fountain in the centre, directly underneath the main dome of the building. Towering on every side were all manner of plant and tree. Quin would have never guessed at the diversity of life had they not heard of it from Benjamin's quiet mouth. It was, however, a collection rather than a natural jungle. Everything was meticulously ordered, labelled and staked into place. It was awe-inspiring but terribly clinical. No sign of a single sprite.

'Let's split up to find it faster,' said Leif.

Branching out into the four arms of the enormous building, the crew moved quickly.

Quin raced to the east. They followed each path that split off to its end before circling back and trying others, looking in every display and garden bed. Leif had said they'd know it when they saw it, and Brun had added they'd know it when they smelt it.

Quin stopped in their tracks. Of course. They were doing this wrong. This was not a garden, but a museum. Where would a prized piece be kept? They took their eyes from the foliage and looked about for something out of the ordinary.

Turning another corner, they saw something. At the end of the path was a sandstone building, the size of a single room house, inside the grand glass structure.

They charged towards it, and found that the door was made of iron, a thick bolt in place to keep it secure – but, strangely, only if you were on the inside. There was no padlock on this side. Why would plants need locking in like this?

Sliding the heavy bolt and needing most of their strength to heave the door, they were not ready for what they saw inside.

A galaxy contained in a room. It took a moment for Quin's eyes to adjust, but their seal-self kicked in, clarifying the shapes in the dark and the beauty became horror.

Sprites: but nothing like those that welcomed Quin to the tavern called *Home*.

Shelves and shelves of tiny silver cages, each with a sprite inside, their bright glows now sickly and dimmed. How long could they survive separated from their plants?

They called into the conservatory, 'Everyone! Come here!' and began wrestling with the cage doors. They were locked and expertly crafted, none of them would open. The commotion was waking the sprites. They stood and moved forward in their cells to look. All about the room their lights grew brighter as they realised that someone was here to free them. Hundreds of tiny creatures, stirring with hope.

The others arrived. The horror on their faces at the sight mirrored what Quin felt.

'What torture is this?' Leif said in a low voice.

Barb let loose a string of expletives and Brun exclaimed, 'Those fuckers!'

They'd come for a heist; to save a single sprite and its plant. They had no idea Slater had captured so many sprites. And for what, a zoo?

Some of the sprites seemed to recognise Leif. They fluttered about their cages now, an excitement spreading among the room, bringing more light.

It was in this light that Quin saw what was in the centre of the room, and a chill ran through them. A sturdy workbench coated in stainless steel, almost empty so they'd ignored it up until now. Yet with fewer shadows, they could now see that on one end of the bench was an assortment of tools. They were not gardening tools. Several scalpels, tweezers, a tiny silver saw, and a collection of shining, six-inch pins. Their stomach turned as they registered their presence and purpose.

Their stillness caught the attention of Barb who followed their gaze. Brun and Leif were next and then all of them were staring in disbelief.

'They will pay for this,' Barb said. She picked up two of the pins. As she turned to the cages, the sprites all screeched in fear, but she was undeterred. Taking to the closest lock with the pins, she made light work of it and the cage had barely sprung open before she was moving onto the next.

Leif and Brun followed her lead, getting their own set of pins and picking locks at a frenzied pace.

'I don't know how to help, there are no locks in the north.'

Through gritted teeth, Leif said, 'I'm pleased to hear it. Tend to the free ones, should they need.' Then, addressing the sprites themselves he called out, 'Find your plants and gather what energy you can. We cannot bring them with us, and the journey is long.'

Those that were freed flew out of the door and into the foliage in search of their own species.

Quin saw that some had not left their cages, despite the doors hanging open. Approaching they saw that the sprites were too weak to fly.

'May I?' they asked extending their cupped hands.

With tiny nods, the sprites allowed themselves to be picked up. Gently as possible, they cradled the sprites in the crook of their arm.

When every one of them was free, and Quin held six of the weakest, they emerged into the greater building, and it was an entirely different sight. Still manicured to the point of dispassionate cleanliness, the Conservatory was now lit from within, glowing with life as lights flitted between the leaves and branches. Flowers burned like lamps, alive and pulsing.

Leif called loudly into the constructed forest, 'Ready yourselves, and wherever possible, hide your light as we travel.' He added to Quin, 'They will be able to rest in the plants on *The Waterlily* while we sail. It's not the same as their birth plant, but they would not be able to fly the distance without resting.'

Then he raced down a path that did not lead to the door.

'Where are you going?' Barb shouted after him.

There was no response, so the other three followed him.

They found him in a small, paved courtyard that had a single plant in its centre in a pot the size of a large barrel. Quin caught their breath at the sight of it and heard Barb and Brun do the same. The titan arum, which Leif had described what felt like a lifetime ago, was even more breathtaking than they had anticipated. It had not bloomed, but the bud was taller even than Brun.

'Leif,' Barb said, not unkindly. 'We cannot. Too much has changed.'

When Leif replied, he did not look away from the plant. 'We cannot leave it to these savages.'

Barb opened her mouth to object, but Brun put out her hand. 'Let's not spend all night having a balanced discussion.' She stepped forward, squatted by the pot and with an almighty grunt she lifted the entire thing. It was the first time Quin had seen her struggle with anything. Through a set jaw she said, 'Just pray you don't need me for fighting.'

Clearly, no one took that suggestion seriously, because when they reached the main entrance, there was the Admiral standing in the doorway. He was dishevelled, sweaty, and clutching his sword. There was a moment when no one said anything as he took in the sight of the four of them and the swarm of sprites filling the conservatory.

Quin let out a loud gasp when they saw a familiar bag slung over his shoulder still. It was all they could do to not rush forward.

'I knew you would come here,' the Admiral said.

Barb spat. 'What do you want? A round of applause?' In the same instant she had drawn her sickle blade. Leif, too, had produced his sword and Brun was slowly lowering the pot to the ground.

Leif's voice was steely when he spoke. 'You should be gutted like a fish.'

Quin inched backwards. They hadn't been given a replacement weapon in all of the changes to their plans. Even if they had, fighting was not in their talent pool. They put a protective hand over the sprites in their arm. The other three formed a defensive stance in front of them and readied for battle.

The Admiral smiled a lazy, careless grin. 'What's wrong with wanting knowledge?' He said it almost casually, like they could have been in a tavern sharing an ale. 'We gather everything so we can know everything.'

Brun said, 'Forgot to gather your crew, then? Or are they enjoying a barbeque?'

The man's smile was gone instantly. 'Your fire has ruined much, and kept my soldiers busy, but you think I can't handle four petty thieves myself?'

'You don't want knowledge,' Leif said, 'you want to control.'

'One is the other.'

'And neither hold understanding.'

The Admiral's voice was ice. 'I will learn how to master those magical scum, even if I have to slice it out of the tiny beasts myself!'

Barb had been moving so slowly no one had noticed. Her patience was up. 'Enough!' she shouted as she flung a throwing knife she'd retrieved from her belt.

The Admiral's reflexes were sharp and he deflected it with a swipe of his sword. And the battle was on.

It was a testament to his skill that he was able to hold the trio at bay, parrying and attacking in equal measure. In the vigorous movement, the bag slipped from his shoulder and landed at his feet.

Quin retreated behind the large pot that Barb had set down. They wanted to help but were out of their depth. They ached for their skin to be returned. That's when they saw something spectacular start to unfold in the titan arum's foliage. The bud at its centre began to unfurl, and inside was a warm, orange glow. Quin had little experience with the plants of the tropics, or flowering plants at all, but they'd never thought a flower could bloom so rapidly and unexpectedly. The petals were thick and elegantly shaped, curling back from the bud like exquisite tongues. With it came the stench of the grave, decay and rot. The parting petals revealed a sprite, sleeping in the centre, their wings full of light and wrapping their body. The clashing of steel woke them, and they made a noise of surprise.

The other sprites responded immediately, flying down and gathering around the newly born one. Quin set the injured ones, which appeared to be gathering strength, on the large pot with the others. Any conversation they might be having was beyond Quin's perception.

Knowing these creatures were more than dancing lights, Quin spoke to them. 'You've been wronged here. Are you able to help us get you home?'

A handful of heartbeats later, the flight of the sprites changed dramatically. Now an angry swarm, they grouped together in an ever-increasing brightness. The combined buzzing of their wings made a sound unlike any Quin had heard. The four that were fighting became aware of the noise and movement, glancing over their shoulder. None were foolish enough to break away from their battle.

The next moment, however, there was no battle to be seen. As one, the sprites flew in a quick angry blast directly at the Admiral. It was so bright Quin had to shield their eyes. Leif, Barb and Brun did the same, throwing an arm up to cover their faces.

The Admiral gave a cry and his sword clattered to the floor, landing in the gravel. The frantic light enclosed him, and then, flew through the door and up into sky as if they were a tiny sun, and the man did not exist.

Quin was able to look again and saw the ball of light explode in the sky and scatter like stars escaping each other. Once they were separated, the sprites looked more like fireflies again and the flitted back down to the Conservatory like embers falling after a fire.

The Admiral was nowhere to be seen.

Quin dashed forward to their skin, lying next to the discarded sword. They held it tight and wept. It felt dry and damaged. The ache for the sea returned, more powerfully than before.

Turning back to the enormous flower, Brun said, 'Wrecks! It smells of death, that's for sure.'

Leif called to them all, 'It's time we get out of here.'

Quin ran for the cliff edge, checked below, and threw themself towards the sea. As they dove through the air, they shook out the skin, releasing the folds tucked in on itself, flapping the length of their body. They got the hood over their head just in time.

Then, they hit the water.

Using the motion to slide their hands inside their skin, they felt everything fall into place, returning it to the shape they were birthed in. The tight sensation of the sealskin fitting closely over their shoulders was a glorious relief. It slid down their body, firming up and becoming whole. Legs and arms swaddled inside, becoming the means to power their tail and fins for swimming. They were off like a shot, deep in the water and out of sight.

–

Floating in the gentle swell, looking at *The Waterlily*, Quin realised that everything had changed. The adrenaline of the blunder-ridden heist had not allowed room to consider life with their form exposed to the crew. Now the group had returned, avoiding the guards who were yet to learn of Slater's demise, they'd loaded the titan arum onto the ship, along with all the sprites.

'There's a seal!' Kip called from the ship.

Quin looked up and saw Kip gazing over the railing at them. The other three joined him and Leif said, 'That's Quin.' There was only a moment's pause before the captain hoisted himself right over the edge, jumping into the water.

He swam closer to Quin, who decided to playfully duck and swim around, appearing behind him, very close. They were suddenly self-conscious of their form. It was the first time anyone had seen them clothed, so to speak, and they felt naked and exposed. Leif turned. The two bobbed in the water, face to seal-face.

Leif studied them, and a smile crept onto his lips.

'It *is* you,' he said.

Quin wanted to say, *Of course it is. How many other seals are around here anymore?* Naturally, though, human speech in this form was impossible.

It was a shock when Leif reached out and touched their cheek, gently brushing their whiskers, letting their fingers trail around their neck and up to their ears. It was a shock of delight but the memory of Benjamin as the last human to touch this form came rushing back in a jolt of joy and loss.

Skin on hide. They closed all three layers of their eyelids and accepted the pleasure of it and the pain of memory. Was this the future they left in search of?

Lowering their head with intention, Quin felt the opening appear on their chest right above their heart. It was like a cleft in seafoam, painless and without a sound. From within, they could use their newly formed arms to open the seam wider and remove the hood. This was always the strangest moment in the sensation of changing, when one head slid away to reveal another, each as vital as the other. With it, the knowledge of their human legs inside the sleeve of skin. They remained this way, human in a seal cloak with the hood removed, floating in the water.

Leif spoke quietly, 'You are a wonder.'

Quin smiled. 'I'm only one of many where I come from. Do not mistake unfamiliar as extraordinary.'

'I only meant—'

'I know, but I will not be fetishised.'

Leif's smile disappeared. 'I had no idea until today, and I think you'll find, I still fucked you.' His tone was defensive.

'And, I hope, you will again.' Quin smiled to ease his worry. 'I simply must speak my mind.'

His face softened and then became serious. 'I will never seek to own you.'

Quin felt the truth of it, as surely as they knew he was worthy of their love.

'Well,' Quin said, 'this whole person wants to see more of your world.'

'*Captain*,' Barb interjected from the deck of the ship. 'Can you keep it in your pants for long enough to remember this isn't the time?'

Quin remembered the others were watching, but no longer cared. They had never heard Barb call him captain before, so knew it was her way of goading him.

Removing the rest of their seal-skin and expertly fashioning it into a sack was a simple movement for Quin. The pair climbed the side of the ship.

'Time for us to leave,' Leif said dripping onto the deck in the moonlight.

Sprites could not fly the distance back to the archipelago, not without resting among plants. As the sprites took up refuge in all the plants *The Waterlily* held, Leif said, 'Dim your lights again, we don't want to be followed.'

'So, all these,' Quin said to him, impressed, 'serve more purpose than aesthetics?'

Leif grinned at them. 'Plants are never just for aesthetics.'

—

Days later, Quin found themselves curled in a corner booth leaning against a sleepy Leif. Barb was beating Kip at darts and Brun kept score.

Mama came over and cleared the empty jug from in front of the pair.

'You found more than work, then?' She said with a knowing smile. Leif's eyes remained closed.

'Yes,' said Quin. 'I found a home.'

Mama's laughter rang out around the room. 'I knew I named this place for a reason.'

HUNGER

VIKA MANA

BEFORE THE PRESENT

Hunger
Huuuunnngeeerrrrr
HUNNNGGEERRRRR
...
...
I
I am starrrving
I crave for songs and prayers
I ache for my name to echo again in this plane
But I am weakkkk
Have I been forgotten?
...
...
...
......
...
...
...
Hungerrrrr
Huuuuuuunnnggeeerrr
HUNNNGEEERRR
It is all I have
...
...
...
...
                              Hmmmmm
...
Who is there!

Hmmmmmmm   hmmmm

Hmmmmmmmm

...

...

Is that ... a prayer?

Hmmmmmmmmmmmmm..........

...

Can... Can you hear me Kabozie?

I've come to ask for your help

A simple request.

And I am starving.

Child, let me feast on your needs.

IN THE BEGINNING, BEFORE IT ALL

When the world was burning, those responsible decided this world was 'not worth saving'. They built underground cities, destroying more of our sacred sites in the process with each new 'kolony,' new colonies made by Kazure Inc, a parent company of many of the world's oil and coal companies. All over the world, we mourned and protested, losing our voices, our throats raw from anger, marching in the streets. They didn't listen. They never listened.

> But those who were never heard, always ignored,
> made sure they did.

It started with what we called the raptures, random attacks happening around the world. First, it was the underwater kolony, off the shore of California, near Miwok territory. It was wiped out entirely, when luminescent giant squids ripped their foundations from the seafloor and dragged the cities into the depths of their homes. Satellite GPS showed they travelled with the skeleton of the city somewhere near Antarctica. Everyone around the world was in shock: how could something like this happen? Why would creatures who only existed in the darkest and deepest part of the ocean travel away from their abode to drag a city that wasn't near them?

The wealthy listed it as a freak accident of Mother Nature, but then the kolony underneath the mountains in Germany was nearly wiped out by ravenous grey wolves and autonomous plants. Scientists and animal specialists claimed that the city could have been located in one of their dens, or destroyed one of their main food supplies by uprooting entire ecosystems where they were based, and that they were starving, hungry, ready to tear flesh apart. But no one could explain the plants. They could move – and do so with a surprising and incredible degree of speed and power. Some of the plants had manifested into beings: some had arms and legs, others had multiple limbs and heads. They erupted from the floor and walls, uprooting themselves, swallowing anyone in their path.

Indigenous people worldwide started talking about their creators, awakening spirits to punish those who contributed to the destruction of the earth. That this was spiritual warfare as well, on those who benefitted from destruction, and those who did not care that they contributed. From observing the casualties, Indigenous people and resistance collectives also concluded that those who were Indigenous were safe from immediate harm. I remember when the Dust Sea, a 'radical' Indigenous collective based in so-called 'Australia', spread the news via encrypted texts and anonymous social media posts.

The only survivors of the German kolony were three families, twenty-one people. They were all Indigenous peoples from around the world, who still practised their cultures. They were only in the city because the breadwinners were service workers who demanded that their families would be able to still be in their care if they migrated into the kolony.

However, this theory was challenged when another attack happened off the shores of Whakatōhea territory, Aotearoa, 'New Zealand', when corpses dug themselves out of the earth and powered through the underground kolony ripping people apart. In the manifest, there were fifty-eight people who identified as being Indigenous; only forty-nine of them survived. People tried to define this anomaly, on our terms of reference but there were always outsiders, and self-proclaimed experts, who wanted to have their say. There was talk about Indigenous people going missing during these attacks as well, their names and bodies missing from the death count and public morgues. Whispers spread of their disappearances, and words lingered in the air about the rich stealing Indigenous people to protect themselves.

Nine of the 753 people who were killed in Aotearoa were Indigenous, but their positions in the kolony contributed to the destruction of the land. Indigenous people worldwide became more vigilant, and wary of their families and treatment of the land. Elders began to warn their kin to seek forgiveness, particularly those who worked for the kolony, to ensure their safety and the safety of their families, especially in light of the footage that was hacked from the Aotearoa servers.

The Aotearoa kolony had a more elaborate security system compared to its sister kolonies, due to the previous raptures. The threat of an incident within the walls of the Aotearoa kolony pushed their board to invest in better safety protocols and technology; yet this would not save them.

The livestream of the raptures continued until Kazure Inc pressured the New Zealand government to shut down the kolony's power and any signal access to it. Working together, they tried their best in addressing the dead, and the endless footage of the rapture. No one could truly stop the animated corpses, as more and more people became infected. The dead didn't roam further from the kolony to the towns nearby, they all stayed within its underground confinements. As if they were being told to, as if this was all by design.

After that, governments around the world started announcing kolony space programs in partnership with Kazure Inc, that were in development before the underground cities were even built. Two fleets of kolony spaceships that were going to establish a new world on a new planet in a nearby solar system. They had spent millions on a future somewhere else instead of investing in protecting our current world.

This time round, in wake of this announcement, people felt the urgency in having to protect the world we were already on, the world we were given, we were born into. More people started realising that they too would be left behind.

—

It was such a bizarre thing to see, being so young and Black, to see people only start caring when they too were affected by the changes of the world. Riots ended governments in some nations, persecuted leaders and they tried their best in halting the programs. South Africa's elected officials were the first to go, but it was too late, the rich were approved for their places in these programs and were already housed in the spaceships. Nationwide lotteries were held, with programs that were ready to begin. It was presumed that they had only held these lotteries in order to appease the demands of rioters and protesters and, for a while, it did, decreasing the numbers of those attendings marches; however, as soon as the ships started filling up, one by one, the intensity of the riots increased, as did the occurrences of raptures.

I remember when my name was announced. I was first in the alphabetised list: *Amina*. Three of my siblings were on the list: Langi, Jakobi and the second youngest of the ten of us, Gracie. Our mother tried her best to hide us so we wouldn't go missing like the rumoured missing Indigenous people and families around the world.

Once the Jackson family from down the road went missing, a Birri Gubba family of seven, we all took off from our small town, to Dad's fishing spot. We were relieved to find two of the oldest Jackson kids, Raven and Thaddeus, with the twins, Malachai and Matai, at the lake.

Raven explained that their parents were taken at the local store. Her dad had been on shift and her mum was shopping for dinner after school. She was with her mother until she scurried off to the milk aisle and heard her mother scream and then her father calling to her to run. Two men, dressed in black suits, had taken them and thrown them into a big black van. Raven had run to the back, called her older brother, Church, to get the twins and Thaddeus out the house. Church had followed her instructions and they all knew about the lake far off the map and the small little fishery house by it. They had all stayed there for a couple of nights, until Church received a message about his girlfriend and her family in the town over. He told his siblings to stay by the lake until he returned.

The twins cried every night for their older brother, whilst Raven and Thaddeus held them. By the time we got there, Mum would stay up to watch over them whilst whispering to her belly, asking our unborn sibling what their name was. We had lived by the lake for three weeks before the Jacksons realised that Church was never coming back. During those weeks, we listened to the radio about the abrupt changes that were happening. People were being rounded up and moved to cluster stations, new man-made cities made to protect citizens as they prepared to leave. It was also where the lottery selections were announced. It was a week before final take off when we were found.

We had been living by the lake for a while until the acid rain started, it had made the lake unsafe and ruined the vegetation that grew nearby. The native plants we lived off were no longer safe to eat. We suspected another rapture was going to occur, so together we planned to go further into the mountains. We were aware that there were other Blackfullas and their families in those mountains because they had been sharing codes over the radio on the sister channel of the local Indigenous radio news show.

So the Jacksons and our family made our way towards the mountains. We originally planned to break into three groups, but Dad decided we should travel in one big group, we were stronger in numbers. We travelled carefully from the lake towards the mountains. We had packed light and had carved weapons just in case. Dad had taken the 'akau-tā, gabagaba and bow and arrows from our house with us when we initially ran. The Jacksons had their father's hunting boomerangs; Hollywood always illustrates boomerangs as lightweight harmless toys, but boomerangs are lethal. If thrown right and carved perfectly, they can take a chunk out of a limb.

We had woken up from our first night of hiking to whistles and barking. We had all rushed out of our gear to run, taking what we could with us. We split up, running in different directions, but the kolony guards caught us one by one. Dad and a few of our younger siblings were able to escape, but we were caught. The guards were scouting the place, trying to find the source of the acid rain, but had found us instead.

We tried to fight them off but they caught us using their taser guns, their lethal weapons and nets. We couldn't do anything except yell out for those not yet caught to run as fast as they could in the opposite direction of our voices. The rest of us were thrown into their trucks, handcuffed, injured and bleeding. They had broken Matai's arm. Thaddeus' whole body was red, blue and swollen. Thaddeus had been the main person who resisted, along with Jakobi and our sweet brother Waru.

Waru was twelve, tall, lanky; he had big soft curls and loved green frogs. He smiled more often than he talked. He saw the world through big brown eyes and lashes, and never raised his voice. He always snuck into my room to tell me what he learnt about the universe online and asked me hard questions like *Where do we go when we die?* I remember telling him where we go, that our souls fly into the sky like stars and visit the people we love before we go to the deadlands. That I remember when Nan came to visit us in all her bright glory and flew off into the night, the sound like a hum, like the beat of a drum, of a tune that I've known forever, had been heard.

Jakobi had tried to get one of the officers off Thaddeus, when they wouldn't stop beating him. Jakobi had thrown one of the boomerangs at the officer's face and the tip of his nose was gone. He fell to his knees. Jakobi had run towards him, ready to make him stay down so Thaddeus could at least make a run for it, but the officer had slipped a blade into his knee and he fell onto the ground. Waru had jumped on the guard, covering his eyes with his small slim hands, screaming for Jakobi to get up, but he was thrown off, and his body – so light, so frail compared to everyone else in our family – flew in the air.

Waru's eyes were wide, never leaving Jakobi's until Waru landed in a ditch, and the sound of bones breaking could be heard, but no scream followed. His big brown eyes probably stayed open, seeing the sky one last time.

Jakobi had crawled to the edge of the ditch, his knee trying its best to hold his leg together. His eyes never saw his brother's whole body, just his arm in a crooked angle. He yelled so urgently at Waru to get up and run that his voice was raw and cracked for days. But lifeless bodies don't usually follow instructions. The guards had left Waru's body there, in the cold, his blood pooling around his head, the leaves and dirt stuck to his skin and curls. The guards had taken us quickly and thrown us into their vehicles.

We mourned in the trucks, kicking and screaming. Langi had managed to stand in the moving truck and tried her best kicking the back doors, as Gracie hid underneath Mum's arm, pleading for Waru. Mum tried to whisper a lullaby, brushing her hair with her hands as Gracie rested her head on her belly, but her grief always interrupted her. The Jacksons surrounded Thaddeus, crying as he held onto them. The twins had been Waru's best friends. They were older than Waru, yet they always played together, and inevitably would talk about the best reptiles and amphibians from their respective countries. The officers, annoyed by our mourning, had demanded we be silent or they'd take Gracie from us and leave her out for the rain. I hissed, protesting, but Jakobi wrapped his fingers in mine and squeezed. My big brother, the protector, looked like a shell of the man I had come to know. All I could do was squeeze his hand in return, and cry silently, like everyone else.

I imagined Dad finding Waru's body, along with our younger siblings Janaya, Alkani, Tesi and Emeni. That they picked his cold body up and hugged him one last time and buried him the way our old people buried our dead. But it had started to rain when we left, and I knew this hopeful comfort could not be fulfilled. The acid would wipe away his brown eyes and the leaves and dirt. We knew we were disposable, we knew that they would continue to wipe us out, even Waru, the kindest soul to have ever existed.

I imagined he'd grow old, taller, lankier and working in the rainforest, giving tours to school children, talking about his favourite frogs and their calls. He used to mimic their sounds around the house, running around with the little ones. I missed his big brown eyes, and running my hands through his hair, as he sat on the kitchen table sketching flora and fauna. His goofy grin lighting up a room as he wore his oversized frog beanie.

That night we arrived at the cluster station exhausted, swollen-faced. Gracie was asking for Waru again as the guards injected DN-8 into our left wrists, oldest to youngest. DN-8s were compulsory black squares the size of a fingernail that transformed into the shape of the sun, a simple outline of a circle and eight lines stretched out once underneath the skin. They were first made as a medical aid device to read vitals, but the kolony changed their prime purpose into tracking people, a digital passport.

—

Once we had our DN-8s injected, they led us to the new citizen quarters. It was just a warehouse with makeshift quarters built by the citizens from local rubbish. I stayed up late, most of us did, only pretending to asleep for the sake of normality in the citizen quarters. There was only one window in our quarters, and I stayed by it, waiting for a star, for the hum of a drum. When it did not come, and the sun rose melting the stars from the sky, I began to mourn again. The guards, this kolony, had taken Waru's afterlife as well.

Food was slop, served every day during the week. Slop was all the out-of-date food thrown into industrial mixers and served to the people. The colours varied every time, and it always tasted like tangy mush. At the end of the few days we spent in the cluster station, the lottery was read, and our family's and the Jacksons' names were called out. We tried to hide, like Mum had instructed us, in and around the civilian quarters, but the guards found us so easily because of our DN-8s. One by one, we were loaded into the kolony spacecrafts, not knowing where we'd sleep, what we'd eat, and where we would stay. All those who lived in the cluster station were packed in, like cattle, in the docks, trying to form single lines passing through detectors, making their way through to cargo. We weren't like the other passengers. We didn't pay for a spot on the kolony, we were stark reminders, remnants of the world the rich contributed to destroying. We were the new underclass, the people they proclaimed to have saved out of the goodness of their hearts, but they needed us, so they could still feel in power, as we'd be working on these ships, and they would not.

After some time waiting at the cargo level's entrance, a cadet, brownskin with short dreadlocks, and honey eyes, finally approached us and made a brief introduction.

'My name is Craydon. I'm a cadet under Sergeant McKenzie.' They looked at each of us with a practised polite smile, nodding as they spoke in an English accent. 'I'll be leading you to your new homes. They've been built whilst we've been docked at this cluster capital. Follow me.'

They turned to lead the way but stopped abruptly, turning back to swiftly add onto their announcement, 'And please, keep up in a timely manner without disturbing others. Don't idle away admiring the scenery, you'll have the opportunity to do so at your own leisure when you're given your job titles.'

They cleared their throat, turning round again to continue towards our unknown destination.

I followed them the closest, Jakobi just behind me, limping, shadowing our mother. The rest were behind us, in a sort of small herd, the older ones around the smaller ones, except Gracie. She sat on the shoulders of Thaddeus, whose bruising was fading from purple to light blues.

When we finally arrived at our quarters, Craydon's voice filled the air again. 'This is for your family, Mrs ...' They shifted their eyes to my mother's wrists and pointed.

'Sorry, may I?'

My mother, used to being inspected by guards now, provided a quick nod and Craydon hovered their hand above her wrist in a circular motion. They smiled, 'Mrs Havea.'

Craydon tapped the metal door, and it slid open to a small quarters. We walked in and the place was barely the size of a stamp. The Jacksons had tried to follow us into our quarters, but Craydon had held their hand up to stop them. Craydon hadn't asked with words that time round. They had just gestured towards Raven's wrist and in response, she had covered it, looking towards Thaddeus. Craydon wasted no time and looked at Thaddeus, hand already in position to scan his DN-8. Thaddeus stuck his hands out and Craydon gestured to their left.

'The Jacksons. Your quarters are just next door.'

With the four of them gone, Gracie blurted out a question: 'How'd they know they were a different family?'

Craydon, still in the doorway, answered as if the question was for them. 'DN-8s are more than what you may think.' They touched their wrist and a blue and orange holographic screen appeared just above it. 'We're upgrading them as we travel through space. Right now, we have beta systems running through personnel. We can read feedback and you can receive feedback, without necessarily knowing that you are going through that process. The process is a compulsory mechanism all new citizens participate in. However, you'll know what information was traded through our DN-8 history tracker.'

Craydon scrolled through their screen and then moved it to stick on their forearm, showing Gracie.

'Soon, these devices will be doing more for our bodies than what we can currently comprehend. One day, you might be writing code for these chips for something groundbreaking, if you're ever selected as a Coder.'

Craydon smiled and left with a last announcement: 'We take off at 0600. Make sure to listen to instructions over the PA system, and to brace yourselves. Dawn will help you with the rest. She'll welcome you to the Titan.'

I looked around the quarters and spied a set of doors in the pattern of the walls. I walked closer and saw they opened to a circular room, a round table in the middle and two sets of doors on the back wall. On the right to each door there was a screen with words that read bathroom and storage.

I opened the storage room and found more beds stacked in the walls. Instead of three beds like the quarters in the front, there were only two beds and a cupboard on the right. These quarters were much smaller than the quarters in the front of our place, so I told everyone this would be mine, the younger ones should be closer to Mum.

'I'll sleep in the storage space with you,' Jakobi said. 'I don't want to take up too much space.'

I was hurt by the thought of him thinking he was taking up space at all. He looked at me, and I could tell he didn't want his words challenged right then, so I insisted that he take the bottom bunk, it would be easier on his knee. After a back and forth, he went silent and just took the bottom bunk, slumping down as he scanned his new home.

Mum and Langi settled in the quarters in the entrance, and Gracie found our rations in compartments hidden in the walls of the middle room. I joined her in investigating what else was hidden in the round room. The walls were cold as I ran my hands over them, trying to find more compartments. I found a kitchenette on the left wall, a couple of drawers with clothes, all in dark grey, the same colour as the room. I took the clothes out and put them on the table and as soon as I did, a hologram loaded in the middle of the table. A voice introduced itself.

'Hello and welcome to your quarters.' A face, with high cheek-bones and long, wavy dark hair appeared in the corner of the holo-graph, a smile lingering on their lips. 'I am Dawn, I am here to welcome you to the *Titan* and to guide you for our trip into the new world. With the kolony, there will always be a new day, a new dawn.'

I smirked and let out a quick huff, amused by it all. But Gracie rushed to my side, all smiles, looking at the hologram.

'Hello Dawn! I'm Gracie.'

Dawn disappeared from the screen, and materialised as a small figure on the table with a smile that felt like she'd just learned how to. 'Hi Gracie! Would you like to be read the laws of the kolony's civilian tier?'

I answered instead. 'Dawn, she's four, she's not interested.'

Gracie's head quickly spun to me, offended. 'Hey, I'm nearly five; I *couldddd* be interested.'

I patted her head and smiled. 'Laws are rules, Gracie. Do you really want to listen to rules?'

Realisation crossed her mind, and probably the memory of the last time she had to listen to rules about the playground, which she always broke.

'Oh.' She turned to Dawn. 'Sorry, I am not interested,' she said as she ran away towards her quarters.

'However, I am.' I walked around the table, reading, looking closer at the words on the holo screen. 'Please tell me everything about the kolony ship.'

'As you like. Due to your status, all the information I can share with you, about our kolony ship, the *Titan*, will take eighteen hours. Would you like to proceed?'

I pulled out a chair from underneath the table and sat down. 'Well, I won't be going anywhere, will I, Dawn?' I gestured around our new home.

Just like that, Dawn proceeded to inform me about the laws of our civilian level, the ration system, the smart tech clothes that shrink to size, the work stations and patrol. Gracie reappeared and disappeared with a ration bar and left me to absorb all we needed to know as a family. The only time Dawn stopped was to warn me that take-off was about to begin in an hour and to secure myself in my quarters.

Before I headed off, I had a quick shower. In one of Dawn's lessons, she had shared that the water on the *Titan* is rationed and recycled, and that any usage that exceeds our rations gets deducted from our wages. I thought about all these new rules as I noticed how dirty the water was, how much grime had stuck on me during my time in the cluster city. I watched the water swirl round and round, like all the new information in my head. My hair was softer now that my kinks were brushed through. Instead of leaving my afro out, I decided to go with a side ponytail. My smart tech was easy to put on, just like Dawn said, just a press onto the skin and the tech did all the work.

I opened the door into my quarters, and noticed Jakobi wincing in his sleep. He hadn't let any of us look at his knee since that day in the woods. Hopefully, when we got to space, he'd let us test the med packs on his knee. They were supposed to completely heal the area they're applied on. I retrieved a bag from our few belongings, which Jakobi had packed in our closet, and took out one of the only family photos we had.

With the photo, I climbed up top, and my bunk strapped me in automatically, just like Dawn promised. She had explained that even in our sleep our bunks would keep us strapped in for lift-off or any turbulence we might encounter. I touched the top of my bunk and the screen came alive, Dawn's face in the top right corner, watching me. I asked Dawn for a clear view of one of the windows in the common areas of the *Titan*.

I wanted to watch us leave, I wanted to say goodbye to Country, I owed it that much. A countdown began and interrupted me trying to think of more words I wanted to share to the world I had promised to protect, the land I was connected to, the waters I was born in.

…10…

…9…

…8…

On the screen I saw the sunrise colours expand on the horizon. I wished I could see it for myself.

…7…

…6…

I whispered to the ocean, touching the screen with my right index finger, as if I was dipping my body in its nurturing waters one last time.

...5...

...4...

I thought of Dad, of Janaya, Tesi, Emeni and Alkani. I thought of never seeing them again, of holding them. I prayed that Country would protect them.

...3...

...2...

I thought of Waru, his big smile and brown eyes. I thought of his small head of hair, always fitting on my shoulder, as we'd watch sunrises like these. I thought of his laugh, and I held onto it. I held onto it because I could not bear the thought of his body, cold, lifeless, in those woods. I wished he was here. I closed my eyes and let the tears go, holding the photo of my family close to my chest.

...1...

I opened my eyes, and watched our world disappear, I felt my Country call for me. I wonder if the spirits could feel us leaving, if they knew that their children were being ripped from them. How would they hear our songs? I pull a vial on a necklace my mum gave me out from under my shirt. It is full of sand from our Country. All of us kids were gifted one, always given at birth when we were named; but being separated, from Country, from each other, by space itself, felt wrong.

All I could do was go to sleep and hope that tomorrow, tomorrow would be better.

That was three years ago and a lot has changed. Mum had our sister Rosie, but the nurses removed Rosie for what they called *newborn analytics and vitals*. After they had taken her, the nurses returned hours later with the patrol, and told Mum she had lost her baby. She demanded to see Rosie's body, but the hospital insisted that protocols had to be followed. They had burned her, my baby sister who had yet to hear her name, cremating her body without her consent or knowledge, and released her ashes through an airlock shoot.

Mum's grief was too much, her heart literally breaking in her hospital bed. She hasn't spoken since, but Gracie speaks to her all the time, and somehow, always knows what she's thinking. Rosie's death wasn't the last newborn or child death from our level. It seemed like, just like on earth, Indigenous people on board were dying fast, being ignored by the healthcare workers and being shuffled off as quickly as possible. The Jacksons nearly lost one of the twins, Matai, but ended up trading in the underground – the last level on the ship that was too packed for the guards to patrol – for a med pack. It turns out med packs were limited on board, the med packs we had in our quarters were the only packs given to families for the entire trip, with the rich hoarding them.

Malachai had traded his life to the air patrol for the additional med packs for his family. The dealers, who would receive a percentage of the wages, had shared that Thaddeus and Raven were undesirable candidates for the *Titan* guards, but Malachai was young enough to mould. Raven protested, begging Malachai to wake up, that the guards were responsible for so many civilian deaths too, and probably behind the disappearances of civilians that were occuring every so often. She didn't want him to trade his soul for that. But Thaddeus held Raven and told her if no one was going to join, Matai would die. They made a choice, and Malachai left their quarters, never to be with his family again.

We saw him now and again on screens: he had worked hard, and made it to the Royal Guard at 17 – the special duty guards that look after those who run the *Titan* and all who live in the Calypso level. Malachai wasn't allowed to travel to the civilian level again as he had dedicated his life to protecting those in charge.

Thaddeus and Langi became bakers at one of the main Bakeries for the civilian levels, and it was here, after my day of labour in the Gardens, I'd sneak in the back to learn more about the tech on the ship and about Dawn. Every store had an admin space, which had an inbuilt computer station and DN-8 registry, to keep track of wages of customers who bought from the store. Thaddeus, being the manager, had full access to admin, and I'd learn new ways to hack into the system, how to change the DN-8s in ways that were useful, how to sneak in a couple of extra wages and rations and so forth. I'd share with the Jacksons, making sure Raven was able to afford rations for their family. It was all confusing at first, I had learnt Python back in high school, but *Titan* used a mixture of coding languages. I taught myself each language by trial and error, and then started implementing beta programs, widgets and commands into my DN-8.

One day Raven suggested that we should randomly gift rations to workers from our level, just to see if the hacks worked for others, and they did. We sent rations to the workers in the Gardens, then the Kitchens, and then Butchers and then eventually to every working department. Soon, we were doing it so often it became a part of our routines; we'd choose a day, and spread the new upgrades, rations and wages anonymously.

Eventually, after months of feeding people, it was Jakobi who jokingly, but affectionately called us Pie-Rats, because we'd all be eating lab-grown meat pies at the bakery, working on a new upgrade together to make the lives of our level a little better. Craydon joined us a few times, and after a while, they just turned up everyday, helping us with the hacks. Eventually, after a few awkward smiles and moments, we started dating. But no matter how sympathetic Craydon was, they were still a guard, so eventually, it ended between us, and they never came back.

The name Rats stuck, and slowly, with the help of a new hack that changed our appearances with holo disguises and voice changers, we gathered a crew. Our avatars made it possible for the Rats to be out in public to talk to people, with an understanding that it wouldn't be shared with authorities. We were for the people, and the people would never turn us in. All the Rats contributed to creating community gatherings, and being physically present, talking to the crowds. All except me. I was the one actively hacking and we had to keep that a secret. The others, their avatars became the face of the Rats. But they always paid tribute to me, their faceless operator as 'the Capricorn' – the nickname Dad gave me for being hard-headed when I was a child, but also Waru's birth sign.

Now I'm here, in the shadows, in the back of a Rats rally. Raven is all in red, handprint smeared on her avatar's face. Langi with her pink bright hair, is with Thaddeus who's all in dark green, behind Raven, and Jakobi is to the side of the makeshift stage, his dark oak cane with a snake carved into that handle, in hand. He chose not to use the med pack all those years ago, refusing to remove a reminder of what happened, of what they took. The underground is packed now, with workers and the new middle class who are still loyal to their roots packing in like sardines.

Raven starts to speak, voice loud, projecting to the back. The crowd is quiet at first, but then they start answering her questions, in unison, like a chant. She sees me and I can feel her adrenaline, and her passion in that moment. Pride radiates from her.

'They're in the crowd tonight, comrades. Our Capricorn!'

People cheer and look around. I cling closer to the wall I'm leaning on, pretending to look around as well.

Raven continues, 'And they have a treat for all who have gathered here tonight.'

I smile and quietly touch my DN-8 to upload new water rations for those within my radius. A series of little blips scatter across the crowd as a litre of water rations is added to their wages. Gasps and louder cheers fill the room, two teenagers nearby talk about how they're going to share with their parents. Another elderly man nearby sighs in relief, looking upward to whichever creator he believes in. Raven continues talking above the noise, about the Rats and our mission. The noise from the crowd gradually subsides but before she can finish, a slow, loud clap just to my left interrupts her, and a clearing of a throat follows. It's a guard, one of the dirties, a dealer. He knows he has no power here yet he wears his uniform and interrupts the rally like we should kiss the ground he's on.

'What a wonderful speech. But we're not really here about just water, right?'

He looks around and people near him shift away. He takes offence.

'Are we not going to speak about what happened in the Calypso? Are we not going to talk about why our water ration system is suddenly no longer working? Are we going to talk about the missing people, or are we going to pretend that that's not happening?'

He stands there, arms crossed, waiting for an answer, but it isn't Raven that gives it. Jakobi speaks from where he stands, all eyes following his voice. His avatar is fifty years older than he really is. I remember the day he showed us all his main disguise: *I'm too easily identifiable as a young person with a cane, but an older person, it'll be harder for anyone to identify me if they tried.*

'We've been looking for our people,' Jakobi says, 'And each time they disappear, it's your people who are disappearing them, are they not?'

The guard is taken aback and Jakobi starts to walk towards him, his cane echoes as he speaks, the snake coming to life on his cane and wrapping itself around his hand.

'Our people have done everything we can with what we have. We share rations, we come together to help when our own die and we continue to demand justice for what they took from us, what they continue to take.' Jakobi is standing right infront of him now, looking down at the guard. 'What have *you* done?' His eyes crinkle into crows feet as he regards him.

The room is full of *mm*s and *ahh*s of agreement. The guard looks away from him.

Jakobi turns to make his way back to where he was standing when the guard speaks again. 'I have footage of what happened in the Calypso, and what is happening up there, will soon happen down here. The Rats can't stop that.' His accent is different to everyone else's, I can't quite place where from in the moment.

It's quiet again, but Jakobi's voice fills up the room as he turns back to the guard. He regards him as he speaks. 'And, what *did* you see?'

The guard answers without missing a beat, his voice different: '*They're* back.'

Confusion is written all over the crowd's faces, except Jakobi, who understands the guard first.

'Like we all saw in Germany all those years ago,' the guard continues, speaking to the whole room now, looking at everyone around him. 'The plants, decorating the walls, turned into a man and killed someone in the Calypso. Someone so important that they're lying about it.'

The room is full of murmurs, and the guard continues, not moving, now locking eyes with Jakobi's Avatar. 'I've only come down here to warn others who would listen, because I was from here. I don't think the Rats can do anything. But I was also curious, curious as to what the Capricorn would do. What the Capricorn *could* do.'

People start looking around now, scared and whispering to their neighbours, with others starting to shuffle off towards the exits.

'Since the Capricorn is in the crowd, tell us.' He turns now, to scan the room. 'What are you going to do when another rapture happens on this very ship?'

Before his eyes even reach my silhouette, a loud familiar noise fills the air, then screams, as people start dispersing, running in different directions, away from the sound. Someone in the crowd yells 'PIGSSSS!' People scramble, and I try my best to track where Raven and the others may be. I stand up straighter, trying to focus on my breathing, and as I look to the far wall, I see Matai opening a panel from inside the wall in the back corner, and Jakobi ushering everyone into the secret passageway.

I know they're safe now, and I tap my DN-8 to go on ghost mode. The upgrade allows me to cloak myself and become invisible to the naked eye and to the eye-tech guards wear. I make my way towards where the guard was. As soon as my boots touch a sticky substance, I know it's his blood.

The crowd had run through it, so my own bloody footprints wouldn't be noticed. Still, I lift my boot out of his blood and walk around the puddle to look at his body. He's limp and unmoving, a new hole is burnt through his forehead, scorch marks still red hot. I try my best to not be horrified, to not feel sick, to not cry. I want to close his eyes, give him some type of respect: he was trying to warn us. But before I can reach down, I hear shuffles to my right. A group of patrolmen is walking toward us. Before they make it, I decide to reach out for the guard's DN-8 instead, swiping all his data with one of my programs. It only takes 10 seconds for his data to transfer and save as a shortcut.

I move backwards, away from them as the small group march, led by a man in a white cape draped over his left shoulder, matching the rest of his uniform, littered in gold and black hems and badges on his right chest. I recognise the symbol on the biggest badge on his chest, *Commander of the Royal Guard*. He stands over the nameless limp body, looking down at him, disgusted. His voice echoes in the emptied common area, 'Make sure to get rid of this dirty, *our way*.' The guard, who sounds British, doesn't look at his co-workers as he gives them orders. But I do, and one of the men, lean and tall, hair short on the sides and brushed back, repeating the same orders to his fellow guardsmen, is barely a man, but Malachai himself.

—

Chiilldddd …
I have eaten but I was beaten
That won't happen again …
Stillllll …
I am hungry

It is quiet. I travel through the shadows, searching and I see her, arriving through the door, worry in her face, as she pulls out a cushion to sit and pray. She starts to sing.

Ahhhhhhh
Ahh ahhhh
Mmmmm mm mm
mmm

I answer the familiar call.

What is it that you need

She's startled by how close I am, but she continues to pray in our language. Her prayers have been working. I grow closer to her and her family, as they wear our Country around their necks. My connection to them, even though they are so far from us, grows stronger. She opens her eyes and looks at me, as if she can see me. I believe that she can.

I need to bring them back.
I need to bring them back.
I think Dawn could help us.

It's all that she whispers. Yet I know what she means, what she needs. And I will provide. For I am hungry for more than just prayers.

When I make it back to our quarters, the Jacksons are there too, all their avatars off, except Langi, all dressed in worry and concern. Raven's the first to walk towards me, her Black hair cascading down her square shoulders to her hips, moving with her as she makes her way closer. She hugs me, and on her skin I can smell the peaches from her fruit-picking duties. I rest my head in the nook of her neck and hold her for a little longer. Thaddeus, not reading the room, joins our embrace, and Raven lets out a low laugh against my chest.

We let go of each other and Thaddeus takes the chance to look me over. 'You right? You took longer than expected, sis.'

'We thought something bad happened ...' Raven's eyes are glassy as she looks at me and reaches for my hand. I hold it and squeeze.

'I'm okay, but I think ... I think we should all sit down for this debrief.'

So that's what the Rats do: Jakobi, Thaddeus, Langi, Raven and Matai squeeze around our table. I tell them the gist of what I learnt going through the shortcut, looking through the data as I made my way home. I shared that there were guards and they were looking for the dirty who was killed tonight, Tyrone Tore. I recognised the last name, I've seen it on one of the missing posters. From his data, I learnt that he was from our level and traded his life for a med pack and additional care for his mother after she was diagnosed with lung cancer. He had come back tonight to warn his mother, but she was missing for weeks now. They were from Aotearoa, that's where the accent was from. Although he was white, his mum was Māori, and she had adopted him when he was five, as she couldn't have children of her own. He had warned her about the disappearances, to be extra vigilant and always let him know she made it back home after her shifts in the Butchers, through an encrypted DN-8 channel. Tonight was the first time he had been able to get down to our level to look for her – but he never found her.

Lastly, I mention the recordings from the night Tyrone described in the Calypso, and he was right, what he witnessed was true.

I let them all sit with this new information, and it's Langi who speaks first. She pushes her pink hair from her face and tucks it behind her ear, her eyes trained on mine, face anxious. 'You think we'll be safe, sis?'

She's not asking outright, but I know what she really means. *We're Indigenous, we should be safe, right?* I just nod, assuring her.

'Did you see who it killed?' Jakobi asks, leaning back on his chair now, one of his thick eyebrows raised. He looks so much like our father now, but his chin is more square, and his cheekbones are chiselled high, leading you to look right into his green eyes. The same eyes all the women in our family have, except me. I have the same brown eyes as my father, the same brown eyes Waru had.

I finally take a seat next to Raven and look around the table. 'I couldn't believe it, I had to pause it and do a quick face recognition against the body.'

I touch my DN-8 and bring up the image of Madame Reece Alexandre, the second biggest donor of the *Titan*, and second-in-command.

Thaddeus looks at me, confused. 'She was on our screens yesterday, sharing public announcements.'

Langi chimes in, 'Yeah, she was sharing something about the Calypso ball happening, and how civilians are now invited.' A smirk appears on her face, her freckles changing into different constellations. 'Which I found quite odd, but especially even more odd since the ball is in two nights. Like what would we wear to the ball, potato bags? It was like she was taunting us, but at the same time, she seemed so ...' She shakes her head, at her own disbelief. 'So genuine. Like it was something that needed to happen.'

A Calypso ball – they've had them every year, but civilians were never invited. We always just heard about what happened through the chitter chatter from the Seamstresses or those who worked in the Kitchens.

Jakobi shifts in his chair. 'Maybe ... it wasn't her.'

We all look at him a little confused, but then I catch on before he can continue. 'Maybe ... They created their own avatar technology. Maybe they can disguise themselves too.' But why would they announce a ball, using her image as an avatar? Why would she invite civilians?

Jakobi realises the same thing I do. 'It's a trap ...'

'Do you think they know about us?' I ask.

Raven shakes her head. 'They shouldn't. We've been proper careful, we've even shared our own rations so we're excluded from potential suspects, we've been anonymous and have kept you out of the limelight. No one from here would rat out the Rats either.'

Another heartbreaking realisation hit me. Of course it wasn't someone from our level who may have said something.

Raven notices the shift in me. 'Hey Mina, you right?'

I nod her off and change the subject quickly before she could catch on.

'There's also something else I need to mention.' I look at Matai, who's been the quietest of us all. 'The guards who came down were being led by the Commander of the Royal Guard. Malachai was here tonight.'

Matai's face transforms from observant to shocked. He asks quickly 'Did he seem ... okay?' His eyes are eager to see the answer fall out of my mouth.

'He seemed like he was doing his best,' I say politely.

Raven nudges my shoulder. 'You know what we mean,' she presses.

I look at her carefully and nod and look back at Matai. 'He looked like a man, proper tired in the eyes, and as if he was trying his best to hide how horrified he was. His eyebrow twitched just like yours does when you're uncomfortable. He's ... doing his best but I can see its toll up close. He's much taller, his baby face is now made of harsh lines. They have trained him hard. He sounds like them now, too.'

Matai is quiet, looking at his reflection on the wall, as if looking to see a hint of Malachai. But the two of them are different now.

Thaddeus stands and walks towards me, grabbing me out the chair, into another hug. 'Thank you, sis.'

Raven just smiles at me, her dimples showing and starry eyed, from her seat. Oh god, how lucky am I.

Gracie, all brunette kinks, rushes into the room and interrupts us, a big smile on her face. 'Mum saved up to buy us lab-grown bacon and eggs for dinner!' She goes to the kitchen wall and takes out dinner with her little hands.

Langi rushes to help her and reminds her that she's the one who we should be taking care of, not the other way around. She just pokes her tongue out and gets plates as I rush to get cutlery for us all. The Jacksons had brought roasted vegetables and we share, talking about trivial and small things that happened throughout our 'normal' days. We steer clear of any more Rats talk in front of Gracie. We all take turns feeding Mum and talking to her directly. After dinner is finished we all agree to touch base again in the morning.

—

I had only slept for a couple of hours before being shaken up by a call on my wrist. I see the name that pops up on the holo screen as I tap my DN-8 but I don't pick it up. Instead, I get out of bed, put my boots back on and make my way to our old secret spot in the Gardens. It only takes me a couple of minutes to reach the spot and I see their silhouette straight away. When I was younger, I remember the butterflies I would get, and my heart's quickening pace, when I saw them waiting for me, in our garden. The small patch of roses we planted together, giggling and drunk on love. It was the place we told each other we loved each other. But now, I am full of disappointment, anger and regret. They turn around and their face is filled with relief and joy. They pull me into their arms before either of us can speak.

'I'm so glad you're ok, Mina.'

They must notice I'm not hugging them back because they release me with a quick apology.

'What do you want, Craydon?'

I think I know what they're going to say, what they're going to tell me. It was them who ratted us out. They were there from the beginning, making pies with us.

'I came to see if you were ok, alive, hell if you were sane!'

Their accent was always alluring to me, it reminded me of the movie adaptations of the books I loved. But at this moment, their accent just makes what they are saying sound condescending.

'What are you on about, Donny?'

Immediately, they soften up to the sound of their nickname. The one I had for them.

'You didn't hear yet? About the Calypso?'

I catch on, they're talking about the potential rapture. 'Yeah, we heard. Tyrone Tore shared the news at our rally only a few hours ago. He seemed a little harsh at first, but the more he talked, the more we could sense his fear.'

Craydon runs their hand through their thick locks, worried. 'Ty came down here? He wasn't supposed to. The guards have been cracking down on our movements in the last couple of weeks. But he wanted to come back, to warn his mum. I came down to warn you and his mum too, but as soon as I got down here, I saw her missing posters. I knew something was wrong, he was so persistent in trying to come back here. So I called you, I need to tell you what happened.'

I interrupted them. 'Did you really come to see me about this, or were you going to tell me that it was you who shared the Rats' identities to the guards?'

Craydon looks at me, offended. They retort, 'It's probably the water you've been skimming that got you caught, Amina. You know the water rations are stricter, you know something is happening with the water. *You* weren't careful enough. I knew it was you when I heard the gossip about the water level changes in the Calypso. *You* thought it was safe, but like I always said, you can't take from them if they're *watching*, and you would know that they were if *you just talked to me.*'

Craydon sighs, defeated. 'Look I came to warn you, but Ty beat me to that. You're holding up well, too. Well, he's probably back in our quarters grieving about his mother. I should probably get back.' They pick up their white emissary guard jacket from a nearby garden stool, and they start to make their way away from me.

'Donny, he's not waiting for you,' I say softly now. They freeze. 'The Royal Guard executed him tonight, one shot between the eyes, from behind. They cleaned up his body.'

Silence fills the air, along with the scent of the nearby roses. They turn to me slowly, tears welling in their eyes. They make their way back to the garden bench and sit down, slumped over, their hands holding their head as they stare at the ground.

'They're going to come for me next, Mina.'

I look at them, confused.

'I was there that night, with Ty. I saw it kill Madame Reece and take the kid.'

I looked at them, even more confused. 'Huh? What kid?'

They look at me. 'Ty didn't tell everyone about the kid?'

I shake my head, even more confused. Craydon reaches for my hands and holds them.

'We didn't have any weapons, so we hid as we watched Madame Reece's body fall from the plantman's vines. It took a kid from her quarters – I told Ty I recognised them. A sibling from one of the families on the civilian level. He must've been silenced on purpose before he could say anything more at the rally.' Craydon glances down at our hands. 'I told him not to come down here.'

I am perplexed as to why this news would necessitate them holding my hands.

'The Royal Guard somehow stabilised the creature with their DN-8s and these round devices they threw around it.' They look back up at me, with tenderness in their eyes. 'They removed the child from its arms without it resisting. After that, the Commander motioned to a guard at his side, and with the press of a button on a controller, the vine creature burst into flames. Dead. They talked about "freezing" the girl. She couldn't have been more than three years old, she looked so tiny, Amina, and so frail.'

'She looked just like you, like the picture of your little brother you showed me. I swear on all things good on this ship, that little girl was Rosie.'

—

This should work this time. They've learned about what we've been doing in the gardens. A lone plantmen didn't work, but this should.

I watch her whisper to the clump of metal in her hands, which is connected to her screen above her bed by what she calls a network of wires. The metal clump rises, hovering above her hand, and a smile spreads across her face. I can feel a connection. She looks at me now.

Told you Dawn could help.

Shall I follow the pathway you created?

Follow it, and take over. You're going to bring a whole new meaning to "A New Day, A New Dawn"

She smiles to herself. I can't help but do the same. Her plans are going to work and I shall eat all that I can. I extend my hand towards the clump of metal and I am immediately inside the machine, like she said. I look around and I see an orange line alight on the floor. This is the pathway. I zoom through the path, passing what she described as codes. A language she was familiar with. At the end of the path, is an enormous orb, white at the edges and pink in the centre.

Hello?

A familiar voice fills the void.

Hello, Dawn

How did you get past the secur—

Before she can finish, I dive into the orb, as I was instructed and my body expands, over numerous channels throughout the ship. I feel the power of the access I have to every part of the Titan. It worked like she said: 'Some of the metals on this ship are from the mines from our country. It's in the Titan guidelines of the ship, specifically the story about how the Titan was built. This ship is a part of you'. It's no wonder I've grown so much stronger. I appear on her screen, and she smiles, wider.

We're going to have to pretend to be Dawn for a couple of days until the ball. But when the time comes, we should be able to stop them, and end it all and get them all back.

I shall feast on all their souls

She smiles and goes back to sleep.

The next morning we have a Rats meeting. I look around the room at everyone, and decide that it's now or never, that this is the perfect time to tell them what Craydon told me. I clear my throat and let the truth free.

'No way! That can't be true. Can it?' Langi is on her feet, pacing the room. She's not asking this question to anyone in particular.

Jakobi, who is unusually silent throughout my whole explanation, asks, 'Did you see her Amina?'

I nod and bring up the footage I had replayed to myself in the early hours of the morning. They all have their mouths agape when they see the little girl in the grips of the vine humanoid.

'It's her. It's definitely her.' Langi's gaze does not leave the screen.

The energy in the room is different and all the Jacksons are silent, trying their best to support us by letting us talk amongst ourselves.

I stand up and look at Jakobi. 'We're going to the ball tomorrow night,' I declare.

He raises an eyebrow, unsure why we'd do so, but like we've always seemed to do, he reads my mind and nods. 'We're going to find Rosie, and we're going to need all the help we can get.'

We plan through the day, scrambling to get ready before the ball. As we get our avatars ready, Gracie pleads non-stop to come, and eventually we cave. We design an avatar for Mum as well for the occasion.

I decide not to wear an avatar, just so if we do find Rosie, she can recognise that we're family. I don't know what tonight will bring, but she will be able to see her face in mine.

—

It's happening tonight, Kabozie.
Are you still hungry?

Starving

*With that, she nods and ties her hair up, and leaves for the
ball, where I will birth more life into the plants. I watch her
leave and make my way through the channels of Dawn to the
Calypso. I go to the secret base behind the ballroom where they
keep them 'frozen', and count the bodies I can see on rotation
in the water purifier. There's seven of them, being drained. I
want to eat those who harmed them, but I remember the plan.
We must distract the others before we can rescue them.*

When we arrive at the Calypso, the level is packed, full of people we don't recognise and people we do. Civilians had shown up in numbers, wearing their digital clothing, speaking to others about how real it all feels. A girl nearby, around Gracie's age, twirls around in her gown, exclaiming that she's always wanted to be a princess. Her parents hold each other, looking at her twirl in awe. I couldn't help but smile at the people enjoying themselves.

Plants hang everywhere from the golden walls. The hallways had paintings after paintings, with an occasional statue or vase on a pedestal decorating the space. But the plants, they're just ... everywhere. I look at my small party and give them a curt nod. Thaddeus and Langi split off together, Matai escorts Gracie and Mum to a station with drinks just behind us and Raven and Jakobi walk off thinking Craydon would be following from behind.

Instead, Craydon makes their way to my side. 'There are more plants on the walls tonight. There's never been this many. Hell, there was a rule about too many plants introduced before launch because one of the founders had allergies.'

'They're probably for the person responsible for the raptures. I still don't get it though. You can't control a rapture, they just happen, right?' I say.

Craydon has fallen silent, and I turn to them to see why. Standing in front of them is the commander of the Royal Guard. Craydon looked like they had seen a ghost. The commander speaks. 'Well, what a wonderful sight. It's so good to finally see you Emissary Gould. I've been meaning to talk with you.'

Before Craydon can respond, the commander turns to look at me, the tone of voice harder. 'Do you mind?' His head tilts, never leaving my gaze.

I quickly counter and bow. 'We were just heading toward the floor for our first dance, Commander. Truly, a wish of mine since

Madame Reece's announcement!' I hold Craydon's arm, trying to walk off, but the commander simply puts his hand out in front of Craydon.

'I believe you can still have your first dance with one of our guards.' He puts his hand down and behind him a familiar boy walks out to stand in front of me, dressed in a maroon tuxedo. 'Malachai, see to it that Emissary Gould's date is able to fulfil her wish of dancing tonight. I need to speak to them urgently, and privately.'

With that, Craydon looks at me with apologetic eyes. I know that something terrible may happen, that this could be the last time I see them. The commander turns for Craydon to follow and I reach out for their arm again, but Malachai quickly pushes it down, as Craydon pleads for me to not do something I'll regret with a quick shake of their head. I watch them leave through the crowd and I pray that they stay protected.

I turn to Malachai who holds his arm out, waiting for me to accept his invitation for a dance. I take it but cannot help myself asking straight away, 'Why'd you do that?'

'For your own good, Amina,' Malachai states. I take his hand. His voice isn't the same, it has more bass, more mature.

'Like you'd know what was good for me,' I counter.

He sighs. He doesn't look at me, as he leads me to the floor where people are waltzing and we begin to mimic those around us. I've never waltzed before. Malachai knows how, so he leads me instead, looking around the ballroom.

'Who else is here tonight, Mina?' His face is scanning each individual; his eye tech is probably searching their identities.

'All of the Rats are.'

'Did she not tell you to leave?'

'What do you mean, Malachai?'

He whispers, his face unsettled, 'Do you not know?'

Is he talking about Raven? What did Raven have to say to me, how did he get into contact with her? I'm the first of the Rats to ever speak to him in years. Before I can answer, the music stops, and the tapping of a mic echoes around us.

Madame Reece speaks from a podium elevated by a stage at the end of the ballroom. She greets everyone to the third ball of the *Titan*. Cheers and applause echo throughout the Calypso. Her smile is unsettling as she waves to the crowd.

Her speech takes an abrupt turn. 'I wish I were here today, alive and well, to celebrate with you all, but unfortunately, a few nights ago, I was murdered by a creature.' Gasps now replace the applause, and so do whispers of confusion. 'You might be thinking, how am I here today? How am I standing on this stage, greeting you all tonight?'

The room stills.

'Well, it's because I am not Madame Reece Alexandre.' The wicked smile of Madame Reece's fades, as the avatar pixels slowly disappear from the face, making their way down the body. Now standing on the stage is a man, blond and pale, smirking. 'It's me, Tristan Titan, your captain and the heart of the *Titan*. I am here tonight, away from the control room, to find Madame Reece Alexandre's killer, and the person responsible for the series of raptures we've had in the Calypso.'

People erupt with questions, in gossip and shock.

'Raptures? Since when could raptures happen in space?' a man says to his dance partner. Another woman is horrified, standing in front of me, looking at her partner. 'The kolony ship was supposed to save us, Edward, what are we to do now?' Tristan claps twice from the podium and looks down at the crowd with hungry eyes. 'Citizens of the *Titan*, do not think so little of me!

I always have a plan. Bring out the girl!'

Behind him, two guards push forward a small child. She's wearing a different nightie to the one she wore in the footage we saw from that night. I go rigid.

'No, this wasn't supposed to happen.' Malachai blurts 'Rosie isn't supposed to be up there.'

I turn to Malachai, eyes wide. How does he know about her?

He curses and continues. 'The guards were supposed to wait for the plants to awaken. That's how they were supposed to know who was behind the raptures. They must know she's here. They're panicking. But this will backfire, Tristan has given Kabozie access to all these plants.' Malachai looks at me, and grabs me by my shoulders. 'Where are the Rats, Amina? I need to find them now, before the guards do.'

'They're here, behind the walls.'

He swears under his breath and looks behind him, towards Matai. 'Just listen to her, we've known it was a trap but we didn't see this coming. I'll find the others, but, listen to her ok. She's been helping me for years now, with her own little hacks Amina, it's time you let her help you.'

Before I can ask for an explanation or who 'she' is, he runs towards the secret chambers which can be accessed at the back of the stage, through the doors on the right.

'Now, will the person responsible come forward, or I'll kill her here and now,' Tristan snarls. Rosie looks up at him, fear in her eyes. She's still just a baby, yet she seems to understand. He looks down at her quivering body. 'I'm so sorry, darling, but you were only adopted to appease Madame Reece. She can't have any rascals herself ... well, couldn't.'

He claps his hands, and one of the guards pushes her to the floor whilst the other aims his gun to the back of Rosie's head.

She starts pushing herself up from the floor, eyes shut tight, tears streaming down her face.

'Hurry now, before the child suffers your consequences,' Tristan declares, scanning the room.

I can't breathe, I feel heavy and light as a feather simultaneously. He can't kill her, not when we've just found her. These people can't take another of my siblings. I push the people in front of me, ready to interject this madness.

Before my voice can even project itself to scream *it was me*, that I deserve these consequences in her place instead, another voice fills the ballroom, one that is familiar and so very young.

'You touch her again, and I'll make sure your death is *long* and *painful*.'

I turn to face the source of the voice, and even though I see her, I can't register that those words came from her mouth and that she is hovering eight feet above the ground. 'Gracie?' is all that comes out of my mouth.

'There she is. Seize her!' Tristan screams, a deranged smile spreading across his face.

Gracie, looks at the plants, and gives a wave. But no vine creatures manifest from the walls.

'Such a pathetic. little. girl. You think we would place real plants in this room?' His smile is sinister.

Panic does not overcome Gracie like it does me as the guards get closer to where she, Matai and Mum are. Instead she returns his smile, with one of her own, as she digs into her pockets throwing seeds on the ground.

She closes her eyes and chants: '*Awaken children, for Kabozie is hungry for the souls who have separated us from our homes, who have destroyed our lands and people. It is time they pay the price.*'

The seeds sprout in an instant and become vine creatures, with an occasional rose sprouting from their vines. She must have been taking these seeds from the Gardens every time she'd visited me with Mum.

A guard pushes past me and I realise how close they really are to her. I gather myself and I run toward him, throwing the boomerang whisper blade I'd hidden beneath my clothes. It goes straight through his back and returns through his chest. He's on the floor now. There's two others running from my left towards Gracie and I touch my DN-8, pushing one of the weapon hacks. From my wrist, to the middle of my forearm, two barrels form for electric shocks to shoot from. I aim at both guards and nick the first one on the waist, sending him crashing to the floor. The next guard gets hit in the neck and he falls on his knees before toppling over the guard in front of him. People scream, running from the ballroom.

'I'll take care of the rest of the guards, you get Rosie,' Gracie says, nodding to me.

I nod back and run at full speed towards the stage.

The two guards on stage fire at me; I dodge as many as I can before flicking my shield on. It reflects one of the lasers and gets the guard right through the heart. He falls backwards off stage. The other guard watches his body fall and screams, 'Lionel!!!'

He looks at me now and jumps off the stage, taking something strapped to his leg and connecting it to his gun. He aims it at me, and I am blown backward by the sheer force of the laser. I get back on my feet quick and watch Tristan take Rosie by the arm, kicking and screaming, leading her towards the chamber where the rest of Rats and Malachai are. I try to make a break towards them, my shield now a dome, but the guard has fired another shot at me. My shield breaks from the impact and sends me flying again, my body slamming into the wall.

I try to get up, but I just fall back down onto my side, my vision doubling. Blood trickles down the side of my head as the guard makes his way towards me. His face is nothing but furious as he gets closer.

'This is for Lionel.' He points his gun at my head.

But before he can pull that trigger, Gracie yells out: 'Kabozie, NOW!'

All the power goes out. Red emergency lights flicker on immediately, and then Dawn appears in front of me, at least seven foot tall.

She picks up the guard with one hand and forces his mouth open with the other as he kicks and squirms. My vision becomes clearer as Dawn opens her own mouth and breathes in, a blue orb escapes from his mouth into hers. His body goes limp in her hands and she drops him. Dawn turns to me and smiles. With a blink of an eye there's two, then four, then eight of her. I think it's my vision getting worse at first, but I realise that Dawn is multiplying to fight off the guards who are making their way towards us. The original Dawn picks me up in their arms and whispers in a deep voice, '**You will be safe with me child. It is me, Kabozie.**'

I remember stories about Kabozie, the spirit who sung lands into existence, who took care of our Country. They were connected to all things, and to our people and somehow, had become Dawn.

Kabozie turns to run in the opposite direction of the secret chamber and towards Gracie instead.

'We're going the wrong direction, Rosie is that way,' I protest, with the strength I have left.

Kabozie simply says, '**I've taken care of that childddd, just resttt.**'

We make it to Gracie's side and Matai rushes towards us, pushing Mum, as Gracie asks Kabozie, 'Can you heal her?'

Kabozie nods. Kabozie places their hand above my face

and starts to whisper something in our language. A feeling of lightness washes over me, I feel it travel to every part of my body, as if making sure everywhere it touches is perfect. My head feels less heavy, and the thumping has disappeared. Kabozie lifts their hand from my face. '**You are healed now**,' they say and place me on the ground. I can stand on my own two feet, and I feel stronger. Matai hugs me and checks if there's anything Kabozie may have missed.

I watch the bloody scene in front of me as he scans my body for any other wounds. Half of the vine creatures are on fire, whilst the others are killing guards, flank after flank, that are trying their best to reach us. The multiple Dawn holograms are wreaking havoc in front of us, but also near the hallways at the back which leads to the secret chamber.

Before I can register the rest of the fighting in front of us, a loud blast comes from behind the stage making a massive hole in the wall. Out from the smoke come multiple Dawns, carrying bodies, bodies I recognise from posters, bodies of people we had laid to rest over the years. Bodies belonging to Indigenous people. In the centre, the Rats walk through the smoke, and it is Malachai who has Rosie in his arms. She looks like Waru, eyes so big and green, with a head full of curls. He holds onto her tight as he runs towards us.

'**Those who sought out harm shall fall**.' Kabozie's voice echoes from Dawn. Guards who have lined up to fire their guns are lifted in the air with a wave of a hand and thrown out of the way. The sound of bones breaking and agony add to the symphony of guttural sounds, and guards yelling orders that fill the ballroom already.

There are only a few guards left, just a little over a dozen, who look around at each other in the ballroom and at the bodies

around them. This is not a rapture they could win, even with the
help of their new devices. The one closest to us throws his weapon
at us, and runs towards the exits. The rest follow and the Rats run
towards us. Raven makes it to us first and jumps in my arms. She
then holds my face and kisses me.

'Please tell me you're ok?' she asks, looking into my eyes.

'I am now,' I tell her.

Langi and Thaddeus follow close behind, carrying missing
children from our level. 'They were in some sort of pool,' Langi
says. 'Their bodies were floating in the water, and they were
plugged into a machine, Amina. It was taking their blood.'

'There's more of them there though, they're frozen, as if waiting
to go on rotation to have their blood drained,' Thaddeus adds.

'We also took a long time because we found someone we
haven't seen in a while.'

Behind them, walking in front of Malachai, is a man who is
a spitting image of the Jackson's father. He's much frailer than
the last time I saw him, but he recognises me, and embraces me.
'Long time no see, Capricorn.' It's Raven's older brother.

'It's good to see you too, Church.'

He releases me and smiles, making his way for a bear hug
with Matai. Raven and Thaddeus are wiping tears away as they
watch their brothers embrace each other. Malachai makes his way
towards us, with Rosie in his arms.

At that moment, the commander of the Royal Guard appears
from the shadows on the right, holding Craydon by their collar.
The commander aims his gun at Malachai and fires, the blast
going straight through both of Malachai's legs, which give way.

'Noooooo!' I scream as I watch both Malachai and Rosie fall
to the ground.

'Well, what do we have here. Is this the infamous group, the

Rats?' He shoves Craydon to the floor. 'Were you a part of this, Emissary Gould? Looks like they might have one less member.'

Malachai crawls towards Rosie and covers her with his whole body, telling her not to move. The commander takes out his gun and goes to add the new attachment to his weapon like the other guard had. Gracie lifts her hands towards the plants, but the commander just laughs.

'They're not going to do anything to me, little girl. I noticed that natives weren't dying during the raptures, and spun up the DN-8 program.' He points to his wrist. 'Why do you think these Dawn holograms won't touch me? These creatures? I stole your blood to immunise myself and everyone on kolony ships from these raptures. Just like my forefathers stole you and did what they wanted. And now, we've found a way to weaponise it.' He reaches into his pocket and takes out the circular device that had been thrown to kill the vine creatures.

Gracie hovers down to join us and tries to take a step closer to me.

'I wouldn't move if I were you, I feel a little too trigger-happy.' He points his gun at Malachai now. 'Ohhh, let's play a game,' he says, enthralled, and goes back and forth between the two. 'Eeny, meeny, miny, moe.'

Craydon winces each time the gun hits the back of their head. 'Catch a tiger by the toe. If he screams, let him go, eeny, meeny, miny, m—'

'There's just one thing wrong with your plan, Commander,' I say.

He stops and looks at me, amused.

I smile at him. 'You forgot that *we're human.*'

I grab my whisper blade and throw it fast, letting it soar straight through the middle of the commander's stomach. I move the handle up so the blade goes higher as it returns, and it whistles straight through his shoulder blade and heart, returning to me. His body drops to the floor, and everyone rushes to Malachai, Rosie and Craydon.

Craydon hugs me. 'Thank you, Mina.'

'It's the least I could do,' I smirk and Craydon softly smiles.

'I'll gather what's left of the guards and tell them things are going to be changed around here,' they say. Everyone agrees to this task, and Craydon runs off, only looking back to wave goodbye.

Kabozie heals Malachai's wounds and all the bumps and scratches on Rosie. When Kabozie finishes, we all wrap our arms around the pair. I let go first, standing next to Mum, and look at Gracie, who is nestled between Jakobi and Langi as they hold onto Rosie.

'Gracie, I really need you to explain everything. Even just a little bit.'

Gracie smiles, walking towards Mum. 'Did you think I followed any rules? I was always listening, Mina. I learnt about coding by looking over your shoulder or listening to you talking about it with everyone. I remember what Mum taught us, what Dad taught us, about our ancestors, about praying, about faith. I started practising and Kabozie came to me. I wanted to help, Amina, but everyone just saw me as the baby. I wanted to look after everyone too.'

I look at her and tenderly say, '*We're* supposed to look after *you*, sissy.' I reach for her cheek and she holds my hand there.

'I can look after myself, Amina, I'm stronger than you think.'

I laugh and look at Rosie. I kneel down and introduce myself.

'Hi little one, I'm Amina. One of your big sisters. You may not remember me, but I remember you, especially the day you were born.' I wait for confusion to wash over her face but Rosie smiles, not scared at all.

Gracie smiles. 'Oh she knows who we are, Amina, Kabozie and I have been telling her about our family for a while now.' Rosie smiles and runs towards our mum and hugs her legs. For a second, it looks like Mum is overcome with tears.

I grin, accepting the fact that Gracie has covered a lot over the years without my knowledge. I stand up to look around. This place will need a lot of cleaning, but all these people from the freezing will need help to find their families. I ask Kabozie if they can help with this, but they say they're already on it.

I look around at the Rats, and I can't help but ask, with a half smile 'So what yas reckon, Rats? What are we going to do next'

Gracie is the first to answer. 'We're going back home, isn't that right, Kabozie?'

One of Kabozie's holo clones appears in front of us and brings up a map of our journey back towards earth.

'We're going back, to save our Country, our people, and to get Dad, Janaya, Tesi, Emeni, and Alkani,' Gracie says, and it's in that moment I truly notice how much she's grown. I think she's finished but she continues.

'But we also have to find Waru.'

I look at her, confused. 'What do you mean, Gracie,' I say.

She looks at me, and at the rest of our family.

'Waru isn't completely gone, he sent Kabozie to me.'

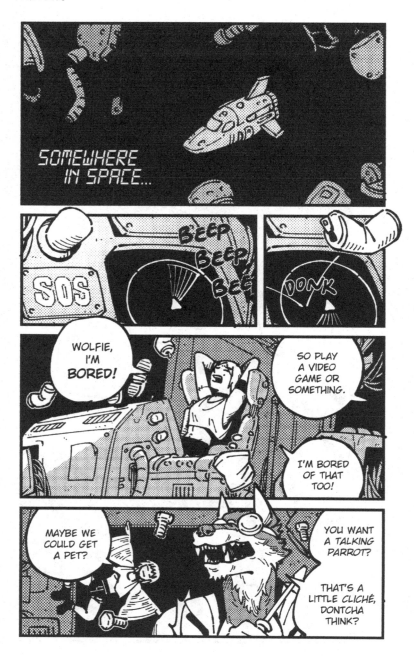

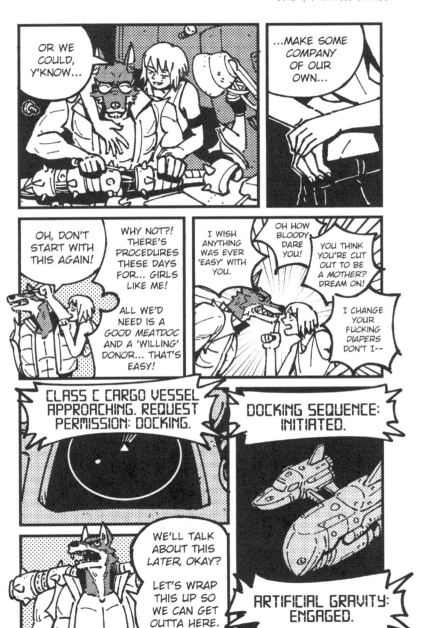

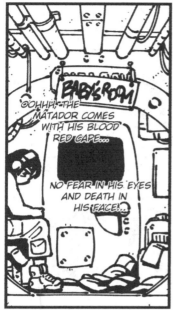

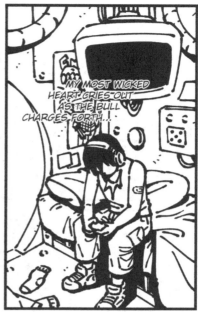

THOSE TWO PEOPLE. ARE THEY YOUR PARENTS?

...NONE OF YOUR BUSINESS.

AND THE PEOPLE ON THE SHIP...

DID YOU KILL THEM?

PFFT. YEAH. SO WHAT?

...GOOD.

...WERE THEY YOUR PARENTS?

NAH. THEY WERE JUST SOME SMUGGLERS.

MY PARENTS TRADED ME TO 'EM FOR A BIG DRILL.

(THEY'RE ASTEROID MINERS.)

DUDE, THAT'S LIKE... REALLY MESSED UP.

DID THEY...

...HURT YOU?

NAH, THEY JUST MADE ME DO THEIR CHORES.

I HAD TO CLEAN THE TOILET. BLEGH!

HAHAHA. EWW!

YEAH, MUM MAKES ME DO THAT TOO. I MEAN, SHE'S KINDA MY MUM.

THEY RAISED ME AND EVERYTHING, SO I *GUESS* THEY'RE, LIKE, MY PARENTS...

BUT THEY DIDN'T HAVE ME, HAVE ME. Y'KNOW?

MUM, SHE'S NOT... SHE CAN'T HAVE KIDS.

AND DAD, HE'S... WELL, HE'S A MUTANT DOG MAN. SO.

WELL, THEY SEEM NICE. NICER THAN MY PARENTS, ANYWA-

THEY'RE NOT GONNA KEEP YOU, YOU KNOW.

THIS ISN'T, LIKE, A CHARITY.

THEY'RE NOT GONNA KEEP SOME DIRTY STOW-AWAY JUST 'CAUSE YOU POUT AND SOOK.

FIRST CHANCE THEY GET, THEY'RE FLUSHING YOU OUT THE AIRLOCK.

...THEY KEPT YOU, DIDN'T THEY?

HEY KIDDO, YOU WANT A JOB?

WE TALKED IT OVER AND--

YOU MEAN I CAN STAY?!

WHAT ARE FALSE STARS TO A GOD?

ALEXANDER TE POHE

Chapter 1

WOODEN ships float through the blushing sky. Thick lines on their underbellies glow a soft purple, painting the figures of a lion, an archer, a ram and all Gods of the constellations. The smaller crafts float around the enormous mother ship and the beating heart of the Fleet – the *Scorpius*. Oliver stares up at Helios' Constellation Fleet in awe. He's grown up with these stars and yet, every time he sees them, he's struck by their majestic beauty.

Someone pokes him in the back. He tips his gaze back down. Back to the procession of groggy kids and adolescents standing in single file. Back to the desert and the swirling dust. He sighs inwardly, wishing more than anything that he was not here in this colourless place. He turns and his twin sister Clementine is frowning at him.

'What?' says Oliver.

'Stop staring at those things,' says Clem with unbridled disdain. She drops her voice and adds, 'They won't be up there for much longer anyway.'

'They're not *things* and, besides, let's see who wins: a crew of grounders or the Celestials.'

Clem's eyes narrow and Oliver knows that if they were at home, their old argument would be recycled again. Clem would say that the Celestials are greedy and deserve to be brought down. Oliver would counter that they are something to aspire to. Their mother Leto would step in and air tales of her time working as an engineer on the *Scorpius*. Oliver had heard them all his life and after a while, he tunes their obvious exaggerations out. Leto always takes Clem's side but at least out here, he doesn't have to listen to their joint tirade again.

'Just focus on the line, okay?' says Clem.

She slicks her short purple hair back and faces forward.

Oliver's eyes stay on the crowd, but his mind flies up past the birds, through the underside of the *Scorpius*, to the gears cranking energy through the veins of the ship, all the way to the upper decks. He imagines glass shoes, long skirts tracing swirling patterns on the floor, delicate puffy sleeves, tall swan-like necks, and eyes focused not up but ahead and outwards seeing all the beauty life offers them and taking it all in.

The line snakes downhill, through flat plains, and over temporary bridges built across deep breaks in the ground. Looking into the chasms, Oliver sees only darkness. From the *Scorpius*, Helios' Domain must look as if many deep cuts have been carved into the land, with more appearing every week. Kids zip just over their heads on their boards, heading home after a long night in the mines. Others walk past, their eyes glazed over or already half closed.

They make it to the front. Line manager Erp ushers them towards the wooden platform with a dozen others. They're forced to squish together, all shoulders, elbows, and feet. This close the scent of soap, sweat, and freshly washed clothes mingles in the air. They all wear the same thing: a helmet, a pair of overalls over a long-sleeved shirt and laced-up boots.

'We haven't been this close since we were in the womb,' Clem says with a little laugh as she shoves her helmet on.

Oliver gives her a look. It's the same joke she makes every day. Sometimes he laughs, but today he's too tired to force it.

'Going down!' shouts the liftman.

The platform shudders as it slowly descends. Oliver watches the ships collapse into the shrinking light above. The lift grinds to a stop in a tunnel. The passage is small and cramped; Oliver has to hunch over to avoid hitting his head on the ceiling. Soon enough he'll quite literally outgrow this job and be assigned elsewhere. With his skills, he could work in the engine rooms in the floating provinces above. It is more likely that he'll be forced to join his mother in her junk shop or the bakery with Luci and her mother. Working in a place where he can't be of use to Empress Selene and her Celestials feels like an insult. Unfortunately, well-paid jobs on ships, ones that require being born above and not below, are rarely given to people like him.

They're loaded onto a tram and after a dull two-hour ride they arrive at their work site. Some kids are already there, slowly picking away at the deep purple Cygnusite. Clem bounds up to them, exchanging greetings, hugs, even bread. Oliver lifts his arm to wave and gets to work on the stone. Deep in the mines time goes slowly. The lights on his helmet do little to illuminate his surroundings and without the sun or stars, the only measure of time is the occasional rumble of a tram. Oliver keeps the Empress Selene and the Constellation Fleet at the forefront of his mind and anytime he feels the walls shrink in he reminds himself that without this stone, without him, those ships would not be able to fly. Antares, the giant stone at *Scorpius'* core, would run out of power and, without that stone, the Fleet would fall. His thoughts fill him with pride and that feeling is enough to cut through the dull and tiring monotony of this place.

Oliver finishes his shift, rests, and the next day after his morning prayer to the Empress it begins all over again. At least, for a little while anyway, he can gaze at the ships floating on burnt sunlight and feel like he is part of something beautiful.

They approach the front of the line, and alongside the line manager is an unusually pale woman. She wears a bright green floor length skirt and a white shirt with sheer sleeves that end at the elbow. She must be a Celestial. People from the Fleet don't frequent the Domain. Their main reason for visiting is Auriga: a race that happens once a decade. Oliver was six years old when the last Auriga took place; he saw Empress Selene for the first time and she appeared to him like a heavenly creature – tall, pale, and ethereal. This Celestial woman with her pearl-coloured skin, straight, long black hair and light green eyes looks like an echo of the Empress herself.

The manager, Allison, gestures for Clem. She's barely taken two steps towards them before the Celestial gestures to her short hair. Allison ushers her towards the elevator and then it's Oliver's turn. The Celestial appraises him as he approaches.

She turns to Allison. 'Who is this?'

'Oliver Mercer of Serpens.'

She makes him take out his low ponytail and he shakes his shoulder-length purple hair out, nervously combing his hands through it as if that will somehow make it look neater.

'No visible imperfections and he looks tall enough. He'll do.' She turns to Oliver. 'Hello, my name is Lily and you have been selected for a new work assignment on the *Scorpius*.'

Joy floods through Oliver's entire being. He can hardly believe what she's saying. This is his chance to leave the mines, take his place with the Celestials, and be closer to the Empress. Clem rushes to his side. 'What are you talking about?'

Lily looks at Clem like dirt under her perfectly painted nails. 'There was an unfortunate incident and we're looking for a new worker for our kitchens on the *Scorpius*. All he has to do is sign the contract.'

Lily hands him the parchment and he hastily reads it. If he works on the ship, he'll have an entire month up there before he's allowed to return. But he'll also be somewhere he's only dreamed about.

Clem squeezes his arm and he meets her gaze. Her eyebrows are drawn together in worry. She hates those ships and the Empress, but this is his dream: a job on a ship and not just any of them but the crowning jewel of the Constellations. Sure, it's not in engineering but it's something. He can't throw it away just because of Clem's opinions.

He signs the agreement. 'When do I start?'

–

Within the hour, Oliver is whisked to the docks. His mother, Leto, walks beside him. When he'd gone home to pack his bags, she was already there waiting for him. They'd argued until Oliver showed her the contract. She'd been silent ever since.

Lily waits beside one of *Scorpius*' Butterflies. The lemon-yellow boat is meant to fit around twenty people and their luggage. After years of reading about the crest of the first Emperor, Oliver can finally see Helios' circular insignia adorning the side of the Butterfly. It resembles a white sun with Helios' side profile outlined in black at the centre. For years, he's woken to the sight of the Empress' framed side portrait on his wall and imagined what Helios looked like. He does resemble the Empress – they have the same small nose and serious gaze. Unlike Empress Selene, the Emperor's chin is tilted slightly upwards and he's staring fiercely towards the sky. Oliver straightens his shoulders and holds his head high. To see the first Emperor's image is an honour only afforded to those that are part of the Fleet. Finally, Oliver's made it.

'Welcome Oliver.' Lily's eyes float over to Leto and her smile falters. 'This must be your ...'

'Mother. I'm Leto,' she says.

'I can see where Oliver got his fine features from. Though it's unfortunate about, well, you know.' She gestures to the scar on Leto's face. The thin line cuts from her forehead, over her left eye, and down her cheek. 'Otherwise, you would have been the perfect candidate for our kitchens.'

Leto smiles thinly with no warmth in her brown eyes. 'I've had the pleasure of working on the *Scorpius* long ago, but I'm quite happy where I am, thank you very much.'

'Yes, yes,' Lily says. She turns back to Oliver and beams at him. 'Say your goodbyes and join me on the boat.'

Oliver embraces Leto. She squeezes him tight and doesn't let go until Lily coughs.

'Be safe, my son,' says Leto. 'I love you.'

She helps him onto the boat, grasping tightly onto his hand. Her skin is calloused and rough and she smells of oil and dirt. It feels like home to him. Lily cranks a gear beside the steering wheel and the boat thrums to life beneath them. Leto's white hair wavers in the breeze. Her face looks much younger and, in her grimy overalls, she reminds him of Clem. As he ascends, he watches her wipe her face and then turn away. His stomach clenches. She's crying? Part of him wants to embrace her, tell her everything will be okay, but another part is brimming with annoyance. She should be happy for him and yet she can't see beyond her own prejudice. He'll be back in a month and by then all her worries will be expelled.

'This is your first time, yes?' says Lily.

Oliver nods. He's been on these boats many times in his dreams, but he could have never imagined the sound of the ocean, the smell of salt, and the feel of the boat swaying underneath him.

'First, always keep your feet firmly planted on the floor. Second, try not to move around too much. You'll end up pitching over the side. Third, if you see a dragon, do not panic. Stick firmly to the first two rules. Your driver will take you to the ship and you'll be safe there. Our sky soldiers will drive away those creatures. Got it?'

Oliver nods, in shock. He's never heard anyone talk about the dragons like that before. Leto has always said that the dragons are Gods, but he's never believed it. Leto would make him pray to them when he was a boy. Since the last Auriga he's prayed to the Empress and looked to the Empress for guidance instead of far-off animals.

Lily grasps the steering wheel and carefully guides the craft into the air. The boat does a wide corkscrew going up and up and up. Oliver grasps onto the side of the boat and stares downwards, not at his feet, but beneath them. His body vibrates with fear and awe. From here he can see everything: the ocean and docks on one side and on the other, the forest and desert with its many entrances to the mine beneath it. They approach the underbelly of the *Scorpius*. From the ground, the undersides are beautiful but, up close, there is so much more detail than Oliver has ever seen from the Domain.

Carved into it is an enormous scorpion with stars at various points across its body.

A hatch beneath the ship above them opens and they enter a large hangar full of Butterflies. Lily lands the boat off to the side and turns the power off by cranking the gear anti-clockwise.

'This is the workers hangar,' says Lily. 'Workers like yourself are restricted to the lower floors. Just stick to the hallways with the mint-coloured wallpaper. If you begin to see blue or, heaven forbid, yellow walls, you've gone too far.'

They leave the hangar and pass through a series of narrow hallways. They are all the same – mint green walls with a floral print. The windows are small, circular, and too high for Oliver to look through. They arrive at a door with white sweet woodruff flowers painted across the panels. Inside, there is an open common area and kitchen and a hallway that leads to the rooms.

'You'll be in room number eight with your fellow dishwasher Oriana,' says Lily. She pushes the door open. The room is small, with two single mattresses and one window. A little less than he'd expected in such a grand ship, but no matter. At least he can see the clouds. 'Normally, we would room the boys together. But I think it's safer for you to be with those of your own kind. Don't you think?'

The comment stings. He isn't 'with his own kind' because he's a boy, not a girl. Everyone's known for years – they'd accepted him ever since he told them that he's not a girl as they'd assumed when he was born. Despite his discomfort, Oliver holds his tongue and shoves those feelings down. He should just focus on the fact that he's made it this far.

Lily hands him his uniform and ushers him into the shared washroom. He washes himself and puts on the uniform – black shoes, white bloomers, a floor-length black skirt, a white waist apron, a sleeveless white shirt, and a black ribbon to tie his hair up with. The outfit feels strange on him: his arms are too exposed and the skirt too airy.

She then takes him to the kitchens. Walking in the skirt takes some getting used to. Somehow, Lily floats as easily as a cloud. He tries to lift his skirt as he goes up stairs and take small, measured steps, but he can't quite match how she moves.

'At the end of your shift laundry will collect your clothes and replace them with clean ones. You get two free uniforms. The cost of additional items and replacements will be deducted from your pay,' says Lily.

They pass similarly dressed people wheeling carts filled with soiled clothes, dishes or covered food waste. Oliver tries to catch their eyes and smile at them. But there are no smiles – just the same grim expressions he saw in the mines. Maybe they're just having a bad day. It has to be that. No-one living this close to Empress Selene could be unhappy.

They arrive at his designated kitchen and Lily introduces him to Oriana – his roommate. She reminds him of a Celestial: she's tall with beige-coloured skin and a slim nose and mouth, but she is wearing a uniform matching his and there is something missing in her dark brown eyes. She looks tired and her gaze distant.

'I'll leave Oliver with you,' says Lily. 'I shall return when I can to check on your progress.'

Oriana bows her head – and Oliver quickly copies her – as Lily walks away.

'The two of us are stationed here,' says Oriana. 'The job is easy: wash and dry everything as quickly as you can.' The two of them weave around servers carrying plates topped with sweet treats, crispy potatoes coated in salt, mussels smothered in a spicy sauce – the scents wash over him and his stomach grumbles. 'We're constantly on the go so if you need a lavatory or food break, let me know so I can cover you for a few minutes. You'll cover me if I need to step away.' Oliver dodges fire erupting from a copper pot and sidesteps cooks sweating in front of open flames.

Oriana nudges him towards a large sink overflowing with dishes. 'Since you turned up so late, we're already behind. Just follow my lead and you'll be fine.'

Oriana throws herself into the job. It's easy to pick up: she scrapes extra food or pours excess liquid down a smaller sink, washes the items, and hands them to Oliver to rinse and dry. They switch every so often. He can't stop himself from cringing every time he has to throw away uneaten food – even entire untouched meals are disposed of. Everyone knows that getting fresh food from *Virgo* is expensive. Not much can survive on the surface.

Oriana catches his look of distaste and laughs dryly.

'What's that face for?' she asks.

'We have to throw out a lot of food. Is that normal?' He doesn't want to speak out of turn on his first day, but within the past hour he's seen enough wasted sandwiches alone to fill the bellies of everyone in his village. It leaves a bitter taste in his mouth.

'Completely normal. My older brother Malachite has worked as a sky soldier on the *Scorpius* for over a decade and he told me that much more is thrown out at night. The Celestials do like their extravagant parties.' She says it with such an air of calm it catches Oliver off-guard.

'Oh, I didn't know.'

She flashes him a small, sad smile. 'You'll learn.'

—

At the end of the day, after supper, Oliver goes back to his room with Oriana. She collapses into bed still in her uniform.

'You should get some rest while you can. The breaks are long but they go by quickly,' says Oriana.

Oliver stands by the circular window. The sun is setting in the distance and a handful of scattered stars have appeared. Seeing the scrap of sky is enough to make the day feel worthwhile.

'I'm not sure I can sleep,' says Oliver.

Oriana rolls over and stares up at him. She must be only a year or two older than him, perhaps eighteen, but her eyes look much older. 'Just try. The sky will be there tomorrow.'

—

Weeks pass and Oliver throws himself into his job. Every dawn and dusk the view from his room is magnificent but once he steps out of his chamber he's not a person but a dishwasher – not even the other people in the kitchen, aside from Oriana, bother to look at him.

His hands become itchy from the potions in the water and his back sore from bending over the sink. It's tough work. Most of his down time is spent resting. He misses the nights when he could argue with Clem about silly things like whether or not the dragons are Gods or if they are just animals with an exaggerated mythology. Even Oriana barely sees her brother despite them both working on the same ship. There is just no time. It doesn't seem fair.

Maybe, one day, he'll be able to work his way up and he won't have to live like this anymore. He might even get to see the Empress in person, even if it's from a distance. Washing dishes is just the beginning, not the end.

Almost a month in, one of the servers falls ill and he's asked to cover for them for a few hours. Excitement runs through his body as he puts on the long-sleeved shirt and gloves Lily gave him to wear. The material is light and soft against his skin. His only instructions are to follow what the others do and to keep his mouth shut. For this chance to spend some time out of the kitchens, he'd do just about anything.

He copies the line of servers in front of him, grabbing the circular wooden tray covered in plates and carrying it out.

They walk apace through narrow hallways. On the higher levels, the walls are blue with a bird print, and yellow with a white sun print. After seeing the green hallways for weeks, the change is delightful; he can't help but grin. He follows the procession of servers through to a tearoom. The Celestials are just as he imagined: tall and elegant like swans and just as graceful. They sit in twos or threes at small circular tables sipping tea and eating cakes, dressed in shades of pastel. Bright light from above dances over their long hands and smiling faces.

A server directs him to a table at the back. He tries to keep his eyes on the tea sandwiches, pastries, and cakes on the tray, but his gaze is drawn to a company of Celestials in long suspender skirts and white blouses, lace gloves, and pearl necklaces on flawless alabaster skin.

He stops at a table. Three young men are seated there, all in similar long plaid skirts with matching waistcoats and white blouses. They don't look up at Oliver and when he places his tray down one of them jokes about the slow service.

Oliver scurries away, an embarrassed blush rising up his neck. He has to be faster, be better; if he makes a good impression maybe Lily will let him be a server instead.

He hurries back downstairs and takes more plates to the tearooms. Upon setting them down, the table of three stand up and leave without a word. They didn't even look at their chocolate cakes and strawberry tarts. He'd only have such food on a special occasion or if his friend Luci gifted them something from her family's bakery – and even then it would be apple flavoured, one of the foods that does grow in abundance in the Domain, and never something as expensive as chocolate or strawberry.

Oliver turns away from the table and someone grabs at his skirt. He jolts backwards, his heart racing. He turns to the Celestial still holding onto his skirt and the woman is sneering at him.

'What took you so long?' she snaps. Before he can even think of an answer, she continues, 'These refreshments are barely edible. Replace them. Immediately.'

He takes her meal, runs back to the kitchens, pleads with the cooks to rush her order to the front of the queue, and rushes back to the tearooms with fresh teacakes and a new pot of peppermint tea. He places it in front of the woman and instead of expressing gratitude, she waves her hand to dismiss him.

He'd expected the handsome Celestials to be softly spoken and warm-hearted. He'd never wanted to believe what Clementine and Leto said about them. Never understood why they wanted to bring the stars down. The image of them as monsters hadn't matched with who he'd needed them to be. All this time he's been wrong – they are cruel and enjoy the cruelty. He's spent his life looking up at them and they've spent theirs looking down at him. If this is what the Celestials are really like, perhaps even the Empress does not care for him or the Domain.

He tries his best to contain his disappointment and finish the shift, but tears prick the corners of his eyes and he can no longer meet the gaze of these Celestials – just being in their presence is breaking his heart.

He barely eats that night and his sleep is restless. He drifts through his final shift for the month and when it's over, he keeps his head down and quickly changes into his regular gear. Relief floods through him once his navy-blue overalls, long-sleeved blue-grey shirt, and black boots are on.

He joins Oriana in the workers hangar and boards a Butterfly with a new weariness.

Oriana pats his arm. In her long-sleeved shirt, suspenders, and black pants she looks much more like a grounder. Even her hair, normally worn in a high ponytail has been neatly wrapped with a simple blue scarf. 'I know. It's like that for all of us.'

'Why didn't you tell me?' he asks, but as the words leave his mouth, he knows that he wouldn't have believed her.

'Because I went through the same thing.' She turns away from him and stares at the Butterflies taking flight around them. 'Malachite started work as a sky soldier when I was ten years old. I dreamed of joining him on the *Scorpius* so when I got my chance to work here, I took it. He was angry at me for a while and it didn't take me long to understand why. The Celestials don't care about us. It doesn't matter what happens to us as long as they get what they want. Even though the Domain is splitting apart, at least if I worked there, the ones I love wouldn't want to die.'

Oliver goes to touch her arm but draws back. 'Did something happen to Malachite?'

'No, not him. It was actually my former roommate. Her name was Avaline.' She takes in a shaky breath and wipes her eyes. 'You see, she died. Being in this place killed her. There was no service or memorial, not even a mention of who she was. They just brought you in the next day.'

Oliver's heart sinks. No wonder none of the other workers speak to him. 'I'm sorry. I didn't know.'

'How could you?'

The Butterfly takes off and joins a procession of other boats heading for the docks. They float along the smoky sky, drinking up the last dregs of light. The mines have always been crushing – physically being in there is to crush your own body, to shrink yourself. He never thought a sky so big could be as suffocating as that.

Chapter 2

CLEMENTINE

THE cramped cavern shakes around Clem. She freezes. In the mines there's nowhere to run when the ground splits. All she can do is wait. She silently says a few words to Jupiter, the God of all Gods, to keep her safe.

When the shaking stops she gets back to work. The usual chatter is absent, leaving only the sound of steel striking stone. The air is thick with shame and guilt. Somewhere out there many people may have just died. And if they did, it would be the fault of every miner.

Clem's shift ends and after a two-hour journey she emerges from the mines. She jogs across the desert on foot, barely stopping to say hello to her fellow workers. Oliver is home for the night. She can finally tell him how thoughtless his decision was. After everything Leto had taught them about Selene, the Celestials, and those ships, he left. She has to convince him to do something to get away from there even if that something is drastic. Leto's accident may have only left her with a white line from her forehead to her chin, but it was enough to get her fired from the *Scorpius*. Perhaps the same could work for Oli.

She crosses into the forest and heads towards Serpens, joining the crowd of people. Only two guards are stationed outside the village gates and they look incredibly bored. She bounds past the guards and up the wooden bridge. The incline feels steeper after a day of hard work, but Clem pushes through. She reaches the centre of Serpens – the village that snakes through the treetops. The marketplace is loud and packed with activity. Throngs of people are crowded around stores and stalls; the stream of people pulse through the markets like a strike of lightning splitting through water.

She passes by The Hearth and Luci is still at the bakery with her mother Hester. Luci's forehead is coated with sweat, her pink overalls are covered in flour, and the ribbon keeping her shoulder length wavy brown hair away from her face is coming undone; she looks exhausted. Somehow her pale grey eyes spot Clem and she flags her down. Clem dives through the crush of people and takes the pastry from Luci's outstretched bronze hand.

'Thank you!' Clem shouts.

She tries to hand her some money but Luci just shoos the paper notes away before moving onto the next customer. Clem heads north-east, shoving apple strudel in her face as quickly as possible.

Clem crosses the bridge to the north-east quarter. There are plumes of smoke coming from the tops of every house as residents prepare supper. Ainsley has put a dozen or so of the orphan kids to work in and around the orphanage. They're busy hanging up washing, putting up the cleaned curtains, sweeping the inside of the house or seated just outside peeling potatoes and preparing vegetables for dinner. Ainsley waves at Clem from the third level of the wooden house. As usual for this time of the day, their short black hair is covered by a blue scarf, and he wears an old white apron. Ainsley grabs something and throws it down. Clem unwraps the white cloth and inside is an uncooked chicken wing.

'We had extra!' yells Ainsley with a huge grin.

Before Clem can return it, Ainsley pops back inside. The scraps Ainsley is gifted by *Virgo* are supposed to be for the children in their care. And yet, he always manages to give what he can to Clem and others in the quarter.

She rewraps the chicken and hurries home. The wooden structure is made up of three levels: a common area and bathing room on the first level, sleeping areas on the second, and the kitchen on top. It's not a fortress like *Aries*, as grand as *Taurus* or even as large as the other houses in the quarter. But it's home – it's safe – and that's all that matters.

Clem discards her dirty boots just inside the door before heading up to the top floor. Leto and Oliver are already sitting on the wooden balcony eating their dinner. Clem expected Oliver to be wearing his *Scorpius* uniform. Instead, he's dressed similarly to her in overalls and a long-sleeved undershirt.

'Oliver! You're back! How are you? How is it up there? Was it as *amazing* as you thought?' she asks.

Oli looks up at her and his eyes are bloodshot and watery.

'It was okay. Nothing special,' says Oli with a half-hearted shrug. 'How have you been?'

All month she's been thinking about what she would say when she saw him again. But she can't quite bring herself to start needling him with her thoughts. He looks worse than upset – he looks destroyed.

'I've been well. I'm just glad you're home.'

Leto spots the parcel in Clem's hands. 'What is that?'

'Ainsley gave us their extras again,' says Clem.

Leto purses her lips. 'I told you to refuse any of his gifts.'

Clem pops inside the pokey kitchen and places the chicken in their cooler. 'The last time I tried, Ainsley grabbed me by the scruff and deposited me back outside.'

'Then I'll go. I'd like to see them do the same to me.'

'Oh, me too.' She grabs some soup and joins her family on the porch. 'Just make sure I'm not at work when you do it.'

Leto laughs. 'Got it.'

'How was the shop today?' asks Clem.

'Busy, but Oliver was there to help me out for a few hours. We had a numerous folks pop in looking for spare parts for Auriga.'

Oli perks up at the mention of the boat race. His interest in it has always been on the Celestials and their boats, never on his fellow grounders. But something in his eyes has changed. The spark of hope has been replaced by something bitter.

Clem scoffs. 'It's a bit late for that.'

Auriga is dominated by Celestials and if any grounders have serious intentions to race, their preparation should have begun well in advance. They'd been working on their boat for years now and planning the build since the last race a decade ago. There's only enough time for final adjustments and practice – just as they will be doing tonight.

'You're talking as if we're playing to win,' says Leto.

She waits for Oliver to say something. Argue that destroying the ships, endangering Selene and her Celestials by bringing down the entire Fleet, is wrong. But he doesn't. His silence is unsettling.

They finish up dinner and once Clem is washed and dressed, she heads for their hidden prayer room. The small room is tucked behind their sleeping quarters. At the head of the space is an old Cygnusite statue of Jupiter. Figures of the dragons have been carved all around: above are Jupiter and Metis, Janus is wrapped around the doorway, Saturn slithers along the floor, Rhea glides behind the statue, and Adrastea and Eris are entwined on the left wall. Long ago, their entire home would have been decorated in such a fashion. Now a space like this is forbidden. As soon as the Celestials took to the skies, even mentions of the ancient Gods were outlawed. Instead, every home in the Domain has Selene's crest painted on the front door and they are all required to have at least one portrait of a Constellation God displayed along with a stack of books about Helios, Selene, and the Fleet.

Clem slips into the room and stops in her tracks. Leto is already seated in front of the statue and strangely, with her, is Oli.

'What are you doing here?' asks Clem.

Leto shakes her head and gestures for Clem to sit. She complies and eyes Oliver suspiciously. He hasn't prayed with them for a decade at least.

Leto raises her voice up in song and Clem joins her. Tonight, they sing a mourning song about the Gods being forced into seclusion. Oliver stays silent but he doesn't leave either. Clem wishes he'd argue or storm out instead. At least that would be normal.

Once their prayers are done, they lock up the room and head off.

Oliver walks them out and lingers around the doorway as they leave. He stands by Selene's crest but without the usual zeal he gets when he sees his Empress.

'Be safe,' says Oli.

There is a strange look in his eyes and Clem can't help but feel that Oli wants to join them.

'We will,' says Clem.

Leto embraces Oliver and then Clem and her mother depart. The two of them travel out of the village and head south-east towards the ocean and in the opposite direction of the docks. The closer to the water they are, the greener their surroundings become. They stick to the dirt path, ducking under webs and stepping over fallen branches. Clem keeps her tread light, making as little noise as possible.

There is a bright flash above. Clem and Leto pause and bow their heads as a sign of respect. Leto's mouth moves in prayer and Clem should join her. Should keep her eyes down and not gaze upon the Gods. But there is something about them, something that draws her in. She looks up and sees two dragons gliding overhead. One of their undersides is deep purple and the other white. When they open their jaws, electric purple lightning strikes out.

In the old stories, it is said that Jupiter's lighting breathed life into the universe and that fragile breath now resides in them all. When Clem was younger, she would be scared whenever she heard a rumble of thunder in the distance – it could bring new life or destruction. But witnessing it now fills Clem with hope. The Gods are still here, watching over them from afar.

Once the dragons are gone, Clem and Leto continue their journey. It takes them a little while, but they make it to the site. Luci, Hester, and Ainsley are already there and have uncovered the boat. It's a relatively basic wooden boat with the name *Caelum* painted on the side in black. Clem doesn't know how it works, but she doesn't need to. Her job is to steer the thing. Out of them all – even their most experienced flier, Hester – Clem was chosen to pilot the *Caelum* because she is the best. She is also the fastest and the shortest and will have the greatest chance of infiltrating the *Scorpius* during the race and destroying Antares. Her crew can handle everything else – she has enough to worry about.

Leto approaches Ainsley. 'I told you not to give us any of your leftovers.'

She takes off Ainsley's black goggles. Though he's taller and more muscular than Leto, he still holds up his hands in defence. 'And hello to you too.'

Hester strides towards them. She looks like an older version of Luci except instead of wavy brown hair hers is white and has been buzzed short. 'Don't be too harsh on the kid. They're doing their best.'

'He's seventeen. Not quite a kid anymore,' says Leto.

'It's okay. Next time, Ainsley will keep the food. Right, Ainsley?' They nod vigorously.

Leto frowns. 'Fine. Let's get started.'

The five of them board the boat. Clem takes her place at the helm, Hester in the pit, and Luci at the bow. Leto and Ainsley go below deck to take care of the engine.

Hester and Luci hoist the sails. 'Ready,' they say in unison.

Clem kicks her boots into their footholds, locking herself in position. She slides on her black googles. 'Ready.'

'Starting the engine.' Leto's voice comes through the speakers at the helm, pit, and bow.

The engine thrums to life beneath her feet. She takes the lever beside the wheel and pulls it towards herself, releasing the brakes. The boat lifts a few feet off the ground.

'Take it nice and slow,' says Leto through the speaker.

'Got it,' says Clem.

Clem carefully guides the boat skyward and then starboard towards the ocean, into the face of the wind.

'All clear ahead,' shouts Luci; her pink scarf has slid off her head and is wavering in the draft.

They cross over the charcoal-black waves. 'We've passed point one. Engage speed two,' says Clem.

Clem feels the gears shifting beneath her feet and the boat

picks up speed. She guides the boat higher and the wind whips at her face. Her heart races but it's not fear she feels, it's exhilaration. She could almost keep going, keep climbing higher and higher, above the clouds and further still.

She turns the boat so they run parallel to the shore.

'Engage speed three!' shouts Clem.

The boat ploughs through the air. Their surroundings fly past them. Clem has the urge to spread her arms like the wings of those dragons. But she contains herself. Now is not the time for dreams, now is the time for action.

There is a loud booming sound from Serpens. Clem turns the boat towards her village just in time to see trees drop away. A sense of dread fills her being. It can only be one thing.

Luci peers through her spyglass. 'It's another split!' she shouts. 'It's cut right through Serpens!'

'Take us there, Clem!' shouts Leto.

They zoom through the sky, hurtling over the air currents, and dipping towards the tree line. Clem's mind swirls with thoughts about Oliver, the orphans, and all the people of Serpens. There's no knowing the extent of the damage until they arrive.

'Speed one!' shouts Clem, her voice shaking with fear.

The boat slows right down. They drift over their village or, at least, where it used to be. An enormous tear has cracked the earth, cutting across their village from south-west to north-east. Without the support of the trees underpinning the village, much of the remaining wooden walkways, houses, and buildings have toppled and fires are spreading across the fallen remains.

Luci falls into her mother's arms, crying. Hester embraces her and runs a hand over Luci's hair.

'Leto,' says Hester, 'the village is gone.' There is a choking noise from the speakers. Clem tries to speak, to move, but she can't.

Her brother, the orphanage children, the villagers, they could all be – no. She can't think it. If she does, if she considers that possibility, she won't be able to go on.

'Stay calm. We don't know who survived. Let's land, then we'll find who we can and get them out.' Leto's voice sounds strained.

With shaking hands, Clem lands the boat in a clearing close to Serpens. She spills out of the boat, followed closely by Hester, Luci, Leto, and Ainsley. She runs through the forest, towards the main entry to their village. The air is thick with the scent of smoke. She ties a handkerchief over her nose and mouth and keeps her flying googles on. Crowds of people are gathered around the gate. All they can do is watch Serpens burn.

'Oliver!' Clem screams.

She hears Leto shouting orders to the confused and weary mass, but continues running, heading towards the east entrance. Oliver has to be there. He has to have survived. Clem followed Oli into this world, he can't go ahead without her, not when there is so much to be done.

She rushes towards the eastern gate and a crowd of distressed people are there too. They stare numbly at the gate and where the bridge up to the village used to be. Past the eastern entry point is only burning rubble.

Hester comes up behind her and orders all able-bodied adults to head north to Ophiuchus, while everyone else goes with her to the *Caelum*. The crowd parts, with the majority heading west towards the ocean to take the long way around the split.

Clem pushes through the gaps in the crowd of moving people. She looks up and around, searching for Oliver's face or a flash of his purple hair. The people around her look grim, some with ash covered faces or with parts of their bodies wrapped in cloth. But none are her brother.

The swarm of people thin out and there, standing with the north-east orphanage children, is Oliver. He looks wide-eyed and a little lost, but he's safe. She runs up to him and throws her arms around her brother; he lightly pats her shoulder in return.

'I thought—'

'I'm okay,' says Oli. One of the littler kids clings to his leg. 'We should get them out of here.'

Clem looks over at the children. Their small faces are frightened, and the older ones look years younger. She wipes her eyes and takes a deep breath. 'Okay, kids. It's not safe here so we have to head towards our boat and from there we'll take you to Ophiuchus. But first, I need all of you to listen very carefully to us. Got that?' As she speaks, she sees the children nodding. A few of them sign to their friends to pass the message on. 'I want all of the older kids to find two to three younger ones. Take their hands or a sleeve, even carry them if you have to.'

The children quickly find their buddies with the very eldest carrying the ones who are unable to walk all the way to the *Caelum*. It'll be slow, but they have to move. Splits like this are always followed by smaller ruptures. Enough to swallow part of a house or an entire person.

Oli leads the way and Clem follows. They pick their way through the forest, heading away from the split first and then back around to the *Caelum*. The kids cry and complain but they also encourage and help each other. Eventually they arrive at the clearing. Instead of the boat they find Ainsley with a small group of children and adults. The orphanage kids rush over to Ainsley. They surround him, hugging him and crying, speaking all at once. Ainsley cries and snot runs down their face. They look relieved and it's no wonder. He grew up in the orphanage and now he works there as a caretaker.

'Where's the boat?' asks Clem.

Ainsley wipes their face with the back of their brown hand. 'Hester and Leto are taking a group ahead along with the other boats. They should be back soon.'

'What about Luci?'

'She's scouting around the Serpens. We needed someone to check if anyone was left behind.'

Clem nods solemnly. The remnants of the village that wasn't swallowed by the split is ablaze now – there is no way others could be alive in there.

Clem looks after the kids with Ainsley and Oli until the boats arrive. They load everyone onto them and then board the *Caelum*. Clem tries to take over steering the boat from Hester, but she's quickly rebuffed.

'Just be a kid for once, okay?' says Hester, raising her thick white brows.

Hester turns her focus back to steering the *Caelum*, effectively ending the conversation. Clem joins Oli and the children at the stern. They say nothing to each other because there is nothing to say. Her home is gone. Their family's dragon statue passed down through the generations is now lost to the depths of the Domain. Nothing will ever be the same again.

The *Caelum* floats high above the trees followed by three larger boats. They pass around the black smoke and head north towards Ophiuchus. The people around them huddle together – Clem can only guess it's for warmth as each has nothing but the clothes they are wearing.

Clem wraps her arms around herself and looks up. The Constellation Fleet glides silently above them, the stars carved into their bellies glowing purple from within.

Chapter 3

OLIVER

WHEN they arrive at Ophiuchus the village is in chaos. Tents are being set up throughout the settlement with many packed tightly together. The wounded are either led or carried away and those too injured to be moved have green tents set up around them. Everyone else is guided to booths where supplies are being given out and tents assigned by Ophiuchus volunteers.

Oliver stands in line and waits for Celestials to appear with more aid: blankets, food, medical supplies, volunteers, anything and anyone would do. But as the hours tick by, not one Celestial appears. Empress Selene was supposed to look after them. A sharp pain stabs through Oliver's chest and he grimaces. He shouldn't be hurt or even surprised that the people he once looked up to have let him down again, but he can't help feeling deeply disappointed.

'Oliver!'

He jumps at the sound of his name and turns. Oriana is rushing towards him. Her long, straight black hair is out as if she's just leapt from her bed.

'What are you doing here?' he asks.

'I've been trying to find you. I wanted to offer you,' her wide eyes flick over to Leto, Clem, Luci, and Hester, 'and your family a place to stay. It'll be cramped, but it's warm.'

Leto steps forward with her arms crossed. 'And you are?'

'Oriana,' says Oliver, 'she works with me on the *Scorpius*.'

Oriana shows her identity papers as proof and only then do Leto and Hester agree that they should all go with her. Once they've collected their supplies, they follow her home. She sets them up in her sleeping quarters on the ground floor and takes herself up to the kitchens on the second floor.

Clem, Leto, Hester, and Luci light a single candle and huddle together. Now that their village is gone, their plan for Auriga has to change and fast. Oliver sits off to the side and listens to their whispered meeting.

Leto unfurls an old piece of parchment in which she's sketched out the interior of the *Scorpius*. Together the four of them hammer out a new plan: Clem will infiltrate the ship from the deck and from there take a workers' passage to Antares – the power source of the Fleet. She will destroy the stone and meet everyone at the collapsed mine not far from Ophiuchus. From there they will head to Navis. Travelling the great distance to Navis and then hiding in the port city will not be easy but it's their best shot of evading capture.

Oliver listens to all of this and upon inspecting the map, he notices a few errors. The placement of the passages seems off and even the workers' hangar is far larger than he would have thought. He clears his throat and everyone stops to look at him.

'Um, t–that's not right,' stutters Oliver.

Clem rolls her eyes. 'What now?'

'Not the plans. It's the ship. This map is wrong.'

'You can't be serious.'

Leto turns to Oliver. The long scar down her face glimmers in the candlelight. 'Show us.'

Oliver explains what he knows about the lower levels and everything that doesn't fit with what he's seen.

'The whole map must be wrong then,' murmurs Leto.

'Then what are we going to do?' asks Luci.

'Maybe we should pull out of the race,' says Hester.

'But what about our plans? It could still work,' says Clem.

Leto sighs. 'Hester's right. There's no room for error here. If you're captured, you'll be killed. Brutally.'

Oliver shivers. He's heard the stories about grounders who have crept aboard one of the ships, been found, and then pushed overboard as punishment.

'But—' begins Clem.

'No,' says Leto. She rolls up the parchment. 'I'll hand in our forfeit tomorrow. We'll try again next time.'

'In ten years! How do we know that we'll survive for that long?'

Leto puts her hand on Clem's shoulder. 'We don't. But we have hope.'

Clem shrugs off Leto's hand and stomps into the bathroom. The rest of them settle into bed and Oliver tries to sleep, but he can't ignore the sound of Clem weeping ever so softly. Not long ago he would have thought that she was overreacting. But after everything, maybe she isn't. Maybe something needs to be done.

'I'll help,' whispers Oliver, his voice barely audible.

Leto sits up. 'What?'

'I want to help.' He shifts into sitting position. 'I think I can remap the interior of the *Scorpius*.'

'Are you sure?' asks Hester. 'We have ten years to figure out another way.'

They can't risk it. It has to be now. 'I'm sure. I want to help.'

Leto stares at him for a few moments as if she's meeting him for the very first time.

'Okay,' she says.

Oliver nods and lies down once more. His heart races in his

chest partly out of fear but also from anticipation. He tries to rest, but as he's finally drifting off there's a loud knock on the door. Oriana runs down the stairs and opens the door. Two soldiers peer at her and then at everyone else. Each of them carries a spontoon and wears a red tunic, white pants, and black boots. They must be from *Aries*.

'Are Oriana Baker and Oliver Mercer here?' asks one of them.

'I'm Oriana, and Oliver is here,' says Oriana.

'The two of you are to depart for the docks in thirty minutes.'

'I don't understand,' she says.

'There may have been some confusion with the recent incident in Serpens. However, both you and Oliver Mercer are obliged to return to *Scorpius* to begin work,' says one of the soldiers; the blade of his spontoon gleams in the morning light. 'If you do not, you will be fined and taken to *Aries* to await your trial. The maximum punishment for evading work is execution.'

–

Oliver rushes to get ready and is out the door with Oriana in ten minutes. They jog through Ophiuchus to the docks and hop straight onto a Butterfly. The view from the boat is still beautiful. The entire Domain is bathed in golden light, and Helios' Constellation Fleet glides silently just above the clouds. But there is an ugliness in the silence too. The Empress could send Celestials from her Fleet to help them, she could do anything to make their lives easier, but she won't. Their lives are not important to her or any of them and the very thought of that makes him feel queasy.

Oliver returns to work and this time, everything is different. In the first week back on the *Scorpius* he spends his nights drawing the paths of every area he knows so far: the hangar, the hallways up to his quarters and over to where he works. In the second, he takes different ways back from the kitchens to the dorms.

Sometimes going down or up a level or two but always staying in the servants' passages. In his uniform, no-one questions where he's going or why.

Halfway through the month Oriana joins Oliver on one of his long after work walks. When they're back in their rooms, she finally says, 'I know what you're doing.'

Oliver's heart rate quickens and he tries to ignore the trickle of fear within him. 'I have no idea what you're talking about.'

'I heard everything that night in Ophiuchus.'

Oliver quickly stands up. He considers tearing apart the maps or even burning them, but he can't make himself move.

Oriana folds her hands in her lap. 'It's okay, Oli. I'm not going to say anything. In fact, I want to help you.'

Before he can give her an answer, she pulls out a piece of crumpled parchment and holds it out to him. It's a partial map of the ship – she's filled in many of the sections in the upper decks, where the Celestials live and work.

'I figured that while you were mapping the servants areas I could do the upper levels. So far, I haven't been stopped. They probably think I'm visiting Malachite.'

'Are you sure?' asks Oliver. With their maps combined, they could finish the entire ship by the end of the month. But the risk of getting caught is great, even for Oriana. Her brother may be a soldier on this ship, but that doesn't make her any less of a target.

'I'm sure. Years ago, I would have snitched on you. But I've changed a lot since I first stepped onboard. I've seen too much – I watched Avaline waste away and perish in this very room. I don't want to lose anyone else.' She clears her throat and swipes a tear away. 'Besides, you need all the help you can get.'

Oliver considers saying no. This is supposed to be a secret and it should be Leto and Hester who decide. But there is no time and

Oriana is proving to be the best friend he's ever had. With her help, he'll have the map done in time for the race.

'Okay, you can help.'

Oriana smiles softly and relief floods through Oliver. These past two weeks have been so lonely. It's nice to finally have someone here on his side.

'I'm sorry about Avaline,' says Oliver. 'What was she like?'

'She was kind and had big dreams,' says Oriana.

'I think we could have been friends.'

Oriana nods, wiping tears away before they can fall.

After Oriana has gone to bed, Oliver whispers a prayer for Avaline and asks that her soul is cared for. He's not sure who he's praying to – the dragons or the Constellation Gods – but he hopes that somehow, someone hears him.

With Oriana's help the process becomes much easier. During the day they work and at night, they add to their ever-expanding map. Every now and then Oriana mentions Avaline, the short woman with a big voice and dark green eyes, and Oliver finds himself laughing and crying with Oriana as he listens to her speak.

On their final night on the *Scorpius*, they pore over the maps of all the levels. Oriana has marked out the checkpoints, of which there are many. Even on a day like Auriga with minimal sky soldiers on duty, it might still be impossible for Clem to journey through the ship undetected. If Clem somehow manages to clear all the checkpoints, she'll arrive at Antares and find that it takes two people to open the door.

Oriana sighs and props up her head with her hand. 'This is hopeless.'

Oliver picks up the maps and goes over them one by one. He can't give up. Not yet. Not when their goal is within reach. He leafs through the parchments and traces routes through the ship with his eyes. None of the paths from the top work. If only they could start from the bottom.

An idea hits him and he pulls out the outline of the bottom level. The workers hangar would be easiest to get into and, once there, Clem could take the servants passages all the way up to the heart without fear of crossing checkpoints. This could work. But Clem would need a uniform and someone on the inside to open the hangar.

Oliver tells Oriana his thoughts.

'Lily has been asking me to work during the Auriga; even with most Celestials gone they still need a skeleton crew. I'll tell her I can so I can let Clem in and help her open the door to Antares,' says Oriana.

'You've already done enough. I'll do it. I'll tell Lily tomorrow,' says Oliver.

'Why don't we both volunteer?' Oriana gathers some of the maps. 'You can let Clem in and I'll cover for you. The hangar door is heavy but I think you can manage it alone. When the job's done, we'll leave by a Butterfly.'

'Are you sure?'

Oriana grins. 'Of course. Someone's got to look out for you.'

Oliver and Oriana hide the parchment in their clothes and retire for the night.

Some small part of him begins to hope that everything will turn out okay. Maybe there is a chance for them after all.

Chapter 4

CLEMENTINE

CLEM steps off the lift, breezes past the guards, and smiles to herself as she leaves the mine behind. On her way out no-one checked her pockets but if they did, they'd find them full of Cygnusite. There is an unspoken rule that none of the miners are to pocket any stone – the truth is, most of them do. Outright purchasing the stone required to power boats and boards is expensive so many people turn to stealing a little here and there. The guards don't suspect a thing as long as daily quotas are met and Cygnusite is sold to the grounders at a steady rate.

Slowly, she makes her way to Serpentis. Serpens' offshoot tent village sits by the ocean at the foot of the latest rift. She should be used to her new home by now, but it just doesn't feel secure.

The bowels of the *Scorpius* open and small Butterflies are released. Oli is on one of those. From there, he should be able to see everything. There is a loud rumble beneath the earth and screaming behind her. Clem watches, frozen in fear and shock, as a crack slices through the ground, heading right for her. Someone bumps into her and she takes off, arms pumping, focusing on her feet, her breath, moving as fast as she can. Her foot slips and she falls, grabbing at the ground above her with one hand. She swings her other up, a few stones fall out of her pockets, and she grasps onto the rock above. Hands grab hold of her and pull her upwards. She barely has time to thank them before the rumbling begins again. She launches herself up and sprints away. There is a loud booming noise like rock striking rock. She looks over her shoulder and streaks of purple light shoot up from within the tear. The light disappears in seconds. Somehow, the tear is gone. She looks round at the people close to her and shares in their astonishment. Leto has told her stories of the meteor that originally struck this planet causing the first break, but the other rifts really began once they started mining the planet for the Cygnusite that grew from where the Domain was hit. Ever since, the ground has kept tearing itself apart. They've tried everything to fix it and nothing has worked. Until now.

Lightning strikes across the sky and she looks up. There, beneath the ships, is a dragon. Clem stops and stares in awe. Everyone around her scatters, running towards the safety of the forest. The creature lands where the tear used to be. He sniffs the ground and turns, training his large dark purple eyes onto her. The creature lowers his enormous head until he is so close she can feel his breath on her face.

She should look away and not meet the gaze of a God, but she doesn't. She meets his stare and senses warmth there. Her heart is steady and a wave of calm washes over her. She reaches out towards the dragon and touches his snout.

Heat radiates up her arm. In her mind she sees a river that runs through the forest from a lake. The dragon jerks his head skyward and the image disappears. Half a dozen red-and-white war boats from *Aries* are heading their way.

The creature leaps into the sky and flies away.

Clem's heart races all the way back to Serpentis. She thinks about the tear, the dragon, and the lake. She passes through the tree line, and everyone has gathered there. Something must have happened in Serpentis during the split. She pushes through the masses until she finds her family huddled together amongst it all.

'Clementine!' says Leto.

She embraces her daughter and then draws back. Her worried eyes scan Clem's face and body as if searching for injuries. 'Are you okay? What happened?'

Clem relays everything – even about the dragon and the vision he showed her.

Oli hugs himself. 'It doesn't make any sense. The rift closing and a dragon appearing. Why now?'

'I don't know, but I'm telling the truth,' says Clem.

Leto leads Clem and Oli to the sands. The tent site is in disarray – a small group of people are picking through the debris to assess the damage. Serpentis was never built to withstand the quakes.

'Do you think you can get to the place the dragon showed you?' asks Leto.

'I think so,' replies Clem. 'Why?'

'Perhaps we should seek the dragons out and ask them for help. What do you both think?'

'I don't know. Is it safe?' asks Oliver.

'No. But where is?' Leto gestures to the fallen tents. 'You can stay here and wait for another quake, or you can meet with the Gods. Which will it be?'

Clem looks at Oli. Firelight flickers in his brown eyes. Mostly, he looks afraid. She lightly touches his arm.

'I know you're scared, but I think we should seek them out. Together,' she says.

He looks to his feet. 'Okay.'

Clem leads them away from Serpentis. In the aftermath of the quake, nobody notices them sneak away from their village. They head south and cross through the blackened forest encircling

Serpens. None of them speak. The air feels tighter here, memories press all round like a second skin. Oliver always craved a life away from their village but for Clem, these trees, these people, the sky from Serpens has always been her home. Walking through it now, it no longer feels like the home of her past. She recognises it only by the path the dragon planted in her mind. And that thought – the very idea that this place is so close and yet so far away – sends a shiver through her.

She keeps walking all the way through to where the forest is full of life, and continues, following a snaking river to a glassy lake.

'Where are they?' asks Leto.

'We have to go in,' says Clem.

Oliver scrunches up his face. 'To the lake?'

She crouches by the edge of the water and touches the surface. Somehow, she senses the dragon there. 'Yes. We'll be able to access their hiding place through it.'

Leto squeezes Clem and Oliver's hands. 'Let's go.'

They wade into the water and swim until they're in the middle of the lake. A soft purple light flickers deep below the surface. Clem takes a deep breath and dives. The waves carry her into the belly of the lake, straight into the light.

She breaks the surface, gasping for air. She finds herself floating – alone – in an enormous underground cavern. Dozens of dragons soar over the lake and around glittering towers of Cygnusite stretching almost to the ceiling. Until today, the closest she'd gotten to them was in her prayer room. Their shadows kept her company for a short time every evening. Seeing their glimmering scales, pointed teeth, and wings outstretched as they fly overhead has left her feeling wonderstruck.

The largest dragon swoops and lands on the surface in front

of her. It's the same one from earlier. He fixes her with a cool and calm stare. The creature lifts a paw and touches her forehead gently with one claw. Suddenly she knows the names of all of the dragons here: the largest and greatest of them all is Jupiter. She's prayed to him every night and seeing him here, with the other Gods, is bewildering. He retreats to the edge of the lake, his paws dipping ever so slightly into the water as he goes. The rest of them soar down and land until she's surrounded on all sides by dragons.

There is a deep rumble in Jupiter's chest and when he opens his mouth, he starts to speak. 'Welcome, young Clementine. I have brought you here as I believe we can help each other.'

Clem shivers. Jupiter's voice is so loud she can feel it shaking the very air and water around her.

'Speak or leave,' says Ananke, a greyish white dragon to Jupiter's left.

'How can *I* help you?' asks Clem.

'Ah,' says Janus, to a bright yellow dragon to Jupiter's right, 'the little one has a big voice.'

'We believe—' begins Jupiter.

'Not I,' says Eris, interrupting Jupiter. The white dragon seems to be permanently displeased.

Jupiter exhales, sending ripples across the surface of the lake. 'You see, I know much about you, Clementine. I know about your plans to bring down those so-called stars. I also know that they will take flight once more unless we control the mines.'

'I-I'm sorry, but I can't help with that,' says Clem, her voice trembling. After all, she's just one person.

'That's where you are wrong, little one. For years, there has been a barrier that prevents us from entering the mines. We need your help to disable it. If you do this for us, we will utilise the Cygnusite to heal these lands – just as you did to close the break that nearly took your life. After it is done, Pluto will guard the mines and no humans shall be granted entry.'

'I don't understand.'

'Think of this planet like an article of clothing and the Cygnusite the materials. Remove each thread and the garment will fall apart. That is the path this planet is on. Surely you have observed this. With our power, we can reverse the breakages. However, we must also be allowed to safeguard the stone from the hands of those who only know cruelty. If we do not, the cycle of destruction that Helios started will begin anew.'

'We will show you how to thrive without the Cygnusite,' says Janus, her bright-yellow scales gleam with hints of reddish brown in the purple light. 'But first this must be done.'

Clem considers sticking with the original plan. Bringing the stars down and running as far away as they can. But, without the help of the Gods, all of their work will simply be undone. They need each other to pull this off.

'I will agree, if you give me one assurance,' says Clem.

Adrastea glares down her snout at Clem with her bright red eyes. 'And what would that be?'

Clem holds her chin up and tries not to show any fear. 'Safety, for everyone living on the ground especially myself and my family and friends.'

'And why should we?' spits Eris. 'It is your very hands that strike out the Cygnusite, the very beating heart of this planet.'

'I know, all the miners know this, we do what we can to survive with little choice otherwise. But I'm putting a lot on the line for this. So, these are my terms if you want my help.'

The dragons murmur to one another for a long while. Her arms and legs become tired from treading water, and she shivers against the cold. Maybe she's gone too far. She, a mere human, asked the Gods for a favour. In the stories they sing of the Gods, the dragons hand down their knowledge and the humans follow through. One simply does not – should not – bargain with a dragon.

The discussion ceases.

'We are willing to make that promise,' says Jupiter.

Jupiter bows his head and all of the dragons follow, even Eris.

'Now, all we need is your face,' says Jupiter.

Chapter 5

CLEMENTINE

CLEM guides the boat over the flat desert to the starting line. Over three dozen boats most much larger than the *Caelum* are already idly floating there. Most entrants are Celestial racers. Their boats are decorated in Cygnusite or gold embellishments; figureheads of horned gods, lions and mercreatures adorn the prows, and murals have been painted across the sides. Any person – Celestial or grounder – can enter; however, grounders have to work with fewer resources, less leisure time to work on their boat, and the very real threat of injury or death.

She joins the flock towards the back. On either side of the *Caelum* the boats are three or four times the size of theirs. They have cannons, more crew members, and the boats are made with thicker, studier wood. They've been built with battle capabilities while the sole purpose of *Caelum* is speed.

A Butterfly hovers at the starting line. Someone onboard waves a large yellow flag, signalling that the race is about to start. There is a roar from the crowd to the right, all people from the ground, and applause from sky people sitting in their private Butterflies and luxury boats. Selene's sleek white boat hovers above the Celestials; she has yet to show her face and may not even be onboard.

Right about now the shape-shifting dragon Proteus should

be using her image to get into the mines. She hopes the workers there don't realise that Clem is supposed to be part of the race.

'Get ready,' shouts Leto through the speakers.

The starter raises the purple flag. Clem grips the wheel with her gloved hands. She hopes and prays that Jupiter is keeping his end of the deal.

The flag drops and Clem drives the boat forward, kicking it immediately to second speed. They glide across the desert flats, passing through green flags arranged into a zig zag pattern across the desert. A dozen Celestial boats pass right by them, going at full speed. She hangs back. The Celestials have fuel to burn, but the *Caelum* does not. And right now she doesn't need to be fast – she just needs to hold on long enough to reach the *Scorpius*.

The course veers right abruptly. They fly over the desert, then the forest, almost clipping the trees, before passing over ocean. The flags are placed close to the surface of the water in a wide arc, forcing Clem to take the boat close to the waves. The *Caelum* skims across the sea flanked by two other boats – both with figureheads of a man with ram horns. They close in on the sides of the boat, forcing them into a choke point.

'What are you doing?' yells Hester.

'Trust me!' yells Clem.

They loom over them like two walls ready to crush the boat to bits. When they're near enough, Clem cranks the brakes, the *Caelum* drops into the water, the boats clear them in an instant and smash into each other. Clem restarts the boat and takes off once more.

They fly over the slowly sinking boats and rejoin the race. She dodges other wrecks, all attended by Butterflies from *Pisces*, and lifts the boat skyward. The twelve Constellation ships are positioned in the sky above them, each one forming a "step" they'll have to pass over. At the very top is the *Scorpius* – one last push and then she'll have made it.

They climb towards the first ship, little *Pisces*. There is loud booming far behind them as gunners fire chain shots. Cannon fire is not allowed close to the Fleet. Here, they just have to fly.

Clem keeps the *Caelum* at second speed all the way up. At the tenth ship, the *Leo*, Clem quickly switches with Hester. She heads port side, picks up the board stashed there, and activates the stone at the centre of the board. She steps into the footholds and holds onto the *Caelum*.

Hester guides the ship towards the *Scorpius* and as it crests over the top, she tips the ship almost to its side. Clem dives, tumbling through the air she straightens her legs and catches an air current, coasting to the belly of the *Scorpius*.

OLIVER

Oliver crouches in the workers hangar. He cranks the hangar doors open just as Oriana showed him. They move inch by inch – even with his strength and stamina, it's still strenuous. When the doors are finally open he twists the wheel until the hatch is locked into place.

Clem tumbles in on her board, landing beside a Butterfly.

He dashes over to her. 'Are you hurt?'

She kicks off her board and grins. 'Never been better.'

He sighs and hands her Oriana's spare uniform. She slips it over her clothes and follows Oliver out.

Oliver's heart races as they quietly make their way through the *Scorpius*. He jumps at the distant sound of cannon fire and nervously stares downwards when they pass another worker. One wrong move and they'll be found out. Clem's appearance alone makes her stand out. Although at a glance she looks as if she belongs, closer inspection would reveal that she lacks the defeated quality that defines most workers here. There is a fire in Clem's eyes, a spark radiating up her spine and across her shoulders, enough to bring this whole ship to the ground.

They approach the double doors that lead to Antares and together, push them open.

An enormous Cygnusite at least three times the size of the *Caelum* floats in the middle of the room. Iris-coloured light flows into the base of the crystal and out of the top through glass veins that cover the interior of the room.

Clem hands Oliver a hammer and chisel and approaches the stone with her own tools. She delivers the first strike and it barely makes a dent. Oliver raises his chisel to the stone, his hands shaking, and brings the hammer down. The smallest of cracks appears and the room quivers. They hit the stone again and again and again – tiny breaks run across the surface of the stone until suddenly, it explodes.

Then, the *Scorpius* begins to fall.

CLEMENTINE

The ship creaks and groans as it drops. Clem runs behind Oliver, following his descent through the spiralling passageways. Other workers join them as they run. She trips over her skirt and immediately kicks it off, throwing the rest of the uniform over her head. With her legs free, she matches pace with Oliver and grabs his hand, urging him to run just that bit faster.

They make it to the hangar, boarding the first available ship. Oliver's head swivels around and he jumps off the Butterfly. The boat thrums to life and Clem jumps over the side as if takes off.

'What are you doing?' asks Clem. 'We gotta get out of here.'

Oliver clenches his shaking hands. 'I have to find Oriana. If she's not up here, she has to be in the kitchen.'

'Oli, wait—'

He pushes his way through the crowd of bodies and leaves the hangar. Clem goes to an empty Butterfly and watches the last of the *Scorpius* crew fly away until only she is left. There are deep rumbles in the distance and Clem can only guess that, without Antares to connect and power them, the rest of the Fleet has already crashed.

Through the open hangar door, Clem watches the shapes below become clear as they approach the surface. She starts the Butterfly and manoeuvres it to the edge. Finally, Oliver bursts through the doors with Oriana and a man that looks similar to her. The three of them jump onto the boat. Clem zooms out, guiding the Butterfly up and away from the *Scorpius*. The boat is slow – made for hauling passengers and not racing – but she pushes it to the maximum speed.

The *Scorpius* explodes beneath them and the entire Butterfly shudders. Clem keeps the boat steady, flying high above the burning remains of what once was the Constellation Fleet.

Now, just one last part remains.

OLIVER

Dragons swoop all around, now free to roam the skies without fear of being shot down. Oliver grips the side of the boat as the one Clem calls Jupiter flies overhead, swooping into an entrance to the mines. Oliver holds his breath.

There is a sound like thunder, so loud that it seems a breath away. Oliver covers his ears. Suddenly purple lightning erupts through the breaks in the earth, shooting upward towards the sky. The sight is spectacular and frightening. It lasts just a few minutes but when the lightning dissipates, all of the rifts are gone and so is a large portion of the desert. Much of it has been replaced by a great forest.

'You did it,' murmurs Oliver.

Clem glances over her shoulder at her brother and smiles. 'We both did.'

Epilogue

CLEMENTINE

CLEM approaches the new and improved Serpens. Janus' yellow serpentine figure has been carved around the entrance gate and up the path. During their village rebuild, in the aftermath of the race, a lot changed. There are no more flying ships, at least not until they figure out a way to fly that doesn't break the planet. Most of the Celestials have been folded into grounder villages and the rest are living with the dragons; she suspects that's where the former Empress Selene went. She spots a few Celestials – many are in their delicate sky clothing – and it's still strange to see them here. Ultimately the dragon Gods, the grounders, and even the Celestials agreed that if the Celestials can live in harmony with the grounders, they can stay.

Clem passes the orphanage and as usual, all the kids are out there with Ainsley cleaning the house and preparing for dinner. He waves at Clem and she waves back. It's nice to see Ainsley happy once more.

She approaches her house and Leto and Oli are seated outside.

'How was the bakery?' asks Leto.

'I think I'm beginning to enjoy it. Luci is teaching me a lot,' says Clem, dusting her hands on her light pink overalls. She hands her mother a loaf of bread and some apple tarts. 'Some leftovers from today. Hester said you can't return them this time.'

Oli grabs one of the tarts and takes a bite. He seems a lot

more relaxed these days. Working with Leto at the junk shop has brought him a lot of joy.

'Well, I suppose I can't refuse now that you're eating them,' says Leto with a laugh.

Oli just smiles around the food in his mouth.

Clem is so glad to finally be home.

OLIVER

After dinner, Oliver creeps into the prayer room. This space is twice the size of their old one, with enough room to fit a carving of Pluto around their new statue of Jupiter.

Oliver sits before Jupiter's wooden statue and unfolds the letter in his pocket. It's from Oriana – they've been exchanging letters regularly. It feels strange, even after the passing of eighteen full moons, to not be by her side each day. She writes that she and the other acolytes Ananke recently accepted are learning a lot about healing, life, and death. Much of it is beyond Oliver, a machine makes sense but the human body, the mind, and spirit, that's complicated. Still, she seems happy and that's the most important thing.

He unrolls a blank piece of parchment, takes out some ink, and sits down to write.

Dear Oriana,

Congratulations on being officially accepted as one of Ananke's acolytes. Avaline would be so proud of you. I'm proud of you, too! It sounds like you're learning so much already. What is Ananke like? From what I've heard from

Clem, she seems tough. Though, after surviving the Scorpius *I think you'll do just fine with a Goddess.*

I haven't told Leto and Clem yet that I'm going visit you or about my planned journey across the Domain. I know, I know, I can see your face already. Clem and I have not been apart since I worked on the Scorpius. *She would only want to follow me. She finally seems to have settled into work at the bakery. This will just upset her. I promise that I'll tell everyone soon. I just want to stay in this bubble for a little bit longer.*

Give my best to Malachite. I've said this many times before, but I hope his recovery is going okay. From what you said in your letter, it seems that it will take a great number of folks time to heal after the fall of the Constellation Fleet. They're very lucky to have you, the other acolytes, and Ananke to help them in this transition period.

I can't wait to see you! By the time this letter reaches you, I will be a day or two away. I'll stay for as long as you'll have me.

From your friend,
Oliver

CHANGELINGS

ALISON EVANS

THE world hushes as the lights appear. Three of them, rotating slowly; my skin tingles, my breath hitches. Slow and steady hovering, then they dart across the night sky to hover again.

I step out of the car, and the lights appear right above me.

Changeling, they say.

I shiver, but then they're gone, and I'm left with a pit in my chest, aching and empty.

—

'I saw things in the sky last night.' My hands shake as I say it, so I keep wiping down the counter. Why they made it glass, I'll never know, fingerprints show up at the lightest touch. 'Like, lights.'

Gwen looks up from the CD booklet she's reading, brushing her black hair behind her ear. 'What, like a UFO?'

'Maybe.' I blush but I hold her gaze. I've been wanting to say this all day, the words rising in my throat, finally released.

She doesn't respond for a couple of seconds. 'You serious, Astro?'

'Maybe it's nothing, but maybe … I dunno.' I swallow. 'I was gonna wake you up when I got home but then I chickened out.' She doesn't say anything. 'Maybe I'm just being a freak.'

'Ooh, good one. Remind me to remember that we need to grab the Silverchair album with "Freak" on it. But you saw aliens, Astro? You saw real-life aliens?'

'I feel like one of us needs to be the Scully in order for this to work,' I reply.

'Get out!' she laughs. 'Let's go tonight. A real UFO!'

'*Maybe* a real UFO … and don't we have *Freak Show* already? It's been out for ages.'

'Only a couple songs. Someone asked for it on the forums last night.'

'You're not closing tonight are ya?'

She shakes her head. 'No pirating today.'

I reach over and grab a scrap piece of paper.

'What're you doing?'

'Just making a list of what we need to take next opportunity.' I write *Freak Show* down, plus a couple others. We take them home when one of us is closing, bring them back next time we're opening. After we re-shrinkwrap them, no one can tell.

'Now, though? We can't afford to get sloppy.'

'It could just be a shopping list, no one's gonna find out. It'll be fine.'

'Alright. But tell me *everything* you saw last night, and you gotta promise to wake me up the next time you think you might've made first contact with aliens.' She whacks me lightly with the back of her hand. 'Bloody hell!'

'Deal.'

As soon as I say it, her eyes widen. 'Red alert,' she whispers, and she pretends to be checking something on the eftpos machine.

I put the list in my pocket and am wiping the counter when a hand clamps down on my shoulder, squeezes.

'How are we today?' John booms. 'Busy?' He looks around at the empty shop, raising his eyebrows.

I'm sure there's a monster inside our boss that wants to scream at us *time to lean, time to clean*, even though right now I'm literally cleaning.

'We're waiting on the deliveries,' I say to him, shifting on my feet to move slightly away.

John places his hands on my clean counter, right in the centre. 'We're having a bit of a problem: I've done the numbers and we're being stolen from.'

Gwen keeps her face passive as she nods. I fiddle with the spray bottle in my hands. I haven't been getting *that* sloppy.

'We're going to have to check the security gates every morning. Make sure they're working. If there's an issue, gimme a buzz.'

'Sure thing,' I say.

'Good girl.' He squeezes my shoulder again and I shudder.

John runs through some tasks to do today, all of which we've already done, and I wish he'd just get out already so we can talk about the lights. He mostly talks to Gwen and treats her like she's the boss of me. We both hate it.

After his spiel he's gone, leaving behind two big, greasy palm prints on my clean counter. We're not out at work, so he calls us by our wrong names. It's annoying and while there's no way we'd correct him, the unpleasantness remains.

'You reckon he knows about the pirating?' Gwen asks.

'Nah, no way.' I flick through the albums we're supposed to play today. Cos John's already been in, we can probably play whatever we want cos I doubt he'll be coming back.

'What was all that about then?'

I scoff. 'Just kids nicking stuff. They're always gonna do that. Plus, anything I don't bring back, the shop has heaps of. I can't see how he'd notice.'

'I dunno, Astro. We should be more careful.'

'We're *so* careful! I think it's fine, honestly. He just wants to exert his power or whatever over us by making us do all this stuff, classic boss manoeuvres.' I wipe away John's handprints from the countertop. 'I don't think we need to worry. So. About the UFO.'

I've got the *Green Guide* spread out on the table checking what's on the telly tonight. Nothing I really wanna watch while we wait for it to be dark enough to go see the UFO. Our other housemates are out.

'What's on?' Gwen asks from her seat in front of the computer.

'Nothing.' I turn to her, she's on the *X-Files* forums we met on. That was a few years back when she used to live in Perth and she was the first trans person I met online and then IRL. She moved here, I got her a job at the CD shop with me, even though it sucks. She let me move in with her and her housemates after my mum kicked me out.

'Any new requests?'

'Yeah, I've written them down.' Gwen types something, clicks the mouse. 'Time for Roger?'

Jolly Roger is my car that's mostly our car, named after the pirate flag.

I look out the window; the sky's definitely got a little darker since we got home. 'Yeah, we can get Macca's on the way.'

—

In the car, Gwen rummages through the tapes. 'What you wanna listen to? *Freak Show*?'

'Maybe a mix?' I say, pulling out of our driveway.

She picks a random tape and puts it into the player. 'Prisoner of Society' by The Living End comes on, the drums building a rhythm in my heart that's fast enough to amp up my nerves.

The dirt road shakes the car like we're driving over corrugated iron and my whole skeleton rattles. 'Weren't they gonna grade the road last week?'

'This week,' she says. She pulls down the shade flap and inspects her hair in the mirror as we get onto a smoother patch of road.

'Do you think it looks good? I can't tell anymore. Thank God for Kurt Cobain making this look fashionable.'

She's been growing out her hair for the last few months after what the psych said.

'It looks nice. I know you miss the short hair, but this looks good too.'

'After I get my pills, I'm buying a wig for my appointments so I don't have to put up with this crap.'

'I was thinking …' And then I just freeze.

'Hm?'

I see her turn to look at me, but I keep looking at the road. 'Do you think there's other people like me?'

More and more, I feel like I've slipped between the cracks, shifting places I don't know the names of. I see it in stranger's faces, the way I slip through their gaze, they can't catch a hold of me. I can't either.

'There's gotta be. I mean look at us, me, Billie, Trev,' she lists our housemates. 'We're all a bit … y'know.'

I know, but it's different.

'Hey, I got you a pressie though.' She reaches over to squeeze my arm. 'I found out about it online, it's a zine from America called *Changelings* but like, in all caps, so like *CHANGELINGS!*' She shouts the last word.

'Changelings,' I repeat, goosebumps rising all over me. That's gotta mean something, right? Like aliens tell me I'm something from the sky, then Gwen getting me this zine. I come back to my body suddenly, remember I'm driving. I clear my throat. 'Like when faeries would snatch away kids or whatever?'

'I guess so. But this is like, a queer thing. About people who are … what did they say. Like on the margins of language or something. Anyway, I got you a subscription a while ago and I was gonna keep it as a surprise. It's in the post.'

'Thanks.' The want claws up my throat, just something, anything, to know I'm not the only one. I've got Gwen, Trev and Billie, but none of them seem to feel as lost as I do.

'Now take me to the aliens!' She drums her hands on her knees in time to a Savage Garden song that fills the car.

We get the usual from Macca's. I stuff a few chips into my mouth and start driving along fields and long stretches of road to where I saw the lights in Pakenham.

'Who knows if they'll even come back,' I say around the chips. They're way too salty today and I can feel a cut on the edge of my mouth stinging. 'Do you reckon they'd come again so soon?'

'Let's just see anyway,' Gwen says.

I park Roger on the side of the highway, angled towards the paddock. Barely any cars pass. We wind down the windows and eat our food, looking out the windscreen, the engine pinging as it cools. I look up at the sky and the emptiness tugs at me.

'So it was just lights in the sky?' Gwen asks. 'No noise?'

'Three lights, I guess sort of rotating, hovering.'

If it had just been that, maybe I could've dismissed it as nothing. But the feel of it, the way it gathered all my joy and brought it up to the surface, the skin-tingling fizziness, the yearning, that was something else. And I can't bring myself to bring up the voices, not even to Gwen.

'I know I've been watching too much *X-Files*.'

'Look, if *you're* watching too much then I'm in deep trouble.'

'Y'know I think it's too cloudy to see anything,' I say.

'Do you think they're below or above the clouds? Like, when you saw them last.'

I chew for a few moments. 'I don't think I noticed. It was hard to tell.'

It gets darker, Roger gets colder, we move to the backseat so we can huddle together.

'Shoulda got apple pies,' I say after a while.

'You reckon we're gonna see them?'

I shrug. 'Maybe we should play them some music, I had the little radio on. Maybe they like Spiderbait.'

Gwen laughs. 'Who doesn't. Where's that radio? Glove box?'

'Batteries're dead,' I say as we clamber back to the front seats. 'We should be prepared next time.' I start Roger. 'I think this is the problem,' I say. 'We can't both be the Mulder. You have to be the Scully.'

'Why do I have to be the Scully?'

'Because I saw them first?'

'Oh shut up. It's more fun if we're both Mulders. We want to believe!'

I chuck a U-ey and head back down the road. I take a detour so we can look down the hill at the lights below, twinkling in the dark suburbs.

'Fairyland, my mum used to call it, this view,' I say.

'Maybe you should talk to her.'

'I don't think she wants me to.'

'Do you wanna talk about it?'

It's like water rushing up through me, like a geyser's just spouting all this want and all this need and then my mouth just slams a lid over it.

'No.'

—

Gwen's getting ready for work without me the next day. She stuffs her work shirt into her bag and sits down at the kitchen table opposite me. She pours herself some cereal.

'Wanna take Roger to look for aliens again when you're back home?' I try to say it lightly, but I want her to see what I saw, to feel it.

'We're going to that party tonight, remember?'

'Ah, right.'

After brekky, I go onto the *X-Files* forums to see if there are any music requests. We've got our own thread for Australians, but the latest posts are from a couple of days ago and those CDs are on the list. The only private messages I've got are just chats. I'm closing tomorrow, so I'll get everything then.

I check the other piracy threads, the US, UK and a few other countries have their own, but the requests are usually filled pretty quickly cos so many people live overseas, they've got easier access to stuff.

My mouse hovers over the spoiler thread. I don't click on it, and just move to the chatbox on the site. It's mostly empty, the Americans are asleep.

astroboy: anyone around?

scully: hey

I've seen scully around online, and everyone on the site knows who she is. I'm pretty sure she's Australian cos we seem to be posting at the same time. There aren't heaps of other Aussies on here, apart from me and Gwen.

scully posted a fanfic a couple of months ago where Mulder and Scully swapped genders after being abducted by aliens. Scully conceded that they were in fact, being abducted by real aliens, and they had to keep living as their other-gendered selves when they returned to Earth. I read it over and over, and even printed it off at work when I was alone.

astroboy: hey I love your fics

scully: thx

scully: asl?

I cringe at the question, but give the answer I've been using for the last few months.

astroboy: 20/!/oz

astroboy: u?

scully: 21 f melb

astroboy: no way! Same

I'm conscious of the way my heart beats in my chest as I wait for her to respond, I refresh the page after a few seconds, but nothing. I sigh, consider going into the spoiler threads, but instead just read everyone's theories about the next season. By the time I've moved to the easter eggs thread to see the latest posts, I see I've got a new DM.

scully: hey, it's so nice to meet someone from melb! Ive lived here my whole life. i'm in the north, where r u?

I type out my reply quickly.

astroboy: So many ppl here are american lol. im way out east in the dandenongs

And I pause here. I'm assuming she's queer because of the fics she writes, but maybe not. I decide to chance it anyway.

astroboy: Me and my housemates are going to a dress-up party tonight in fitzroy, at the bookshop, hares n hyenas. Do u go to them? mayb weve met before

Sometimes I want to live in the north cos there are so many queers there, and it's where all the art and music stuff seems to happen. But I love the trees, the space, out here. The stars from our roof are astounding.

scully: I've been a couple of times. I'll try and come down for a bit tonight

We keep chatting, making plans and talking about fics and what we reckon will happen in the next season.

—

We leave with our housemates Trev and Billie, all dressed up. Gwen drives Roger, and I've got the bag of burnt CDs that our DJ mate Davey asked for in exchange for tickets. It feels weird trading them for something, cos we never take any payment at all for this, but I do want the free tickets.

'Do you think this is a little on the nose?' I ask, holding my feathery pirate's hat in my lap.

'Yar, nar,' Gwen replies in a pirate voice. 'It's funny.'

'And also way too late now,' Billie says. He's painted a little beard onto his face.

'I was talking to scu— er, the Scully on the forums who uses the double ones in her handle. She's coming tonight.'

'What!' Gwen shrieks. 'A celeb!'

'Well, she said she'll try.'

'Who's this?' Trev asks from the back seat. He's got just about every piece of leather on that he owns, like he was born to dress up as a pirate.

'A fanfic writer Astro has a crush on,' Gwen says.

'No I don't.'

'You're blushing,' Billie teases.

I look out the window as my cheeks burn.

—

Gwen parks Roger a few streets away from the party and when the four of us enter the bookshop, Davey gives us a wave.

'If it isn't the pirate queen herself,' Davey says, bringing me into a hug. 'What've you got for me?'

I pass over the bag. 'Everything you asked for, and then some stuff I found on the net that I think you'll like.'

He flicks through the CDs, grinning. 'Yes! Amazing. This is gonna be sick as. Hey listen, I've gotta go chat to Crusader before I start but I'll catch you round, yeah?'

And then he's gone. I'm in the crowd alone momentarily, eyes searching for Gwen and the others. But instead I see someone dressed as Dana Scully. Apart from the clothes, scully doesn't look like Dana at all, she's got dark brown hair that's close-clipped to her head, she's tall, she's got tattoos everywhere. Her shirt is unbuttoned so her bra is showing. I give her a wave and when she sees me, she smiles.

'What should I call you IRL?' I ask.

'I dunno. I guess you can call me Sophie.'

'I use Astro,' I say, blushing harder even though I'm not embarrassed. 'Better than my other name.'

'Astro's cool.' She smiles. 'So you live with all these pirates?'

'Yeah, one of them is GwenIsOutThere, from the forums.'

'You together?' Sophie asks, her finger tracing the top of her glass.

'No, more like platonic soul mates.' We joke about it, but I think it's true.

'Good to know.'

Before I can answer, someone butts in.

'Hey Astro, you reckon you can grab me Lawnsmell's CD?' It's a guy who I've met maybe twice before. I'm surprised he knows my name. 'Davey said you'd hooked him up.'

'We don't do local indies,' I say. 'You gotta buy that.'

'C'mon.'

'No.' I turn back to Sophie, and I hear him muttering about how I'm a bitch.

'What's all that?'

'Me and Gwen work at a CD shop. I've been giving Davey the DJ burnt CDs for free tickets.'

'Oh! Is *that* you doing that on the forums? I've got some great stuff on there, thank you.'

Gwen appears from the crowd and hands me a drink. 'Let's boogie. Oh! Are you the double-ones-Scully? GwenIsOutThere, pleased to meetcha.' Gwen gives a curtsey, as much as the crowd will allow. She takes my hand, leads me to where people are dancing, and Sophie follows.

The way Sophie's and my body fit together when we're dancing, the salt on her lips when she brings me in.

—

Up here, everything's quiet. I reach out and gather the stars in my hands, dust trickling through my fingers into the dark surrounding. Earth is so small, beautiful and blue. I've always imagined what it would be like to look at the whole of it, every person alive, but I never thought it would be like this.

Over their systems I hear Silverchair.

The aliens gave me a bag of marbles because they look like Earth. I hold them up one by one, compare them all to Earth, but the shades of blue are wrong, there's not enough green.

After an age, I return inside, breathe the oxygen they give us.

—

I'm woken up by Sophie rolling over to face me. Her hair's all tousled, her make-up smudged. 'I've gotta go to work,' she says. 'Come with me to work, I'll make you a coffee?'

'Sure.' I kiss her, she pulls me closer. My breath catches and she giggles.

'Not now, I'll be late.'

She gets up and starts gathering her things, takes off her make-up.

'Oh my god,' I groan as I reach for my clothes. 'I'm dressed as a fucken pirate.'

'You want to borrow some clothes?'

—

At the end of the day I pull the rollers shut and immediately unbutton my work shirt, stuffing it and my nametag in my bag. We're in the shopping centre so it's never too hot to wear two t-shirts. I have a look at the CDs on the list, crosscheck them with the ones in my bag. Sophie chose a couple after we hung out again. Close up the till, don't bother to vacuum, then I get outta there.

One the way home, I empty out our PO box and there's a pink envelope in there. It's addressed to me and it's got an international stamp on it. My heart jumps to my throat and I scurry back to the car, throwing the rest of the mail onto the passenger seat as I hold the pink envelope in my hands.

I tear it open and pull the zine out. It's pretty thick, a lone staple struggles to keep all the pages together. The cover has the word CHANGELINGS repeated over and over in different handwriting.

It's filled with little essays and art by different people, all black and white, photocopied together.

This is a genderfuck manifesto one of them begins, and I don't know what that means but I know it's me. The writer goes on, saying how they're not a man or a woman, something else, a genderqueer, a changeling. My heart's beating too fast and I can feel my hands shaking.

I AM A HOMOCORE ALIENSEXUAL FREAK another page screams out in all-caps written in thick marker. *Gay is Good and Transexuals are Terrific*, another says.

My hands are still shaking so I put the zine down and drive home. Gwen's out so I just go straight to my room, chuck my bag on the floor and lie on the bed.

I read the zine cover to cover, and then again. There's a shift in me, I feel it. I feel like the tides coming in and out, leaving salt on the shore. Where is Gwen?

In the lounge, Trev is playing a racing game on the telly. He swears, swerves his whole body to make a corner, and I watch his car explode into flames on the screen.

'What's up?' he asks. Trev's a couple years older than me, always wears a flanno, has a ciggie tucked behind his ear. He's trans but psychs keep denying him hormones because he still "might want to have children". 'Your boss being a cunt again?'

'Do you know where Gwen is?' My hands are still shaking, I keep them in my pockets.

He shakes his head. 'Nah. Wanna play?' He offers me the controller.

I've always been shit at racing games. 'This on hard mode?' I ask after a couple minutes.

Trev laughs. 'Easy.'

'Really? No way.'

'True as the deep dark blue, Astro.' He takes the controller back when I finish my race and we go into two-player mode.

'Nick any CDs today? I wanna get some stuff, actually. Can I give you a list?'

'Sure, just lemme know,' I say. 'I might be able to find some online but. I got some good stuff today though, check it out.' I go grab my bag from where I dropped it, and pull out the CDs. When I get back to the lounge, I see two of the plastic cases are cracked. 'Ah shit.' I hold up the broken cases.

'Surely those things crack all the time.'

We play for a bit longer, then I get sick of being shit at it so I go to the computer. I start ripping the CD and the computer hums loudly, I can smell the plastic and the metal heating up. The first time we did this I freaked out, but Gwen assured me it was okay. Reckon why that's why they called it burning CDs.

In the forums, the longest thread is a word-association game, so I muck around on there for a bit. I read the start of a fanfic where Mulder and Scully are getting ready to go to a FBI ball, but it's way too out of character for me so I close it, end up just looking through the music threads to see if there's anything new I wanna download until the CDs are all ripped.

Gwen gets home just as I'm finishing and I show her the broken cases.

'Shit,' she says. 'We're gonna have to buy them.'

'You reckon?' I ask, examining the thing. But the corner's completely broken off, so the cover doesn't stay on anymore.

Gwen raises her eyebrows at me. 'We can't muck around, Astro. John's gonna find out and then we're both done for.'

'It'll be fine,' I say.

'Then why's he all suspicious?' she asks. 'C'mon. Don't be a dickhead.'

'Yeah look, fair enough. Sorry. I just got them cos Sophie asked.'

'Ooh Sooophie.' Gwen makes kissing noises. 'Well, you listened to these yet?'

I shake my head, and we chuck one on. It's noisy, everything clashing together in a way that kind of works, though I feel like it shouldn't.

Gwen pauses it. 'Dunno about all that.' She opens up one of the booklets and leafs through the pages. 'Oi, Astro,' Gwen says. 'This one's a local band.' She holds up one of the cases to show the label's info. It's a tiny label, too. 'Did you buy it?'

'Shit.' A chill runs through my body. The code.

'You know we don't do that.'

'I know, I know. I'm sorry. Look, I'll buy it when I'm in next.'

'Alright. Just … we have to be careful, Astro. That's how we've got this far, y'know?'

—

We have dinner with Trev and Billie, watch some telly, and then when it's dark, I turn to the others. 'Aliens?'

'Hm?' Billie asks. Billie's a butch lesbian and isn't as home as much as the rest of us, he's always out at the bars and then asking for a lift from the station at midnight.

'Me and Astro have been looking for aliens,' Gwen explains. 'There's lights in Pakenham.'

Billie laughs. 'What?'

'You've found extra-terrestrial life and you haven't been sharing?' Trev asks, turning the TV off.

'I mean, *maybe*,' I say. 'I saw some lights the other night, like a UFO. Gwen hasn't seen anything yet.'

'Well we gotta see this,' Trev says.

—

Tonight is clear with a crisp view of the stars. I feel a bit restless, fiddling with a loose string in my sleeve as we all sit around on a picnic blanket.

'Do you ever wish you were a robot?' I ask as we watch Billie put four big batteries in the back of his CD player. 'Y'know like, impenetrable skin; instead of sleep you could just charge yourself, or you could like, upload your consciousness to the web …'

'No way,' Trev says. 'What if got a virus or something? Remember when Billie downloaded whatever it was and we got pop-ups everywhere?'

'Hey, it was a pretty legit scam,' Billie protests.

'I just feel like I need two bodies,' I say, thinking of the zine. 'That way I could have two robot bodies, and just like, switch between them.'

'I guess sometimes I feel a bit like that,' Gwen says. 'But I mean, robots can't have sex. Or eat.'

'Shht—' I squeak out, tapping Gwen on the arm frantically. 'Look.'

We see the lights, the same three as before, hovering, and there's a moment of silence before Gwen shouts. I realise I'm on my feet when I start jumping up and down, and then we're yelling all kinds of shit into the sky like *come back! we love you! take us away!*

Not today changelings, I hear.

I feel my pulse quicken through my whole body, throbbing, and the air's whooshed out of my lungs as Gwen pulls me into a hug. Billie and Trev squish in and we all yell up at the sky again. No words this time, just noise, at the lights now gone.

'What the hell!' Billie says when we break apart. 'That was definitely aliens!' He laughs, shakes Trev by his shoulder.

'I dunno,' Trev says. 'Could be anything—'

'Aw, come on,' Gwen says. 'That was *so* aliens! Did you see the way they were watching us?'

'For harvest,' Billie says.

'For *science*,' Gwen replies. 'They're gonna make first contact!'

'Why'd they choose us?' I ask, but no one knows how to respond.

—

The phone rings the next day and it's Sophie, asking if I want to do something soon.

'We saw a UFO,' I blurt.

'What?' she laughs.

'Yeah!' I nod enthusiastically, though I know she can't see me. 'A UFO, like a real one. It was just these lights in the sky.'

'Are you making fun of me?' she asks without malice.

'No!' I say. 'This was real, I swear to God. My housemates saw it too. It was amazing.'

'I think I'd need more evidence,' she says, and I can hear the smile in her voice.

'If you saw it, you'd think the same.'

She snorts. 'Sure.'

I frown. 'I'm not joking, I promise.'

There's a tiny pause before she replies. 'Nah yeah, I know. I'll see you soon though, yeah?'

—

A few days later, John's called a staff meeting. It's me, Gwen and my least favourite coworker Amber, plus a few people I haven't worked with a lot. I can't believe I had to get out of bed for this. It's hard enough keeping my feet on the ground.

'We're gonna do a stocktake every Sunday,' he tells us.

My jaw drops. 'Are you serious?' I say before I can stop myself. Gwen nudges me.

'Extremely,' John says. 'We've got a new roster too.' He hands out sheets of paper. I've only got one shift with Gwen now.

'We've got two staff but we have to do a stocktake?' I ask. 'How is that possible?'

'Start early,' he shrugs.

'I've never done a stocktake before,' Amber says. Even she looks trepidatious. 'What are we supposed to do?'

'We have to scan every CD in the shop. John, how is it supposed to be accurate if customers are rummaging through everything?'

'It'll be fine,' he says. 'We're gonna do one together, and you'll see how it's done. And I've got these instructions from head office.'

He plonks down a thick booklet. We all stare at it.

As soon as we start, he has to suddenly go and make a phone call, so he stands behind the counter while we work.

Me and Gwen take the rock section, scanning each CD case. I recognise a lot of these as stuff we've nicked. 'Man, this roster sucks. I can't believe I'm on with Amber,' I say quietly, writing down the titles of the CDs in the racks. 'She's so uptight and she *loves* John. Like,' I mime spewing, 'kill me now.'

'Maybe we should stop pirating,' Gwen says quietly.

'Hell no,' I reply. 'What about the music?'

'I don't want us to get fired,' Gwen says. She counts a huge stack of Powderfinger CDs. 'Where else is gonna take two losers like us?' She grins as she says it. 'Look, we can just leave it to the others.'

I sigh. 'We'll be fine, Gwenny.'

She looks over my shoulder. 'We better look like we're both miserable, John's watching us.'

—

'Why do you reckon Scully is still so adamant their cases are mundane?' Gwen asks as I park Roger next to a field. Sophie came over to watch the *X-Files*, but we persuaded her to come see the aliens.

'Like, at this point it's been *years* since she started working with Mulder,' Gwen continues. 'She knows that supernatural stuff exists.'

'She's pretty smart too, like …' Sophie pauses as we all get out of the car. 'She does admit that the supernatural ones are supernatural when it's clear there's no other explanation.'

'I reckon it's like, we must be seeing five per cent of their cases,' I say. 'And the other ninety-five per cent are all mundane, Mulder keeps trying to make her see the aliens or whatever. But in the show we're only seeing a sliver of their lives. So she's just tired at this point.'

'I love that,' Gwen says. 'I reckon that's what it is.'

'So these lights, mundane or alien?' Sophie asks.

'Time will tell,' Gwen says at the same time as I say, 'Aliens.' Gwen grins at me; Sophie's eyebrows rise.

'Well, really I think it's a UFO,' Gwen says.

'Next time,' I say, and Sophie laughs, though I don't see why.

This time, we brought some cushions. We spread them out on the picnic blanket and Sophie sits close to me, where our skin is touching is warm and I can't concentrate on what anyone's saying.

Gwen gets out Billie's CD player. She puts on Spiderbait first, and we wait and watch the sky.

'How long do you reckon this'll take?' Sophie asks after a bit, just as hairs start to lift on my forearms. 'I've gotta get up early tomorrow to get to work on time.'

'I can feel it, something's coming,' I say.

Everything hushes, the sound of the cars falls away. Then through the clouds, the lights descend and I tremble as they come closer, the movement so slick and silent.

Changeling changeling changeling.

'Holy shit,' Gwen swears. We lock eyes and she grins. 'Again.'

When the lights are right above us, Gwen whispers, 'Are we about to be harvested?'

I wish I'd brought a camera for proof. My heart swells as the lights get closer, the voices get louder.

The song ends, and the lights spin, and then they're gone. I feel like a stone dropped into the ocean. Gwen pulls me into a hug as she laughs and I come back to my body, fleshy and solid, I grip her tight.

'You reckon they'll choose us?' I ask, my arms still all goosebumpy. 'What about you, Soph, what do you reckon?'

She shifts, looking away from me. 'I dunno ... it could be

anything. The government's probably testing out some kind of new airplane or something.'

Sophie at least, hasn't heard the voices. I look back up at the sky, the blackness stretching once more.

'It was totally aliens,' I say. 'I'm with Mulder on this.'

—

When I'm on my next closing shift a few days later, I'm stuck with Amber. Being at work without Gwen is torture enough, especially when we can't talk about the aliens. I made a thread on the forums about sightings, but no one's really replied. It's less cool to be a believer than a sceptic, I guess.

When it's finally time to pull the shutters down at the shop, I sigh in relief. As Amber counts the till, I tidy the shop, vacuuming and straightening all the stock. I take off my work shirt and bundle it in my hands, slipping past the alt section to grab one of the CDs that's been asked for, hiding it in the shirt in my hands.

I go into the staff area to grab my bag, shove the shirt and the CD into my bag, and when I come back into the shop proper Amber's watching me.

'You right?' I ask.

She gestures to the money, her hand's shaking slightly. 'Till's out by five dollars,' she says.

'Let me count it,' I say. I count the money as she gets her bag and then come to the same conclusion.

'What if it's been stolen?' she says, looking significantly at me when she says the last word. 'Should we call John?'

'I don't think John cares about five bucks.'

She keeps looking at me, eyes narrowed just a bit.

'Well, I didn't steal it,' I say. 'Jesus. Just leave a note for tomorrow and put it in the log book.' I know she's anxious about it and maybe I should cut her some slack, but the constant wanting of John's approval just makes me wanna spew.

She writes the note in a huff, and I wipe the counter down so it's squeaky clean for the morning.

We leave together, so I make sure I walk through the right security gate. I turned it off on Amber's lunch break so I could take stuff tonight. I should've grabbed the CDs then too, but I couldn't get them all before customers kept interrupting.

It goes off. I yelp, I can feel my face heating up so I know I can't play it cool, put a hand to my chest.

'I wish they weren't so buggy,' I say.

Amber looks at me but says nothing. We walk out the same way but thankfully she says she has to go to the toilet, and we part ways. I rush all the way back to Roger and get in, breathing in and out slowly as my heart pounds.

When I get home, I don't tell Gwen about what happened. We're going to another party, and I want to go, but I want to go see the aliens more.

'I don't know what to wear,' I say. 'I want to look more ... Changeling-y.'

'I knew you'd love the zine,' she says. She clicks something and the computer starts whirring like it's gonna take off, the familiar smell of burning CDs floats into the air. 'You should take some of Trev's clothes maybe.'

'I don't wanna look like a guy,' I reply. 'I just want to look less ... like I am now.'

'Should we cut your hair?' Gwen says. 'Billie will know what to do.'

I grab my ponytail self-consciously. 'Oh. Maybe?'

'Billie!' Gwen yells, 'Astro needs a haircut.'

'What do you want done?' Billie asks, poking his head into the loungeroom.

I shrug. 'I dunno. Something.'

Gwen checks the time. 'We've got an hour and a half.'

'Easy peasy.'

—

I emerge from the bathroom so much lighter. I move my head around, side to side, my hair swished up. It doesn't touch my neck.

'Oh you look like just like Jack in *Titanic*,' Gwen says when Billie shows me off. 'Dreamboat.'

'I'll dress you up,' Billie says.

I get this big purple jacket, fancy billowy pants and a plain white t-shirt. It's a bit eighties, but I like it.

'Looking cool,' Billie says.

'Thanks for this,' I say. 'I feel really ... me.'

Billie claps me on the back. 'One more thing.' He reaches up to my ears and takes out my earrings, plops them into my hands. He takes out his own little silver stud and puts it into my ear.

'Is that the gay ear?' I ask.

'Oh shut up.' He laughs. 'Come on. Let's see if Gwen's ready.'

Gwen's in her classic jeans and black t-shirt, hair falling onto her shoulders. 'Don't tell my therapist I dare to not wear a dress,' she says.

'We all ready?' Trev appears from the kitchen.

'Jesus,' Gwen puts a hand on her chest. 'Stop sneaking up on us.'

'Oh Gwen, did you burn Davey's pile?' I ask.

'Hm?'

'The pile on the desk—' But it's in my bag. 'Ah fuck. I'll just loan him the CDs, I promised them for tonight.'

We're running a little late by the time we get to the venue, but it's all good. The place is electric, the air's thick with sweat.

I find Davey, give him the CDs.

'I've gotta get that back before I leave,' I yell at him over the music. 'I need to take them back to work.'

He gives me a thumbs up but I'm not sure if he actually heard me.

Billie drags me outside to the beer garden, I dunno where Gwen and Trev have gone, but then Billie starts talking to this femme so I excuse myself, lost in the sea of people I should know but for some reason, not tonight. Everyone's a stranger, I'm adrift in the crowd.

I see Sophie in the sea of faces and I wave for her to come over. Someone touches my shoulder, their arm slinking across my chest. My skin heating under their touch. When I turn, I don't know who they are, taller than me, but there's familiarity there, the way their face resists any understanding I try to pin to them. When I can't, the fluidity is a relief. We're the same.

Behind them, I see Sophie getting closer.

Bye changeling, they say into my ear, breath hot, and then they're gone. Emptiness enters my body.

When Sophie gets to me, I kiss her, pull her close, so she doesn't see my eyes well up, my face burn.

Sophie anchors me after that, we dance, we sit, she takes me outside to a dark corner. We dance with Gwen and Trev after, Billie's disappeared, and then Trev drives us all home in the dark as the sea of trees stretches on and on and on.

'Why do we live out here?' I ask as the sky spins above, heaving.

'Cos my parents own this place and the rent is cheap,' Trev says, the same time as Gwen says 'Where else are we gonna live?'

'I think it's cute,' Sophie says to me like a secret, jewels on her tongue. 'Just us and the trees, no one to disturb anything.'

When we get back, I can hear Gwen and Trev talking in the kitchen as me and Sophie go to my room, find each other in the dark.

—

'Ah fuck,' I say to Gwen as we walk through the empty shopping centre to our next shift. 'I might have messed up a bit.'

'What?' Gwen asks, counting the float before we open the doors. She fumbles the pile of coins she's holding and they clatter across the counter, onto the floor.

I help pick them up. 'I didn't get those CDs back from Davey.'

'What?' Gwen repeats, this time the word is heavy. 'That massive pile?'

'I didn't have time to burn them.'

'John's already suspicious of you, Astro. I was on shift with Amber last week and she was calling John to dob you in. She didn't have any evidence or anything, but—'

'Oh god.' I think back to yesterday, with the gates. My insides seize up. 'Okay. That's fine. I can just pay for them.'

But when I open my wallet, I've got barely any money left; pay day's two days away. Gwen's out too.

'This is why I need a credit card,' I say weakly, but Gwen's not having it.

'Fuck's sake,' she hisses. 'Come on, let's just get this shitshow on the road.'

I bring the roller up as she wheels the display of stock out the front, and then I go grab us some coffees from the food court. I get her a doughnut too, one of those ones that look like a dinosaur, but her face remains hard.

'We've got rules for a reason,' she says as we stand behind the counter. 'No more breaking them, okay? Especially when Amber's around.'

'You're right,' I say. 'I won't.'

After that, we're busy till lunchtime. Gwen goes on break first, and I'm straightening the stock on the bargains table when John comes in, face thunderous and red.

'Hey John,' I say weakly.

'You taking the piss?' he says to me, poking me in the chest.

I wince, but don't say anything. A few customers turn around to see what's going on. They all look away.

'I never shoulda hired you,' he hisses, his eyes catching on my new haircut, and I know what he sees, what he's seen the whole time. 'Gave you a chance. How long have you been sneaking CDs, you little weirdo?'

'You don't have any proof,' I say.

'I don't care. Get out of my shop. You're fired.'

—

The hum of the ship is gentle on my cheek as I lie on the warm floor. The ship moulds itself to my body, I'm cradled in its arms. Out the window, I see spiralling arms of stardust rotate slow, slowly, barely perceptible.

I watch a galaxy expand and contract, changing, swift and sure and millennia go by.

The changelings show me time, the way it weaves together and separates, but the emptiness within me fills. They show me how they create themselves too, just like me. They give me everything my body needs here, but I still feel nothing.

—

The next day I lie in bed until my bladder's about to burst. I drag myself to the shops to go buy a coffee with change that's scattered around my room, my only money till my last pay comes in. I get to the bakery and must look wrecked as, cos they give me a free cinnamon doughnut.

'Cheers,' I say. The server gives me a smile before she walks off.

At the first sip, my mouth scrunches up. The coffee's burnt, but I keep drinking anyway. I scoff the doughnut and wish I was anywhere else.

I go to the op shop and flick through CDs. There's some good stuff there, but it's not the same as stealing from work. Appropriating. Besides, you can't just steal from a charity, that's just mean.

—

The Centrelink guy sucks in air through his teeth before he asks why I'm here. I wish I'd got the other guy, the one who looks like Santa.

'I need to go on the dole,' I say.

'Why?' He asks it in a way like no one's ever said this to him before, eyebrows raised to the roof as he crosses his arms.

'I was unfairly dismissed.'

He clicks something on his computer and frowns. Even he's disappointed in me.

We go through the questions and he types in my answers one finger at a time. I dig my fingernails into my palms to stop myself from fidgeting, though I can't help but keep crossing and uncrossing my legs over and over and over.

'You'll be notified if you're approved or not,' he says dryly at the end, handing me the printout.

'Cheers,' I say, taking the paper.

At home, I go on the forums and I see Sophie's posted a new fic. Only the first chapter is up, but both Mulder and Scully get abducted. I read it through, wishing there was more, then go back to bed.

—

A couple nights later, Sophie comes over and we go through me and Gwen's music collection to see if she wants to burn anything.

'Do you ever worry about like ... stealing from the musicians?' she asks.

I shrug. 'The CEO of Warner music made ten million dollars last year. You reckon he deserves all that money? The way I see it, he's stealing way more from them than I ever could.'

'Fair point.'

'And I mean, how many times can you copy a file? That's infinity. I don't take the actual file.'

'Youse wanna come for a drive?' Gwen asks, coming into the lounge room. She's in her PJs, and now her hair's long enough to tie up.

I go to say yes, but then Sophie shakes her head a tiny bit.

'Can we just hang out?' she says, quiet.

'Nah,' I say to Gwen, who gives me a thumbs up. 'Have fun.'

'We'll let you know if we get abducted,' Gwen says, poking out her tongue before she disappears. I hear the jingle of the car keys and then the others leave, taking Roger.

I show Sophie Yothu Yindi and she gets me to listen to The Superjesus, which we have to download off the internet cos we don't have the CD yet. I wonder if the others are seeing the aliens right now.

—

'Where do you go?' Sophie asks me, rolling onto her side towards me later.

'Hm?' I ask.

She's propped her head up with her arm, staring at me.

'Like now. You always seem so far away.'

'Do I?'

She moves closer, our legs touching. She's just shaved her legs so her skin's smooth and cool.

'Yeah. You're always off in dreamland. I feel like you're always looking for something better instead of like, I dunno. Being present.'

'I dunno if that's what I'm doing. Not exactly. I think it's just like. I can't stop thinking about the lights.'

'The UFO lights?' She frowns.

I nod, wishing I hadn't said anything.

'You know that's not real, right?' she says slowly. 'Like, you don't think it's really a UFO up there?'

'Would that be so silly?' I'm trying not to let my cheeks warm, but they do.

'Yes!' she says, half-laughing. 'Everyone knows aliens aren't real.'

'Well then, what are we seeing?' I ask, sitting up.

She sits up as well, pulling the sheets up. 'I dunno, Astro, just lights. It could be anything. The world is a strange place.'

'The universe is a strange place,' I say. 'What makes it so weird that aliens exist? It's a huge universe, the thought of us being alone in it … doesn't that make less sense?'

'Okay, so say aliens are real. Why the hell are they interested in Pakenham?'

'I dunno, why not? Like what makes Pakenham so unspecial?'

She scoffs. 'It's Pakenham. It's just farmland.'

'It's not *just* anything,' I say. 'It's a place where life grows. It's not more or less special than anywhere.'

She rolls her eyes. 'Look, I'm gonna go. I have work tomorrow.' She gets out of bed and pulls on her shirt.

'It's late already, are you sure you wanna drive?'

'I'll be fine.' She finishes dressing. 'I'll catch you round, Astro.'

'Soph,' I start, but she walks out of my room, closing the door behind her. I scramble into a shirt and undies, but by the time I'm ready I hear the front door open and close.

I grab a jumper and climb onto the roof. Dusty swathes of stars shine above, and something in me stirs. The endless black, the glitter of other suns. Would we be the only ones? Could we?

—

Roger pulls up and, after a while, I hear a scrambling behind me and I turn, see Gwen climbing up onto the roof.

'What's going on?' she asks. 'When you come up here alone, something's wrong.'

I sigh. 'Nothing.' I look back up and I see a satellite, blinking in and out of existence as it moves across the sky slowly. 'Do you think it's right, to believe in other life out there?'

'Right?' Gwen repeats.

'Mm. Like, isn't it a bit childish? Why not just focus on what we've got here, instead of always looking away?'

'Did Sophie say something about our trips?' Gwen asks, touching my arm.

'No.' I look at her, look away. 'Don't worry.' Shouldn't Sophie be more important than trying to find little green men in the sky? I close my eyes, weight pressing against my chest.

'What's brought this all on?' Gwen asks, I hear her move closer to me, her boots crunching against the metal roof, covered in dried gum leaves.

'Like should we be doing more with our lives than stealing from work and looking for aliens that don't even exist?'

'I think it's fun. Where's your anti-capitalist spirit?' she asks lightly.

'Where's your sense of reality? You think I really want to waste all this time going to some random spot in Pakenham?'

When I look at her, her face is crumpled and it mirrors how I feel.

'I dunno what Sophie said—'

'It's not about Sophie, Gwen,' I snap. 'This is all just a fucking joke.'

'Is it?' she asks.

I watch a cloud pass over the stars, my hand pressed to my chest to keep it all in.

'You don't need to worry about what other people think about this,' Gwen says. 'It's just us …'

'Well maybe I need something more,' I say. 'Maybe I don't wanna be stuck in a shitty job out in the middle of the fucken bush.'

Gwen's face goes stony. 'I dunno what could be more than this, but okay.'

And then she gets up and leaves. The stars move overhead, and I'm alone with only the rest of the universe for company.

—

Gwen and I sit in front of the huge windows on the side of the ship. Earth is now one of the small white dots in the sky.

'So this is space. Y'know, I'd always kind of… imagined it to be more.'

'I miss fresh air,' she says, even though we're breathing the cleanest air we ever have before.

'Do you think they'd take us back?' I ask.

'Do you think it'd feel like home?'

When I go to reply to her, I'm alone.

—

Trev's making pancakes when I come into the kitchen, heavy from sleep, but I jolt awake when I see Gwen's sitting at the table.

I don't look at her, my face burning from shame.

'You look like shit,' Trev says.

'Cheers,' I croak.

'I better go to my dead-end job,' Gwen says. She pushes her chair back forcefully. 'Maybe you can sweep the kitchen, unless you've got something better to do?'

'Sure,' I say quietly as she leaves.

'What are you and Gwen fighting about?' Trev asks.

'We're not fighting.'

He flips a pancake. 'Did something happen at work? Like are you fighting cos you got fired?'

'Trev, look. It's … it's nothing.'

He holds my gaze for just a sec, and that breaks me.

'I messed everything up with the pirating,' I say. 'John found out, and that's why I got fired, which is why Gwen doesn't bring home CDs anymore, and then I was mean to her because I was so obsessed with what Sophie thought, and now I'm like, is looking for aliens just like, babyish? Like do I need to grow up?'

Trev puts the last pancake on the plate and sits down opposite me. We squeeze lemon juice onto them and dust powdered sugar over.

'Do you think Gwen hates me?' I ask, my mouth full of food.

He shakes his head. 'Just talk to her, Astro.'

I roll up my pancake and take a bite. I chew but the more I eat, the emptier I feel.

'I could drive you to her work,' Trev says. 'I could steal some CDs for you.'

'Don't worry,' I say, but I do smile a little. 'I'll figure it out.'

—

After pancakes, I go back to bed and sleep until noon. Trev and Billie are both out of the house, so I end up driving to check the

PO box. There's another pink envelope in there. The next issue of CHANGELINGS is all pictures. People who shift and switch genders and form, fey and malleable, like ocean tides, everyone is something else. They're laughing together, kissing, fucking, hugging. The middle page spread is the one that gets me – a room full of trans people dancing.

I cry in front of the post boxes and a woman hurries her children away from me. Fat, salty tears dripping down my face, into my mouth, onto my shirt. I take myself back to the car and look through the zine again. This time slowly, taking everything in.

Tonight it's so foggy the headlights barely let me see anything more than a metre in front. It's not the same, driving Roger by myself. She needs her crew, Gwen would say.

I wait under the stars, but either the fog is too dense, or they're not coming. I play them Spiderbait, Powderfinger, The Living End … every tape I've got in the car and the CDs I brought in my bag.

One the drive home, *Changeling, changeling, changeling* echoes in my mind, but no one is speaking to me.

—

When I get home, Gwen's on the phone

'What?' she's saying, voice strained.

I turn around and she's turned too, she's got the cord tangled all up in her fingers, her knuckles white as she grips the phone, and then it's like she doesn't see me at all, she's so far away.

'Okay,' she says, and that's all, she hangs up.

Her face falls, and I go to her, pull her into a hug.

It's only after I've made her a tea and we're sitting on the couch that she tells me what's happened.

'My dad's left Mum, he's taken heaps of her stuff, she doesn't know where he's gone, but she knows he was sleeping with someone from work.'

'I'm so sorry,' I say. We never talk about her family, we never talk about my family, and I don't know how she is with them.

She takes a deep, shaky breath. 'I need to go to Perth.'

'I'll come with you,' I say immediately.

'You would?'

'Of course.'

'She doesn't know,' she says.

'Do you ... are you going to tell her?'

'I could try and hide it, but,' she says. 'I dunno, I don't know if I can anymore, or if I even want to. You know, he was the reason I came here, the other side of the bloody country.' She sighs, drains her tea cup. 'We should go to bed, it's almost four.'

—

The next morning, we get up way too early and Gwen calls work to say she'll be away for the next week, and then she calls her mum to say I'm coming too. We book our flights, Gwen's mum gives her money so she pays for me.

—

On the plane we share a discman. I flick through the huge CD wallet to figure out what to listen to next, but I can't choose.

'Here,' Gwen says. 'I'll close my eyes and you just tell me when to stop.'

She takes the wallet and flicks through it, I wait, watch her, and eventually she opens her eyes.

'You gotta say stop,' she says, and I burst out laughing.

'I was gonna.'

'What in like, ten years?' She laughs. 'Come on. Do it quick.'

She flicks through again and we end up on a mix that Sophie

made. It's in her handwriting. I didn't tell her I'm going to Perth, but Billie or Trev will let her know if she calls, I guess.

'It *is* a good mix,' Gwen says, and puts it on.

I've never been on a plane before, and I didn't realise how small they are, how it feels like being on a train or something, but you still sort of feel panicked the whole time like you know it's wrong that humans are in the sky.

'Do you reckon I shoulda worn a dress?' Gwen says. 'To see Mum.'

'You never do.'

'I know. Too late now, anyway.'

I pause for a moment, looking out at the clouds. Thinking about the sky, aliens, CHANGELINGS, I say, 'In that zine you got me ... There was someone who said she was a she but also a he. I think maybe that's ... me.'

Gwen swallows what she's eating and nods. 'That makes sense.'

'It does?'

'Yeah.'

A knot loosens inside me. The flight is long and we listen to the mix CD in silence. Gwen falls asleep; I watch the clouds as the plane takes us further from home than I've ever been.

—

Gwen's mum picks us up at the airport and Gwen's the spitting image of her. She gathers us both into hugs and introduces herself to me as Pam.

'Thanks for letting me stay with you,' I say.

She waves a hand. 'Don't even mention it. Thanks for coming all this way.' Her smile falters a bit, but she starts walking to the car. The drive to Pam's isn't too long, and soon she's got us having a cuppa at the table.

'How are you, Mum?' Gwen asks.

And then Pam bursts into tears. I excuse myself as Gwen takes her mum's hand across the table, and then I try to not overhear them talking when I retreat into the room that used to be Gwen's when she was little. The walls are paper thin though, and I hear everything. I go to put in the discman headphones when I hear Gwen tell her mum her real name.

My breath pauses for the moments of silence, and then Pam starts crying more.

I poke my head out into the hallway, ready to go to Gwen, but then I see they're hugging again. They break apart, Pam's smiling and wiping away tears.

—

A few nights later, we take Gwen's mum's car and drive. It's not long before we're out of the city and the sky stretches over us, endless black. Gwen pulls into a petrol station after I don't know how long, we fill up the tank and buy some chips and a chocolate bar inside, park the car out of the way and lean against the side, looking up at the sky.

'I didn't think I would care this much,' she says to me.

'About aliens?'

'About Dad leaving. Realising how much I'd missed my mum.' There's a moment before she laughs, then her eyes well up.

I hug her close and kiss her cheek. 'You never really know with these things.' I open up the bag of chips and offer some to her.

'You reckon we'll see aliens out here?'

'Maybe not our aliens. Perth's a bit far from Pakenham.'

She laughs, short and sharp. 'Yeah, maybe not.' She takes a deep sigh, stretching her arms outwards.

'I miss my mum too,' I say. Maybe because we're so far from home, I can let myself feel it. 'Seeing you with Pam, it's ...'

'Do you wanna call her?'

'I dunno.'

Gwen raises her eyebrows, nudges her shoulder to mine.

'Alright,' I say. 'I do. I will.'

The sky is clear and bright, there are way more stars visible here than home.

'Look at it all,' I say, turning my face to the sky, drinking in all the darkness. 'You reckon we'll get out there one day?'

'Like, as in be abducted or like *Star Trek* style?'

'*Star Trek*. Journeying out there. Meeting other species.'

'Fucking all the aliens.'

'Look, if they need a volunteer.' I giggle, nudging her. 'You wanna head back?'

'Not yet. Let's just sit out here a bit.'

The longer we stay there, the colder it gets. We move closer together, and I lean into her shoulder, she puts an arm around me.

'I don't want to fight with you again,' she says.

'Me either.'

—

When we get home, I leave my blow-up mattress alone and we both get into the single bed that's set up in the spare room. It's squishy, but nice. I press the side of my face into her back and close my eyes, wrap an arm around her. She falls asleep after five minutes but I lie awake for hours, listening to her breathe, trying to think of what I could say to Mum.

—

I dial Mum's number on Pam's phone. When it starts ringing, I nod at Gwen and then she goes to help her mum with rearranging the lounge room because Gwen's dad took the nice couch.

The phone keeps ringing and I pray that no one answers, and then I hear her voice.

'Hello?' she says.

It's too long before I say, 'Hey, Mum.'

For a moment, I think she's hung up, but then I hear her suck in a breath.

'Why are you calling?'

'Just to see how you were. And Dad, and Jeremy.'

She's silent again and I can feel cold sweat all over. I'm shaking.

'I miss you,' I say.

'Have you thought about what I said? It would do you a lot of good, darling. You know Maria's son went to one and now he's got a beautiful baby girl.'

'Mum.' I grip the phone harder. Gwen pokes her head around the corner, but I turn away from her. 'I can't do that.'

I can imagine her pursed lips at my words, and her clipped answer comes, 'I don't think it's a good idea for you to call here. Jeremy's very impressionable and we just can't have someone like you around if you refuse to see the options.'

'Can I give you my phone number? Just so you can get in touch?'

'I have to go.'

She hangs up and the dead tone sounds out. I stay on the phone because as long as I'm listening to it, maybe the phone call isn't over, and I don't have to tell Gwen what's happened.

The tone stops eventually, so I hang up the phone. In the lounge, there's a cuppa waiting for me.

'At least now I know,' I say. My voice sounds so far away.

Gwen touches my arm, tries to anchor me.

—

On the flight home, the sun's setting and the clouds around us are bathed in brilliant red.

The CD we're listening to finishes, Gwen offers me the wallet to choose a new one.

'Thanks for coming with me,' Gwen says.

'Thanks for letting me.'

After a few days, I give Sophie a ring and we meet at a cafe near hers. The food comes out and the smell of it makes my stomach cramp and I feel ill. Sophie tucks into hers straight away, cutting the egg so the yolk spills over everything.

I pick up my burger and I know I'm going to like it, so I make myself bite into it. We eat in silence for a while.

'How was Perth?' Sophie asks eventually. 'Is Gwen okay?'

I nod. 'Okay as she can be.'

The silence falls down again.

'I don't think we should keep seeing each other,' I say to Sophie. My voice scratches over itself. 'I really like you, but I just don't think we fit.'

Sophie looks at me, smiles sadly. 'I know,' she says quietly. 'You really believe, don't you?'

I nod. We both don't know where to look.

'We should've done that after we'd finished eating.' I try to smile.

'Totally.' She pushes a bit of food around her plate. 'The food is good, though.'

'The food's great.'

After the cafe, we end up at her place. She pulls me into her room and our bodies push and pull, breathing each other in. My fingers slip into her, her wetness coats my mouth.

We kiss goodbye, clinging to each other, and then I walk alone to the train station.

—

'So how was your first day?' Gwen asks as we take Roger out to the fields again. We've got our Macca's, Billie's CD player, and heaps of CDs.

'Obviously not as good as working with you,' I say. 'But I did borrow this.' I show her a few CDs that I'm pretty sure we don't have yet. 'Range is way better than John's.'

'What should we give the aliens tonight?' Gwen says. 'The Gurge?'

'Always a good option ... I was thinking maybe Bachelor Girl. Something new.'

We get out of the car and Gwen turns on the CD player and the music starts. There are a few puffy clouds in the sky, but behind them it's clear as. Only three songs play before the hairs on my arm stand up.

The lights appear brighter than ever, zipping across the sky to rest above us for a few moments, for an age. The uncut grass in front of us whips back and forth in the wind and the rest of the world falls away under the bright lights. I take a hold of Gwen's hand and she squeezes mine.

The lights land in the field in front of us shimmering through blue, green, back to white, and we have to shield our eyes. Steam whooshes out across the field as I peek through my fingers, and warmth washes over me.

Changelings, the voices say. *It's time.*

CONTRIBUTORS

MICHAEL EARP is a non-binary writer living in Naarm (Melbourne, Australia), the editor of *Everything Under The Moon: Fairy Tales in a Queerer Light, Kindred: 12 Queer #LoveOzYA Stories* and co-editor of A*vast! Pirate Stories from Transgender Authors* with Alison Evans. With a teaching degree and a Master's in children's literature, they have worked between bookselling and publishing for twenty years as a children's literature specialist. Managing The Little Bookroom saw them named ABA Bookseller of the year in 2021. Their writing has also appeared in *Archer, The Age, PopMatters, The Victorian Write, Aurealis* and *Underdog: #LoveOzYA Short Stories.*

ALISON EVANS is an award-winning novelist, zinester and writer of short stories living on Wurundjeri Land. Their novels for teenagers, *Euphoria Kids, Highway Bodies* and *Ida*, are speculative, magical and queer. Their first book *Ida* was described as a 'landmark book in Australian YA'. Their shorter work can be found in the anthologies *Everything Under the Moon, Hometown Haunts* and *Kindred*, as well as places like *Going Down Swinging* and *Bramble*. You can find out more at **alisonwritesthings.com**.

Alison would like to thank Crusader from Hare Hole for their help with research.

MADISON GODFREY is the author of two poetry collections *How To Be Held* (Burning Eye Books, 2018) and *Dress Rehearsals* (Allen & Unwin Imprint JOAN, March 2023). They write and teach on Whadjuk Noongar land, where they live with a rescue cat named Sylvia. Find out more at **maddiegodfrey.com**.

MELEIKA GESA-FATAFEHI AKA VIKA MANA is a Torres Strait Islander and Tongan storyteller that takes many forms. They descend from the Zagareb and Dauareb tribes of Mer Island and the village of Fahefa in Tonga. They've written for *Overland*, *The Big Issue*, *The Saturday Paper* and other publications at home and internationally. Vika is also a part of the FAMILI collective, rapping about Afros and abolition. In 2019, Meleika became one of ten writers that were chosen to be a part of The Next Chapter run by the Wheeler Centre. Find them **@endlessyarning**

MIA NIE is a Chinese-Australian comic artist, essayist, illustrator, zine-maker and award-nominated ex-poet living on unceded Wurundjeri country. In 2020, she was a participant in The Wheeler Centre's The Next Chapter program, and her comics have been nominated for the National Cartoonist Society's Reuben Awards. She is currently working on her self-published serial webcomic, *Samsara Dreamin'*. Mia can be found at **girlwithhorn.wordpress.com**.

MX MADDISON STOFF (she/her) is a neurodivergent non-binary essayist, independent musician and author from Melbourne, Australia. She writes unapologetically leftist, feminist, & queer fiction set in a continuous universe which blurs the line between experimental literature & pulp sci-fi. You can find more of her short fiction on Patreon (@thedescenters), or linked via her website at **maddisonstoff.com**. Her work has also appeared in *Aurealis*, *Overland*, and *Andromeda Spaceways*.

ALEXANDER TE POHE is a Māori trans man living on Whadjuk Noongar Land. His prose and poetry can be found in the collections *To Hold The Clouds* (Centre For Stories, 2020), *Australian Poetry Anthology* (Volume 9, 2021–2022) and *An Unexpected Party* (Fremantle Press, 2023), as well as publications such as *Djed Press*, *Portside Review* and *Strange Horizons*.

MORE GREAT ANTHOLOGIES

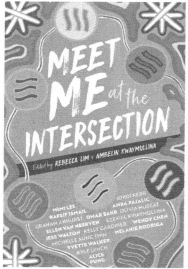

FROM FREMANTLEPRESS.COM.AU